Chapter One

Taiyo stood in the shadows by the window, her back to the room. From her vantage position on the third floor of the building where their flat was located, she had a bird's view of the sprawling town. The rising sun shone on rooftops, giving them a yellowish tinge. Across the roads that criss-crossed the town, diminutive figures of men and women hurried briskly as they went to their places of work. Uniformed school children, rucksacks on their backs, jostled boisterously as they alighted from one matatu and boarded another. Beneath her, down at the courtyard, she could see the shortened figure of her father, stocky, brisk moving and fussy. He was organizing and directing, with obvious shortness of temper, the loading of two ten-ton lorries. He was yelling, barking and gesticulating violently, apparently reprimanding loaders for being slow and inept in carrying out the task before them.

Taiyo knew her father well. He was not a man who cared to have his well-laid work-plans delayed or disrupted. She had noticed that he had become even more belligerent ever since the family learnt that he had been retrenched and they were now being forced to vacate the house and relocate to the rural town he had left many years back. Although the distance would not allow her to hear what he was telling the loaders, Taiyo felt a mild but quite genuine twinge of sympathy for the poor fellows down there, for she knew the sting of her father's tongue.

It reminded her of her own recent battle with him when he denied her permission to travel to Mombasa with

other young men and women who had been selected by an F.M Radio Station to attend an extravaganza. She had stubbornly put up a spirited struggle with him but the battle was so predictably and utterly lost. And that had left a wound in her heart that was still too raw to probe. Her rage, she realized, then, was still seething within her and that the simple faith and certainty of childhood upon which her life until then had been found, had failed her. Her trust that her father would give her whatever she requested for, had been badly shaken.

Stemming those thoughts out of her mind, she lifted her head and looked out through the morning sunbeams that gleamed brightly across the rooftops of Nakuru town. That was the beloved town of Nakuru which was the mother of all flamingos. It was the town she loved so much and which she was now about to leave. Tears welled in her eyes. She blinked suddenly and rapidly.

Taiyo did not hear her younger sister Resian approach. Briefly and in silence they stood by the window, side by side in the empty room. As far back as the two sisters could remember, they had always stood by that window every Sunday morning before they went to church. But their little habit of observing what went on below there at the streets of the town was made poignant that morning by the knowledge that it was going to be the last time they would do this.

Resian leaned forward and lifted her face to look into her sister's large brown eyes. She spoke very softly but her words were distinct and her voice very clear in the silent empty room.

"Taiyo— e – yeiyo, what do you think life is going to be

like in Nasila?"

"For heaven's sake, Resian," Taiyo said, turning round to face her sister. She made a small sound, affectionate and exasperated. "How am I supposed to know?"

"I suppose it's going to be very different from the kind of life we are used to here, isn't it?"

"Most likely so, yes."

"It seems so very strange, doesn't it?" Resian pressed on relentlessly. "To be leaving Nakuru town."

"We have always known that it was our father's plan to end up in Nasila," Taiyo told her sister, trying hard not to answer her directly. "That is why he built that shop that he has always spoken about. Now that he has been retrenched..." she hesitated a moment. It transpired that the more she spoke of the relocation, the harder reality hit her that she was about to leave Nakuru town for good. The twenty years of her life had been spent there. She loved its crowded streets, the bustle and excitement of its wholesale and retail markets, and the boisterous bus stage. But the most painful to leave behind was her boyfriend Lenjirr, the lanky dark-haired, blunt-faced young man whose big languid brown eyes had always smiled at her warmly, fostering in her the dreams of young womanhood.

"Taiyo-e-yeiyo?" Resian called, lifting her head to look up suspiciously into the face of her tall sister. "Is something amiss?"

"No, nothing is amiss."

"I am somehow worried, dear sister." Resian's voice dropped a little with apprehension. "What do you think will happen to us if the shop father intends to open does not become as successful as he hopes?"

"Resian-e-yeiyo, I don't know any better than you! Father thinks the shop will be a success. I overheard him tell one of his friends that he was going to stock agricultural inputs such as fertilizer, seeds, animal drugs and chemicals. Nasila is an agricultural area and business is bound to do well. I am sure he must be right. Let us have faith in him and hope for the best."

"I don't want to work at the shop," Resian declared, her pretty face hardening and her voice sounding petulant. "I want to come back to Nakuru and join Egerton University. I want to take a course in Veterinary Science. I like to become a Veterinary doctor. I want to read everything that there is to be read and put on the graduation regalia at the end of four years. Yes, I like to be called Dr. Resian Kaelo. You aren't laughing, are you? I mean it."

"I am not laughing, little sister," Taiyo said fervently, "you know too well that it is also my ardent ambition to join the university. How nice it would be if father were to allow the two of us to join. I would love it!"

"It would be wonderful, dear sister." Resian said excitedly, the elation evident in her voice. "You will then persuade father to allow us to come back to Nakuru and join the university, won't you, Taiyo-e-yeiyo?"

"I can't promise that with certainty," Taiyo said and tore her look away from her sister's face. "You know the stubborn nature of father." She looked down into the courtyard where their father was still busy moving from one lorry to the other, making sure that their furniture was loaded as fittingly as possible so that it did not break on the way. When she heard him yell at one of the workers,

4

a cold knot of anger and resentment tightened in the pit of her stomach, a flash of almost physical pain. She wondered what made her sister think she would be able to persuade their father to allow them come back to Nakuru and join the university if that was not his intention. Once more she recalled with bitterness how her father's adamant refusal to allow her to go to Mombasa and participate in the musical extravaganza had nearly fatally damaged the father-daughter relationship that had always been remarkably close.

"I know you will try to talk to him, won't you Taiyo-e-yeiyo?" Resian pleaded persuasively. "He always listens to you and this time round he will. Just try."

"I'll try," Taiyo said doubtfully to close the delicate subject.

Behind them and from the adjacent room, their mother's voice rose, the edge of complaint in it making them take keener interest on what was happening down there at the courtyard. At that very moment, their father craned his neck and looked up, as if to see what they were doing at the window.

"Taiyo, what on the earth are you doing there at the window instead of helping me pack the bags?" their mother asked sharply. And to Resian, "run downstairs and check what is happening. Are we never to leave?"

"They have completed loading the lorries, Yeiyo," Taiyo said nonchalantly. Turning to her sister and nudging her urgently, she added, "here comes *papa,* quick let's go! We better be found in the company of Yeiyo when he comes, otherwise he will spoil our day with his sharp tongue!" They giggled as they rushed out.

The two girls were with their mother gathering suitcases, placing them at the doorway ready to carry them downstairs, when their father entered the now empty living room.

"Ready to go?" Kaelo asked, addressing no one in particular. "We must start our journey straightaway if we are to get to Nasila early enough to offload the trucks and arrange the furniture in our new house."

That short speech poignantly brought reality to them that they were now about to leave Nakuru town for good. Kaelo cleared his throat loudly. His wife, Mama Milanoi, took out a handkerchief from her pocket and blew her nose. The four of them stood there for a moment in a sudden silence, each one of them keeping their thought to themselves. But one thing that was clear to all of them was that the flat that had been their home for so many years, stripped of all furniture, of all personal possessions, all books, pictures and ornaments, now looked bleak and shabby.

"Well," Mama Milanoi's voice wavered a little. "Let us pray that the Good Lord gives us journey mercies." And she prayed.

At the end of the prayer the four stood briefly in silence. Then, with a last glance about her, Mama Milanoi got hold of one of the suitcases and led the way out of the flat. Her husband followed and together they preceded their daughters out of that flat. Taiyo was the last to leave. She turned at the doorway, stood for a long moment looking back into the room that she had seen all of her childhood. Then, with tears in her eyes, firmly closed the door and followed the others down the stairs.

Minutes later when all of them were settled in the fourteen seater minibus that Kaelo had hired for them, the journey began in earnest. Father and mother sat in the front seat while the girls shared the back seat with suitcases and other hand luggage. The two lorries preceded them. And they were off.

When Mama Milanoi was settled in her seat and the vehicle was speeding steadily out of Nakuru town, she gave thought to the bigger picture of their relocation. At first when her husband broke the news that he had been retrenched, she was shocked and dumbfounded. It was as though a thunderbolt had struck her out of a midday blue sky. Ever since she got married to Kaelo twenty-two years earlier, Agribix Limited had been her husband's employer and the sole source of her family's livelihood. Now that it was closing its door on them, she felt as if providence itself was turning off the valve that supplied the vital air that sustained their lives. But her husband had received the distressing news philosophically. He had said it was an inevitability that was always coming. It began its journey the day he was engaged and now, like a baby who must be born at the fullness of time, this had come to pass. He counselled and convinced her that she had nothing to fear for he had prepared for that eventuality. He maintained that they could as well take the opportunity offered to them by the cessation of employment, to go back home and find an entry point into the flow of life of their community.

Once she was convinced that relocation would enable them begin a new phase of life, she became unflaggingly enthusiastic. She began to see in her mind how a brand new house and a big, well stocked shop that her husband promised to set up on the right side of Nasila town, predictably offered glamour and a chance to be associated with the great and the powerful of the land. She saw a chance for her family sharing the good fortune enjoyed by those who were already happily settled in the rural town. But above all, she saw a chance to marry off her two girls to greater prospects in the new town than were to be found – or so she thought – in the melting pot that Nakuru town had become. 'Yes, two sons-in-law from reputable families in the land could easily catapult them right into the centre of the affairs of the community. That could be the re-entry point into the community that they had been thinking about,' she thought contentedly.

There was, however, a dark spot in the whole affair. Women friends from Nasila who had visited her in the past had asked her very intrusive questions regarding her daughters. At that time she dismissed them as busybodies who enjoyed intrusion into other people's affairs. But it now dawned on her that those could be the mothers of her would be sons-in-law. The words they used to describe the status of her daughters came back to haunt her like demented spirits of a past that was better forgotten; *Intoiye Nemengalana** they had called them contemptuously.

On his part, Parsimei Ole Kaelo sat quietly beside his wife, his mind roaming the distant past in reminiscence. He knew that he had worked his fingers to the bone over the years, preparing for that day when he was no longer going to be employed. He was on his way to opening up his business. Not that he felt any particular excitement or pleasure; he was a man to whom disappointment came more easily and naturally than contentment. And that

---

*See glossary on page 292

latter attribute fired his ambition to always strive for the stars. It was characteristic of him that, surrounded by what other men would have considered evidence of a well-earned successful life, he felt nothing but the need to strive even harder to achieve better results.

He had a contentious mind that seemed to question every aspect of his life. Although he was blessed with a shrewd brain and a pugnacious obstinacy that had stood him in good stead in his struggle to rise through the ranks, from a clerk to the coveted position of Commercial Manager of the Agribix Ltd, he still saw only the greater successes of others. Even on the family front, he felt himself cheated by nature, for although it had been his prayer to get at least three boys, he had ended up with two girls. But even more obnoxious to him was the fact that despite all his achievements, it seemed to him that his younger brother, Simiren, who remained in Nasila, had been more appreciated and was considered the cultural head of the Kaelos by the community. That hurt him. But it did not worry him. Since childhood he had been aware, without self-pity, that no one really liked him. That, too, did not bother him since in his mind, to pursue the easy and worthless admiration of others was a sign of weakness of character.

Nature had not, however, been totally inconsiderate. It rewarded him with a gem in the form of his wife – Jane Milanoi. When he first saw her at a church service at Nasila, he was stunned. She was then hardly eighteen. Her body had now ripened to a sensual womanhood completely at odds with her childish face. She wore her jet black hair in braids that accentuated her wide eyes. Her

9

breasts were full and heavy, her waist slender, her hips wide and seductively curved. And the dress she wore, a simple red frock, fitted well her tall shapely figure. From the moment he saw her, he had been obsessed. And against all odds and despite all efforts, he was still so obsessed twenty-two years later. His marriage to her had been a great success.

His two daughters occupied separate parts of his heart. Taiyo, his eldest, was his pride. When she was born twenty-years earlier, his heart was enthralled. She was the proof of his fatherhood. When his wife got pregnant the second time, he prayed for a healthy baby boy who would carry the Kaelo's name to the next generation. But that was not to be. Against his expectation, and to his utter disappointment, nature had given him another baby girl. From the moment she was born, mute and helpless, he detested her. The very sight of her enraged him. Her arrival and her continued stay in her father's home, remained unwelcome and detested. And right from her cradle, baby Resian instinctively detected the absence of love from her father. She grew up sullen, bewildered and resentful. As a result, her nature was darkened by melancholy. Self-doubt made her awkward and very difficult to deal with. And that made him detest her even more.

Even her physical appearance angered her father. Like her sister Taiyo, at eighteen, she had grown almost as tall as her father, but unlike Taiyo who was still skinny and symmetrical in formation, Resian's body had blossomed early. Signs of early womanhood were evident. The earlier he disposed of her, he declared to himself angrily, the better.

A few kilometres to Nasila, one of the lorries developed a mechanical problem and broke down. The other two vehicles stopped behind it, the crew alighted and immediately swung into action to repair the fault. While Kaelo fussed around the vehicles, cursing and muttering expletives under his breath, Mama Milanoi and her daughters alighted and stood beside the vehicle. They huddled stoically together, eyes downcast, saying little. They knew thieves, robbers, rapists, car-jackers and hooligans lurked everywhere and could strike at any moment. They therefore stood there waiting with fatalistic resignation for the worst. Taiyo and Resian, both head and shoulder taller than their mother, stood on each side to protect her more from the cold blowing wind than from the fear of the marauding thugs.

"Here comes *Papaai*," Taiyo said with relief. "He is waving at us to get back into the vehicle. I think they have fixed the fault."

Soon the vehicles roared and within no time they were rolling into the small town of Nasila. Taiyo and Resian strained their eyes into the darkness of the evening to see the town that was to be their new home.

Their arrival came sooner than expected. The gates of their uncle Simiren's homestead where they were received swung open and a crowd of jubilant relatives who had been waiting to welcome them surged forward to greet them. When they stepped out of the vehicle, the girls were hugged, kissed and their heads touched by uncles, cousins, aunts and other relatives they had never met. There was so much noise, laughter, singing and dancing, that the girls, who least expected such a reception, were confused and dumbfounded. Soon, they were all seated around a bright fire lit in the middle of the homestead, enjoying pieces of roasted meat that were passed around.

For the thirty years or so that Parsimei Ole Kaelo was away in Nakuru, his younger brother Simiren acted as the head of the Kaelo family. He ably represented the family in the Ilmolelian clan to which they belonged. When there were *intalengo* to be performed, such as the initiation of girls, the circumcision of boys or betrothal ceremonies, he was always there representing his elder brother and his clan. And he was a strict adherent to his people's customs and traditions, for which reason he was respected and appreciated by the elders.

There had never been any argument or rivalry between him and his brother. Ever since they were young, and as they grew up, Simiren had always accepted his position to be subordinate to his elder brother. The fact that he had four wives and sixteen children while his brother had only one and two children, did not make any difference. Parsimei Ole Kaelo was still the *Olmorijoi* and he still humbled himself before him.

During Parsimei Ole Kaelo's absence, Simiren ran all kinds of errands for him. Many times he sent him money to purchase livestock alongside his own. He drove them to Dagoretti cattle market where he sold them at a profit and brought back the money to him. Seeing the rate at which his money multiplied made Parsimei Ole Kaelo appreciate and respect his younger brother's experience as an *Olkunchai*. When Parsimei Ole Kaelo put up two buildings in Nasila – a shop and residential house - his brother participated fully in the construction.

12

As Simiren and the clan elders sat around the fire, entertaining his elder brother, he thought quietly over how things might change. And as chunks of meat were passed around, he furtively looked at his brother as he selected a piece from the tray and wondered what was going through his mind. He hoped that Parsimei would appreciate that the weighty burden of matters pertaining to the Kaelo family would henceforth rest squarely on his able and mature shoulders. He however, envisaged some problems. He had informed Parsimei Ole Kaelo on many occasions, in the past, that there were murmurs in the clan about him. Elders had termed reckless his decision to remain married to only one wife, who only bore him two daughters. They had likened him to a mono-eyed giant who stood on legs of straw. Parsimei had got angry and called the clan elders megalomaniacs who were still trapped in archaic customs and traditions that were better buried and forgotten. Simiren did not argue with him then nor would he do so now. He would rather have matters take their own course.

There was however a more sensitive and controversial matter that had not been broached; it had to do with his daughters. He had hardly given thought to their age earlier, but when he saw them that evening he knew they should have left home long ago. It would take not long before his brother earned himself the derogatory name of the father of *intoiye nemengalana*.

Chapter Two

Taiyo and her sister Resian were woken up by a lively chatter of birds in the trees surrounding the house and by the intermittent crowing of roosters. What a contrast to what they were used to in Nakuru! They were always woken up by a rowdy clatter that assailed their ears at dawn: what with matatu drivers hooting and revving their engines noisily, touts shouting themselves hoarse while incessantly banging the body-works of their vehicles. For the first time in their lives they experienced a rare atmosphere of tranquillity and serenity they had never known to exist.

Taiyo lazily got out of bed and sleepily dragged herself to the window. When she opened the shutter, bright morning sunlight suddenly flooded the room. A cool fresh breeze swept in and caressed her face soothingly. From a distant, she could hear a bustle of activity within the homestead. She could also hear the mooing of cattle and bleating of sheep not far from the homestead. But what captivated her most was the cool natural environment that was created by giant trees that grew between houses.

Wondering what could have entranced her sister so much that she kept gazing unblinkingly at a spot outside the house, Resian too stealthily left her bed and joined Taiyo at the window. Standing behind her sister, Resian noticed features at their uncle's homestead that she had not seen the previous night when they arrived.

Apart from that house in which they had spent the night, three main houses stood within a well-tended and evenly-trimmed kei-apple perimeter hedge. She guessed that the four houses must belong to their four aunts who, they were informed the previous night, were the wives of their uncle. Between the houses stood smaller buildings that were overshadowed by massive yellow- trunked acacia trees. Interspersed were olive-green *iloirienito* trees whose fragrant foliage filled the air with their aromatic scent. Flights of birds flashed between the trees and the air was alive with their constant motion and cheerful calls.

"Hope our home will look like this," said Resian with enthusiasm.

"It is so calm and peaceful here. It is the kind of home one would look forward to come back to at the end of the college semester."

"Children," a woman's voice called from an adjacent room. "If you are up, come out and have your tea."

They quickly dressed up and within no time, they were out of the house and one of their aunts was leading them to the next house to join the rest of the family for morning tea.

The three crossed the courtyard talking happily, the girls walking closely behind their aunt. Like the house they had slept in, the next two houses they walked past were built of heavy cedar slabs, had similar wooden shutters for windows and were roofed with green painted corrugated iron sheets. Standing beside each house, on raised platforms made of strong cedar beams, were large, black, plastic water tanks that collected rain water from the roofs. Chicken clucked and scratched in the cool shade underneath. Clusters of bushes of O*lobaai* with their shinny dark-green leaves and tiny yellow flowers scattered the compound. *Ilkilenya* climbers grew around the beams that supported the water tanks and climbed over the walls of the houses, making

15

them look cool and comfortable.

The last house on the row was next to the main gate through which they had entered the homestead the previous night. It was different from the previous three. It was larger and was built of stone and had glass windows and like the others, its corrugated iron-sheet roof was painted green. Its front door was ajar and standing smilingly next to it was a stout woman of forty-five or so who greeted the girls affectionately and eyed them curiously as they responded to the greetings. She introduced herself as *Yeiyoo-botorr* which meant she was their senior-most aunt and the eldest wife of their uncle.

They were led to a spacious living room whose large open glass windows faced the east allowing in bright morning sunlight. The light shone on the young faces whose innocent wide opened eyes stared unashamedly at the two young women who *Yeiyoo-botorr* was introducing as their sisters. The sixteen or so children aged between three and sixteen were perched on benches, stools and chairs around the room, each holding a steaming enamel tea mug on one hand and a slice of bread on the other. Their mothers were there too and so was Mama Milanoi who sat placidly admiring the composure of her own daughters. It was only after the children were reassured that their new sisters were not visitors and that they would be seeing them often, that calm returned and they resumed taking their tea and bread. Room was created at the table and Taiyo and Resian sat with their cousins.

Seeing that they had the whole morning to themselves after breakfast, Taiyo and Resian told their mother they wanted to sightsee around the neighbourhood. She allowed them but cautioned care and wariness of strangers who might take advantage of their unfamiliarity. The girls looked at one another and giggled as they dismissed their mother's misplaced fears as born of the misconception by the old people that girls were weaklings, incapable of deciding what was right.

Their mother watched them as they walked leisurely and happily down the path out of their uncle's homestead. For reasons she did not understand, a pang of a strange premonition twisted her nerves unpleasantly. A creepy feeling kept on gnawing at her conscience regarding her daughters' status of being *intoiye nemengalana*, in the midst of a community that cherished girl child circumcision. She however, dismissed the feeling and relegated it to the back of her mind.

"What do you make of our uncle Simiren's home?" Resian asked her sister quietly as they walked down the path. "Honestly, I don't think all is well. Beneath the veneer of apparent happiness, I think I detected some apprehension, a subtle rivalry of some sort, between the four houses."

"What a terrible person you are my dear sister!" Taiyo rebuked her sister mildly. "You are not worth being a guest in anyone's home. How dare you make judgement on a family's way of life that seems to suit them perfectly?"

"Easy, easy, big sister," said Resian teasingly. "Don't be so harsh on me. All I have done is to make an observation. Am I not entitled to that?"

"Of course," Taiyo agreed and flicked an affectionate smile at her sister. "But do you know that the rivalry and apprehension that you say you detected could simply be a figment of your own fertile imagination?"

"That could be true," Resian added and smiled pleasantly. "But can you honestly claim, if you were one of the sixteen little fellows taking tea from enamel mugs in that crowded room this morning, to be content?"

"Perhaps I would be happy," she answered thoughtfully. "You know happiness is relative. One could be happy in a family of twenty and another may fail to find happiness in a family where he or she is an only child."

"Did you notice that two of our aunts are expectant?" Resian asked mischievously, slanting a look at her sister. "At that rate..."

"Come off it!" Taiyo said sternly. "There are better things to discuss. Parents have the right to have as many children as they desire. You will have that right yourself when your turn comes."

"Who? Not me," Resian said vehemently "I don't want to be a parent. At least not in the foreseable future. I want to study. When I'll have obtained my degree, other peripheral matters such as a husband, children and such may be considered."

They were walking back to the homestead talking animatedly when they were accosted by a tall heavyset young man with a thick dark beard and moustache. He wore a pair of faded jeans and a dirty blue shirt. On his face was a wide impudent grin. Taiyo glanced at the young man and looked away. She moved closer to Resian and nudged her to change direction. But the man walked directly to Taiyo. On seeing the man approaching, a heavy knobkerry in his hand, Resian almost fainted.

"Please do not harm us," she pleaded. "We do not have any money with us."

"Who told you I want any money?" the man jeered as he strode menacingly towards them. "Are you not the *intoiye nemengalana* from Nakuru town?" he asked laughing contemptuously. "I want to have a good look at you and know what kind of stuff you are made of!" And he roughly grabbed Taiyo's arm.

"Leave my sister alone!" Resian hissed indignantly lifting her eyes and glaring into his. "Let go her arm at once!"

"Let go of my hand," Taiyo demanded, trembling with anger. "We are not the kind of women you have in mind!"

"What women!" the man retorted acidly. "Soon, you will be able to differentiate decent women from *intoiye nemengalana.*"

Taiyo tried to wrestle her arm from the man's grip without success. But suddenly, he seemed to change his mind. With a sour smile, he spat and glared at the girls. Then, releasing Taiyo's hand, he told them: "You have not seen the last of me. Soon you will come to know that there is no place in our society for women of your ilk." He turned and disappeared down the road as suddenly as he had appeared.

The two girls sighed heavily and shook their heads as they watched him walk away. Although they had put up brave faces, they were terribly scared and shaken. "Thank God his intention was not to rape us," Resian said tears streaming down her face. "We would have been helpless in the hands of such a brute."

Taiyo bit her lower lip struggling to maintain control. "His intention could have been worse than rape," she said, tears of anger and indignation welling up in her eyes. They quickened their steps as they walked back to their uncle's home. True, the incident had taken the sparkle from the day that had begun so joyfully, but they reasoned that it could have been worse.

The girls debated as to whether to inform their parents or not. They knew their mother would understand and empathize with them. But judging from past experience, their father would be less supportive. He would blame them for having dared venture into an unknown territory without his approval. Finally, they decided to keep the incident to themselves.

When he finished supervising the off-loading of the lorries and arranging of furniture and other personal effects in his new house, Ole Kaelo set out to meet his mentor Soin ole Supeyo. He was a much older man, possibly sixty-five or seventy years old, a member of the *Ilmolelian* clan and a respected elder of *Ilnyangusi* age-set. He was known to be shrewd, scrupulous and honest, attributes that saw him rise from an ordinary *Olkunchai* who drove his three or four heads of cattle for hundreds of kilometers to the cattle market at Dagoretti, to the now immensely rich man that he was. He was reputed to own the largest ranch in Nasila and his beef herd and sheep were said to be in tens of thousands. His business empire comprised a fleet of buses, lorries and shops, beside numerous business premises and residential houses that he rented out.

As he drove his pick-up towards Ole Supeyo's farm, Ole Kaelo gave thought to the old man. When he was in primary school, Ole Supeyo was already a famous cattle trader. He would buy cattle from Nasila and drive them all the way to Dagoretti market where he would sell them and come back laden.

In those days money was still a new concept to many up-coming illiterate traders. He would find it difficult to add up the notes and was forced to arrive at an aggregate of what he actually owned. Ole Supeyo had to fetch Ole Kaelo and together they would walk deep into the forest where they would find a safe place. He would then remove one of the blankets that he wore and spread it on the grass, take out his pouch and from it fish out a large bundle of notes and coins. He would ask his friend to count the money, while he stood tense, waiting, and would only relax when Ole Kaelo told him the actual amount and it tallied with the figure he had in mind.

They carried out that exercise at least twice a month and he came to trust and depend on Ole Kaelo. The two became close and their friendship developed even as Ole Supeyo became a very wealthy businessman and farmer. Ole Kaelo respected him and considered him his mentor.

Although Ole Supeyo did not attend school, Ole Kaelo thought he was one of those intelligent old men who were able to embrace modern culture, balance it appropriately, and make it run parallel to the old Nasila culture. He had six wives and about thirty children. He had sent all his sons to school and two of them had reached university level. All his daughters were circumcised and married off to prominent elders in Nasila.

Ole Kaelo had witnessed Ole Supeyo's incense only on one occasion. A certain woman known as Minik *ene* Nkoitoi, the *Emakererei,* a manager at a certain Sheep Ranch called Intare-Naaju, and a known crusader against girl circumcision, had come to persuade him not to circumcise his daughters. But Ole Supeyo would hear none of it. When the crusader insisted on having her way, he got angry and forcefully ejected her out of his homestead, threatening to clobber her.

Later, he told Ole Kaelo, the woman, whom he referred to as a wasp, was a great threat to the Maa culture. Female circumcision, he said, was not only an honoured rite of passage that had been in existence from time immemorial, but an important practice that tamed an otherwise wild gender. Like cattle that required to be dehorned, to reduce accidental injuries to each other, a certain measure of docility was also necessary to keep more than one wife in one homestead. And Ole Kaelo agreed with him, recalling the adage that: two women in one homestead were two potent pots of poison.

Ole Supeyo's homesteads, sheep pens and cattle enclosures were at the centre of an expansive farm that extended for many kilometers in all directions. Ole Kaelo first glimpsed at the glimmer of the corrugated iron sheet rooftops from the top of a low hill some ten kilometers away. The *manyattas* that long ago used to dot the area among scrubby trees and bush had given way to modern sprawling buildings. The trees had been cut down and the bush cleared so that in one direction, the land was now an expansive plain of thick rich grass that stretched as far as the eye could see, while towards the other direction, thousands of acres of wheat and barley lay.

When he arrived at the homestead, Ole Kaelo parked his pick-up outside the gate. Looking at the modernity of that homestead, he appreciated how far his friend had travelled from being a simple cattle trader, to the wealthy man who owned that massive homestead accomodating eight large houses. The first wife's house was the largest and was built amongst tall *iloiraga* trees.

He walked towards the gate thinking of the man he continually drew his inspiration from. He yearned to grow in business to be like him. He had therefore considered it opportune to make his home the first port of call before he put his hand to the plough.

Ole Supeyo came out of the house to welcome his friend. He had only just woken from his siesta and his eyes were still smarting from sleep. As he walked down the steps in front of the house, he lifted a corner of his shirt and scratched his belly, while his other hand stroked the stubble on his chin.

"Come in, my brother!" Supeyo said happily, "Welcome! Welcome! Welcome! Come right inside." They shook hands warmly and Ole Kaelo was led into the spacious living room that was not strange to him as he had been there on numerous occasions.

As they talked casually over a cup of tea, Supeyo glanced furtively at his friend, his black eyes gleaming in the afternoon sunshine. He certainly liked him, he told himself quietly, and he would have liked him to succeed in the business he had set himself to do. He however considered Ole Kaelo a bore and sometimes a pompous one, although he did not doubt his intelligence. Little did he know that his friend was much more advanced when it came to the murky business of the underworld.

"I hope all is well with your business arrangements," Supeyo commented nonchalantly.

"Everything is moving on smoothly," said Kaelo contentedly. "I hope to open the doors of the shop at the onset of the rains."

"Good," said Supeyo cheerfully. "You will soon find out that, unlike in Agribix where somebody else provides the finances, another does the books, yet another runs up and down making sales, you will have to carry all those tasks single-handedly. And sales will be the most challenging."

Kaelo's pride was wounded. How could the old fellow think he was so naïve as not to know how to organize his sales? Perhaps, he thought sourly, his clansmate had not known that in his earlier years in Agribix, he had been sent out to open sales depots in remote places which he quickly developed into expanding profitable modern branches. Maybe it was time he showed the ageing businessman that younger bulls were raring to go and the old ones would better start skirting the pastures. He threw caution to the wind.

"The sales are already taken care of," Kaelo said pompously. "Sales of about three hundred thousand bags of fertilizer, half a million bags of seeds plus insecticides, fungicides and herbicides are as good as bagged and secured. You see that?"

"My goodness," Supeyo exclaimed. "How did you manage such a feat?"

"I am about to sign a four years' contract to supply all

24

government institutions in Nasila with agricultural inputs," Kaelo said confidently.

Once he had spoken those words, Kaelo felt guilty. Ever since he began negotiating for the supply of the inputs, he had told no one of the deal. It was a secret that he kept close to his heart. It had already cost him a fortune but if the deal went through, he thought apprehensively, it would make all the difference. He now felt rueful. It was as though by speaking about it, he had broken the spell that would have brought the good fortune. He grew anxious, leaned back on his seat, crossed his legs, trying to firmly suppress his own distaste for corruption that was entrenched in those contract giving offices. He had long realized that the choice was between remaining a nobody, self-righteously and accepting, sensibly, that the man with the meat was also the same man with the knife. Whoever wanted to eat meat, must of necessity dance to the music of the man who held the two.

"My brother Kaelo," Supeyo called amidst malicious laughter that had a touch of friendly mockery. "Tell me, who have you been corrupting?"

"Nobody really," Kaelo answered angrily, his teeth set on edge. "I only made contact with…" he hesitated, then gaining his composure continued, "I made contact with a man called Oloisudori. I met the man in Nakuru…"

"Do you know Oloisudori?" interrupted Supeyo sharply. "Do you really know what you have gotten yourself into? *Taba*!" He leaned forward, elbows on the table, his eyes growing into sudden sharp needle-points of interest. He remained so for a moment, then sunk back into his chair, smiling mirthlessly. "My dear brother, here in Nasila, everyone knows anyone who is corrupt. And Oloisudori is probably the most corrupt of them all. What a head start! I'll be glad to share some of those contracts should you run out of supplies. They are quite a bite, I dare say!"

The mockery did not escape Kaelo. But to hear the man he had all along considered to be his mentor pour cold water on what he regarded as his grand entry into big business was not only frightening but disconcerting. He wondered whether his friend, who he had regarded as his inspiration and guiding star, was not a hypocrite. He could be, he concluded, one of those selfish people who, after crossing a river, would destroy the bridge so that others did not use it. He lifted his eyes to look at his friend and shifted in his seat uneasily.

"In your opinion," he said and hesitated quite embarrassed. Then he continued, "do you think Oloisudori will deliver what he promised?"

Supeyo shrugged his shoulders. "My brother, you are not naïve nor are you new in business," he said candidly. "Oloisudori is in business and wants to continue being in business. If you have fulfilled your part, he will do his, especially if it suits him."

"So, he is a man of integrity?" asked Kaelo, a flicker of hope rising in his heart.

"A man of integrity indeed." Supeyo said a scornful smile twisting his lips. "Don't trust him any further than you would a hyena in your homestead." Then lowering his voice as if he was letting him into a guarded secret, he whispered mischievously. "And my friend, keep the fellow away from your daughters. He has a reputation that would rival that of a randy he-goat!" With that advice, Kaelo left his friend. Though feeling discomfited, he was nonetheless the wiser, or so he thought.

In the afternoon, the Kaelo family left Simiren's homestead to be driven the one kilometre distance to their new home. They rode almost in silence, each wrapped in thoughts they did not care to share with others. Mama Milanoi, dazzled by dreams of eventual fulfillment failed to notice that her husband's silence was ominous. She even forgot the premonition that had earlier gnawed her conscience. Taiyo had not recovered fully from the traumatic experience they had gone through. She still felt as if the threatening hostility the evil young man displayed had not dissipated and that the sense of foreboding from the threat was still hanging in the air like the sword of Domocles. Her arm, which the man had roughed up, still felt unclean and could still feel the touch of his heavy callous hand. She drew in a deep, trembling breath and released it in a sigh as she silently sat at the back of the pick-up with her sister. Resian also sat there silently.

At last they were home. Before them was the solid, stone-built, red-tiled roofed house that was going to be their home. It was built on a hill that allowed a command of a breathtakingly beautiful scene all around it.

While his wife and daughters jumped out of the pick-up excitedly and scrambled to the gate of their new house jubilantly, Parsimei Ole Kaelo remained behind for a few minutes. Ole Supeyo's words still nettled him. Truly, he had known Oloisudori to be a notorious criminal, but was not everybody doing business with him? Was he really that bad? He wondered. Or was it the usual business rivalry and envy? Try as he did to justify his business deal with

Oloisudori, something inside him told him it was not right. He thought an old man of Ole Supeyo's seniority did not use the word *Taba* lightly.

Chapter Three

When their father pointed out their house amongst other red tiled ones on top of a hill, the girls could hardly believe their eyes. That imposing huge building enclosed in a stonewalled perimeter fence, could not be their home! They nudged one another excitedly as they giggled and threw furtive glances at their father. The oppressive gloom that had weighed upon their hearts as they drove down the road suddenly lifted and dissipated. An atmosphere of excitement and anticipation pervaded their hearts. Their faces were radiant and their feet quickened as they walked the remaining distance with bated breath.

Mama Milanoi was also happy. Although she had not seen the house before then, she knew it must be excellent. She had always trusted her husband to do the best for her and her children. There was no reason, therefore, for her to have doubted him. When she married him twenty-two years earlier, she not only did so, as was expected by the Nasila people, but she had needed someone to look after her and her children.

And true to her expectation, Kaelo had always been responsible. Even as she sat happily beside him that sunny afternoon, she let her mind travel fancifully into her past. She recalled with amusement the excitement and pride of her father and mother when the parents of one Parsimei Ole Kaelo, accompanied by other elders came into their home to engage her. Her parents were all along determined to find a well-to-do son-in-law, preferably from a well known family.

When the suitor happened to be a young man who was

reputed to be an up-coming businessman, her parents were satisfied that their daughter would not only be in safe hands, but that their grandchildren would have a dependable protector. After what appeared to her to be lengthy protracted negotiations, the parties agreed and she was betrothed.

She accepted him without any resistance. Tradition did not allow her to offer any and as expected of her, she did not resist. So at eighteen, after undergoing the mandatory initiation rituals, she had married Parsimei Ole Kaelo who was then twenty-four years old. And although over the years he had scolded and bullied her, like a halfwitted child, she knew he was a good man, a great provider, a foresighted planner and a man with a will to succeed in whatever he put his mind on. She also knew that he loved her genuinely. For even after all those years of marriage he still pampered her. She loved him too and had a childlike dependence on him. She, however, knew that she had failed miserably by not giving him the sons that he had so much looked forward to. But she also knew it was still not too late. God could still favour her with a son or two. And now that she had gone back to the home of the gods of motherhood, she was going to join the rest of Nasila women in their ancestral prayer, song and praise: *Enkai Aomon Entomono*, a prayer exhorting God to open women's wombs.

She turned and looked at her daughters. They were full of animation as they walked hurriedly down the road that led to the gate. That made her happy. She was even happier to see Resian who was often a pessimist, looking exuberant that afternoon. She hoped they would always be that happy. But she knew things had not been easy for them. At that delicate stage of their lives, she knew relocation to an extremely harsh environment that was devoid of their friends and all that they had known throughout their lives was not only trying, but cruel. But she feared even a worse looming scenario and which they were soon likely to encounter. Poor innocent things! How she wished she could shield and protect them. But could she? She knew Nasila people were extremely intolerant of those who ignored their cherished cultural sensibilities. And the case of her daughters was no exception.

Mama Milanoi was so engrossed in her thoughts that she hardly noticed that they had arrived at the gate of their new home. Her husband's voice jolted her back to reality.

"Lanoo-ai-nayorr," the endearing diminutive that he rarely used to call her and which he only used in the most intimate of circumstances, stopped her in her tracks. She straightened up and her eyes widened. "This is the home that I have always dreamed I would one day build for you and my beloved daughters," he said emotionally and dramatically dipped his hand into his coat-pocket removing a key. For a brief moment the air around them was expectantly taut as the girls stood there breathless staring fixedly at the gate.

The whole episode seemed magical. And like a magician, Ole Kaelo stood there beaming ecstatically, his hands ready to unveil the object of his magic. He inserted the key into the key hole, turned it and as it clicked open, he swung the gate open to reveal a home that was so breathtakingly beautiful that they could have only imagined it in a fantastic dream. They were stunned.

"Father of all creation!" Mama Milanoi exclaimed loudly. "This is but a dream."

"It is magnificent!" enthused Taiyo in an ecstasy of delight, "*Enkai supat.*"

"I have never seen anything like it!" completed Resian, enthralled, "*Eitu aikata adol...*"

The air of excitement that danced about the Kaelo family was so exhilarating and riveting that it transfixed them. And for a long moment none of them moved and their eyes were glued to the exquisite house before them.

Ole Kaelo ushered them into the sprawling homestead with its lush well-tended lawn. Here and there were squat robust *ilopon* trees. Clusters of *Oleleshua*, *Osinoni* and *Olkirrpanyany* bushes dotted the compound, while beyond the house, hanging on the stone perimeter wall, was a blaze of bougainvillea climbers that burnt red, cream and purple.

When they got to the front of the house, they could hardly believe their eyes! Truly, their new house was a real dream come true. Resian looked about her with eager fascinated eyes while Taiyo, itching to enter and see for herself, took the lead and proceeded to mount the graceful sweep of steps, walking through the verandah before reaching the front door. And when their father opened the door they were breathless.

They filed through the door into a spacious hallway that led to a large living room lavishly furnished with familiar furniture. The girls ran from room to room curiously trying to find their orientation. Surprisingly, they found that the house looked familiar. What they did not know was that their father had the house plan designed after the flat they occupied in Nakuru. All the rooms were a replica of those rooms of their former house in Nakuru. It was not easy to distinguish it from the Nakuru flat.

Back in the living room, Taiyo, Resian and their mother began to speak at once. They spoke of its size, its convenience and the furniture fitting.

After a hurriedly prepared dinner, the girls retired to their bedroom to arrange and tidy it up. Cartons of their clothes, bedding, books and other personal effects were still piled up on their unmade bed. Curtains were yet to be hung as were their pictures and decorations. Taiyo removed her cardigan and immediately swung into action. She loosened the ropes that tied cartons, emptied their contents onto the floor and sorted them. After some time, the large room that held their big bed was in shambles. Shoes lay strewn all over, books were stacked in heaps on the floor and clothes and bedding were scattered on the bed. Exhausted, she straightened up and stood, hands on her hips, eyeing in growing exasperation her sister who sat on a chair at one corner of the room reading a book.

"Surely, Resian," she complained to her sharply. "Is this the time to read a book with all this mess around us?"

"Do your bit now and I will do mine tomorrow," Resian replied with a nonchalant carelessness.
"I insist that you get up right now and get to work" Taiyo raised her voice. "We need to arrange this room before we get to bed."

Resian grunted and grumbled. She reluctantly laid the book down and went to work. They reviewed the events of the last two days as they tried to bring order to the room.

"What a contrast between Nakuru and this place," said Taiyo quietly. "It is so quiet and tranquil here."

"I don't know, but I feel an oppressive silence," Resian said defiantly. "A little noise is not all that bad."

"Don't befuddle me with your weird kind of reasoning," said Taiyo getting impatient. "Do you prefer the Nakuru bus stage to this serene atmosphere?"

"No, not at all." Resian said seriously. "I would rather live in the most noisy place on earth, than live anywhere near a vagabond who would accost me in the most quiet and serene atmosphere with the intention of mutilating my sexuality!"

"Of course I also don't care whether I am counted among *intoiye nemengalana*," an embarrassed Taiyo said as she began to fold clothes, not looking at her sister. "What I know is that my body belongs to me. I belong to myself." She picked a pillow, tossed it onto the bed, plumbed it up and looking around said fiercely, "only when I am dead would anybody mutilate my body."

"Don't you think they can force us to undergo the ritual?" Resian asked fearfully. "What do you think will happen to us if *Papaai* is forced by his clansmen to embrace the archaic culture that would require us to get the cut?

"Resian-e-yeiyo, I hope nothing of that sort happens, for if it does..." she shrugged her shoulders and pulled an expressive face. "I don't know what would happen to us."

"That's why it's imperative that you persuade *Papaai* to allow us go back to Nakuru and enroll at the university," said Resian vehemently as she threw herself onto the bed, her arms behind her head. "We must beat them to it. We must convince him to allow us to go before they prevail upon him to embrace the primitive, backward, outdated and archaic traditions."

"I'll do that soonest, dear sister," said Taiyo thoughtfully. "I'll try to persuade him to see our way."

"How soon is soonest, dear big sister?" Resian cried out resignedly and added petulantly, "I would never want to be confronted again by a deranged vagabond in this wild and frightening jungle that *Papaai* has thrown us into."

"Hush little sister, please don't cry," Taiyo cooed soothingly as if singing a lullaby to a crying baby. "Your big sister will make sure that no harm comes anywhere near you and that you get what you yearn for. Just wait and see."

Taiyo stood by the bed for a while watching her sister who lay forlorn, staring through the window into the brightly moonlit sky outside. Then she sat on the bed beside her and reassuringly touched Resian's cheek gently with the back of her hand. Ever since they were young, attending nursery school, she had been fiercely and protectively devoted to her sister. When they went to primary school, Resian clung to her for protection from bigger girls who wanted to bully her. And in their growing years, even at secondary school, Taiyo always sensed her sister's yearning.

She had made it her duty to mop her younger sister's tears, sooth her anger and gently reassure her when she was badly shaken; as often happened after the frequent tongue lashing from their father. For reasons she did not understand, she had always found their father strangely and harshly impatient towards Resian. She was sure it was that inexplicable attitude of her father towards Resian that had contributed to her tempestuous disposition. Even stranger was their mother's failure to come to Resian's defence. It was as if her motherly instincts could not extend her protective wings to cover Resian.

And so, in the absence of their mother's protection and in the face of their father's constant provocation and intimidation, Resian's dependence on Taiyo strengthened. And Taiyo would have been irked by her sister's ever present nagging complaints had she not been so deeply aware of her never ending unhappiness.

Although Resian had a lot to complain and grumble about life in their new environment, Taiyo found it tolerable. For instance, she gladly discovered that mornings at their new home began with a lively chatter of birds in the trees surrounding their house. That gave the home an atmosphere of tranquillity and peace.

However, one of the unpleasant aspects that the girls had to live with was the constant violation of their privacy. In Nasila, they soon discovered, the home belonged to all clan members. It was not an unusual thing to get up in the morning to find the living room full of men and women who came that early, not for any tangible business, but simply to share a sumptuous breakfast with their kith and kin. Taiyo and Resian were soon to get used to hearing an urgent knock at the door very early in the morning. On opening, they would invariably be met by a grinning group of men and women who would unashamedly ask them what they were doing in bed that late in the morning. They would proceed to take seats in the livingroom and order them to serve them with breakfast.

When they got used to what they first considered to be negative aspects of Nasila culture, Taiyo and Resian adjusted accordingly and soon they began to live harmoniously with the people. Their father was out of the homestead most of the time working at the shop and organizing other business matters. His absence also meant the absence of his irksome and corrosive remarks that always heightened tension in the house. In his absence, the house was a continuous joy with comfort and conveniences, and the girls found it a pleasure to keep it clean and well arranged.

Mingling with the women folk, the girls learnt a great deal about the hilarious, the absurd and the weird aspects of Nasila culture. They also met a variety of women. Although most of the women who visited the Parsimei's home did so for entertainment purposes, others visited with definite purposes. A great number of them came to survey and get to know the girls well, so that they could have sufficient information on which to decide whether they were marriageable, and commendable to their husbands to be married as their *inkainito* (co-wives). Others came looking for potential wives for their sons while *enkaitoyoni* (midwife) and *enkamuratani* (circumciser) came to make acquaintance with potential clients.

So when their father announced one evening that he was planning a home coming ceremony, the girls and especially Taiyo no longer felt like strangers.

Chapter Four

Parsimei Ole Kaelo planned his homecoming ceremony meticulously. He had wanted the occasion to be remarkably memorable, preferably taking the form of the traditional *enkang-o-ntalengo*. He however, knew that having been away from Nasila for many years he had lost touch with the cultural sensibilities of the people.

To re-establish the severed links, he enlisted the help of his brother Simiren and several senior elders of the community who were the custodians of his people's culture. He was prepared to get down to the bedrock and find out at which point he lost the way. He had known that *Odomongi* and *Orok-kiteng*, the legendary twin homesteads of the founder that begot the five clans of Nasila: *Ilmolelian, Ilmakesen, Ilukumae, Ilaiser* and *Iltarrosero*, were the cradle of the Nasila people.

He not only desired to reunite with Nasila people but also needed their blessings. He had therefore dispatched people to all corners of Nasila to invite representatives of all the five clans to the grand party, which was going to be his re-entry point into the cultural life of his people.

When he gave thought to the clans, Ole Kaelo could not help but laugh silently when he recalled the stereotyped anecdotes that used to be told when he was young. They were made up by rival groups with the intention of lowering the esteem of their adversaries. He recalled with amusement that his own clan of *Ilmolelian* was said to be made up of ludicrously generous men who would slaughter a bull and foolishly share out all the meat to others leaving themselves without any. They would then happily and ridiculously raise up their arms to show to all and sundry that they had not hidden any meat under their armpits. But for the *Ilmakesen* clan, it was exactly the opposite. The clansmen were said to be so miserly stingy that they would deny a dog the afterbirth of a she-goat. It was said that they would opt to sleep hungry rather than share food they had in the house with a sojourner who dropped in unannounced. Interestingly, Ole Kaelo was a member of the supposedly generous *Ilmolelian* clan, and his wife Milanoi was the daughter of the close-fisted *Ilmakesen* clan.

When the party was finally thrown, it was nothing short of ostentatious. And true to the *Ilmolelian* spirit and tradition, Ole Kaelo held nothing back. He slaughtered a fattened ox, six rams and four he-goats. In the living room stood four long tables spread with the most astounding array of food Nasila had ever seen. There were large trays laden with huge chunks of boiled meat whose tantalizing aroma filled the room. Lamb chops grilled to a golden brown colour glistered appetizingly on chop-boards. Succulent pieces of pink-roasted liver lay arranged on leaves of *Oloirepirepi* weed to preserve moisture and taste. Then there were other choice pieces of meat on skewers and others wrapped up in sacred *Oloirien* leaves that were the preserve of the elders who were to bless the home of *Intalengo*. It was only after such blessings that Nasila would receive back their son who had gone out to hunt for fortunes and returned safely. The elders would also bless the wife, children and property that he brought back and which were all henceforth going to be the wealth of the *Ilmolelian* clan.

That day had begun early for Ole Kaelo. He had left his bed at cock crow, the time that was known in Nasila as *Tolakira-lole-Kasaale*. He was to see to it that every detail about the impending homecoming ceremony was taken care of without exception and absolutely nothing was to be left to chance. There was little for him to do that morning though, for all preparations and arrangements had earlier been made, systems had been set, and all that was left to be done was to implement what had been agreed upon and ensure that everything was running without a hitch.

Days earlier, with the help of his brother Simiren and his wives, he had gathered a retinue of young men and women from his *Ilmolelian* clan and charged them with the responsibility of organizing the activities and chores of the ceremonial day. And true to their calling, the young men and women immediately swung into a variety of activities with zest. Those who belonged to the sub-clan of *Iloorasha-kineji*, to which Kaelo also belonged, felt that the responsibility to have the occasion succeed rested on their shoulders. Led by a young local primary school music teacher called Joseph Parmuat, they took charge of the entire ceremony. Members of the other sub-clan of *Lelema* readily and graciously accepted the leadership of Joseph Parmuat and their other cousins and all worked harmoniously and tirelessly, to bring about the success that was already evident that morning.

From the verandah of his house, Kaelo surveyed with utter satisfaction all that was happening in his homestead. He was most grateful and felt humbled by the fact that in that ancestral land to which he had finally returned and to which he belonged, body and soul, honour, brotherhood and selflessness were still virtues. Where he had been, only the promise of monetary payment would have induced such a large number of young men and women to turn up. With trembling lips and with tears welling in his eyes, he swore under his breath that never again in his life, would he ever abandon the culture of his people or live outside his clan *Ilmolelian*. Its twin sub-clans of *Iloorasha-kineji* and *lelema,* would always be like two chambers of his heart that incessantly pumped the blood that sustained him. Regaining his composure, he walked back into the house.

Mama Milanoi was at the tables ensuring that the trays that came out of the kitchen laden with meat delicacies, were sorted out and arranged appropriately. Taiyo was busy slicing chunks of oxtongue into manageable pieces, a job she did with dexterous fingers. When their father opened the door to let himself into the livingroom, Resian was busy transferring glasses from the sideboard onto a nearby table. The moment she saw him enter, her fingers became clumsy and she nearly dropped a glass.

"Would you ever do anything right, child?" her father reprimanded her severely. "I hope you have not broken any glasses this morning."

"I am terribly sorry, *Papaai*," Resian said remorsefully, her eyes downcast. "But I have not broken any."
But sensing that her father's eyes were still upon her, she felt out of place. Just then, her braided hair fell free of its pins and over her face. She tried to tuck a strand behind her ear, but in the process lost the grip of the two glasses dropping them on the floor. Her father winced, grimaced and struggled to control his temper for, he reasoned, that

was not a day to get angry. But all the same, he wondered where in the world they fetched that awkward, overblown, stupid child. Her gracelessness appalled him. And the very look in her eyes, half-fearful, half-defiant and wholly troubled, was always enough to raise his temper to the highest pitch. He clicked his tongue irritably and quickly left the room.

At noon, Ole Kaelo's spacious homestead was nearly full to capacity. There was pomp all over and a carnival atmosphere resonant with song and dance hung in the air. A bevy of beautiful young women stepped forward, their necks bedecked with layer after layer of exquisite multicoloured bead ornaments. The bright-coloured *lesos* they wore over their shoulders fluttered in the windy afternoon air as they moved sedately, heads poised, chests heaving forwards and backwards, knees bobbing, voices raised melodiously, as they glided smoothly into an exciting traditional dance.

Two young men out of a group of about twenty began to sing in their light melodic voices. The rest joined in, their deep guttural voices mingling with those of the young women. The moment the voices mingled and fused, the dance changed subtly. The men's group broke into two, each with a light quick springy jumping movement. They skipped away as they skirted the compound, then they joined again into one group amidst shrieks of excitement. The young women repeated their dance. Their light steps were sedate, their backs and shoulders held straight and their heads haughty and graceful. And as they sang, the young men, leapt to the centre. They jumped high into the air, each one of them vying to outdo the other.

Taiyo and Resian who had joined the throng of spectators were ecstatic. Their eyes were glued to the handsome, arrogantly athletic figures of the *morans*. One particular young man caught Taiyo's eye. He was a lithe, tall dark-haired young man in red *shukas*, who leapt higher with more grace than the rest. She involuntarily gasped, her gaze still riveted upon his handsome face.

"Look at that young man," Taiyo told her sister urgently, excitedly pointing at him." Isn't he handsome?"

Resian followed her sister's gaze. "Yes, he is," she said trying to scrutinize his face from that distance. "He is doubtlessly good-looking."

Even as they gazed at the young man, he broke out of the group he had been singing with and walked out of the gate. Moments later he came back leading a group of uniformed school children, boys and girls who he quickly arranged into four short lines, one following the other. Soon the air was resonant with their vibrant voices as they sang an exciting heart-lifting song, whose words had been carefully selected to commemorate Kaelo's return.

Tenining iltualan loo nkishu ang,	If you listen to the tinkling bells of our cattle,
Niyolou tenaa naapuo linka ashu nar ukunye ang.	You will know whether the cattle are going out to pastures, or on their way back home.
Tenaa napuo linka, shomo taanyu tenaituyupaki	If they are on their way to the pastures, wait for them, at the hills of Naituyupaki

Tenaa narukunye ang, taanyu te kishomi Ole Kaelo.	If they are streaming back home, wait for them at the homestead of Ole Kaelo.
Eterewa apa ole Kaelo inkishu enyenak linka,	Ole Kaelo took his cattle out to the pastures,
Nenyaaka areu pookin ang elulunga	And brought them back home
Tenininig iltualan loonkishu enyenak	without losing any.
Niyolou ajo iltualan lookishu narukunye ang	If you listen to the tinkling bells of his cattle, You will know it is the sound of cattle coming back home
Oiye kuldo murran lolmolelian,	You young men of *Ilmolelian,*
Enchom entanangare oltungani linyi olotu ang	Go out and meet your returning hero.
Entoboinu inkishu enyenak metijinga kishomi	Direct his cattle to enter his homestead,
Eniningo iltualan loonkishu Ole Kaelo	Listen to the tinkling bells of the cattle of Kaelo.

Then the children broke into a quick exciting dance. The boys formed a semicircle while the girls formed themselves into a line. They wove into an intricate pattern, hands touching and dropping, their eyes demurely, down cast. The boys chanted and sang a refrain while the girls moved with a grace that brought instant applaud from all those present, their tiny steps gliding smoothly, like ducks upon water. Then the boys changed their dance style. They leapt, one by one, into the centre of the circle they had formed and amidst shrieks and chants, jumped high in the air, while whirling, spinning and clicking their heels. The girls responded by singing a melodious praise song.

As they sang, they gyrated their hips creating a certain rippling movement of their abdomens that was seductive and pleasant to watch.

From the children's performance, it was evident that the cherished Nasila traditional dance would stand the test of time. Those in the compound came closer to watch. Several began to clap in time to the music as the tempo of the girls' gyration speeded up.

Taiyo was stupefied. She clapped until her hands hurt. And all along she was lost in thought. The sight of those young school children singing and dancing so joyfully brought back the memories of her high school days. Her heart warmed up with elation when she recalled the numerous occasions when she excelled in music festivals and was awarded and garlanded. Broadcasting stations recognised her talent and encouraged her to take music as a career. She had taken for granted that her parents who on several occasions applauded her when she won trophies on account of her performance, would not have any objection if she pursued the desire of her heart as her future career. An F.M Radio Station that had for a long time followed her music development keenly, offered her a chance to discover and explore the worth of her talent by enabling her attend a music extravaganza in Mombasa at their cost. Thereafter, she was to attend a short course after which her abilities and suitability were to be gauged.

When she broke the news, which she thought would delight her parents, her father was furious. He curtly refused to grant her permission and angrily disallowed any further discussion on the matter, effectively crushing any hopes she may have developed of making music her career.

He stated categorically that no daughter of Ole Kaelo would so demean herself and her family as to perform in public in exchange of monetary gain. It was one thing to perform in a school festival, he reasoned, but to perform to a public gallery was one short step to harlotry. No amount of persuasion would change her father's mind.

She knew without any doubt in her heart that she still loved music. She always told herself that music was in her blood. How she wished she would meet that young man who coached those young children to sing and perform so enthrallingly well.

It wasn't until three in the afternoon that the carnival mood that had been getting merrier by the hour, exploded into a frenzied celebration. The exultant crowd in the homestead broke into an exciting rhythm of exuberant song and dance. Taiyo and Resian, who by then had retreated into the shadow of a spreading *Oloponi* tree, from where they watched the colourful movement of the throng of dancers, could not resist the urge to join them. They quickly stepped into the crowd and began to dance. And so did their mother who, tugging their aunt, *yeiyoo-botor* also joined other dancers who were already heaving their chests forward and backward as they chanted the refrain. Before long, they spotted their three other aunts who too were amongst the crowd of dancers. Uncle Simiren was there too, dancing, his bald head shinning like a piece of iron sheet in the afternoon sun. Then they saw their father.

"Look at *Papaai*!" said Taiyo giggling as she pointed out their father amidst a group of dancing elders. He held himself stiffly as he danced awkwardly.

"He doesn't seem to know how to dance," commented Resian jokingly and then added mischievously. "He should ask uncle Simiren to coach him."

They laughed heartily as they hid their faces behind other dancers so that they did not come face to face with him lest they embarrassed him.

Just then, a shadowy figure suddenly appeared and swiftly walked past them. They simultaneously looked up and saw a man stare piercingly at them. He sneered at them contemptuously then quickly walked past the dancers and disappeared out of the gate. But that was not before they positively recognized him to be the young man who accosted and terrorised them on their first day in Nasila. They were shocked and suddenly, all the happiness and serenity that had hitherto pervaded their hearts dissipated. They now felt angry, terrified and isolated even when they were in the midst of the happy throng of revellers that was oblivious of what had befallen them.

It was at five o'clock when Simiren charmingly invited all those present to savour his brother's lavish hospitality. The elders and their wives were ushered into Ole Kaelo's spacious living room while the young men, young women and the children mingled happily in the lush, sprawling, well tended lawn.

Soon the ever dutiful daughters of *Ilmolelian* moved to and fro among the chattering throng with trays heavily laden with choice pieces of meat that the revellers ate ravenously to their fill. When beverages had been distributed all round and everyone had had their share, the young people departed having acknowledged that a true descendant of *Ilmolelian* had finally arrived and taken his rightful position in the clan.

At seven o'clock in the evening after the lights had been put on, and the traditional *esuguroi* drink had been served in generous measures, tongues loosened and hearts gladdened. Soon after, the party gathered momentum and voices rose. Within no time, one could hardly be heard over the hubbub of talk and laughter. And as the pleasurable and lively celebration progressed, voices became animated; hands and arms gesticulated more vigorously while heads turned more often as eyes searched out acquaintances within the throng of revellers.

And it was all pomp and gaiety as ivory adorned and bejewelled fingers fluttered; bare shoulders gleamed in the light; multicoloured bead ornaments glittered upon elaborately bedecked necks; pendulous *Ilmiintoni* of all colours dangled loosely down extended ear-lobes; and the bright colours of *lesos, kangas, red shukas* and multicoloured blankets, all turned the Kaelo living room into a kaleidoscope of shifting light and colour.

That evening, Mama Milanoi, the perfect hostess, was a woman with glamour. She was resplendently dressed in purple silk and moved happily from one group to the other talking cheerfully: her laughter ringing out pleasantly. That was her home and that was her evening. And she intended that no one present in that living room would leave with any shred of doubt in his or her heart as to who was *Enopeny enkang* of the Kaelo homestead.

Taiyo was watching with amusement as her mother moved from one group of revellers to another when suddenly her eye caught sight of a tall man who was advancing across the room towards her direction. She recognized him and her heart missed a beat. Momentarily his bright eyes met hers. They were perfectly set on a young and handsome face that was above an equally impressive attire of red *shukas*.

Across the room, maternal instincts directed Mama Milanoi to look at the direction of her daughter, Taiyo, in time to see two events happening simultaneously: a handsome young man striding towards her daughter and her husband sending a seemingly corrosive glance in the direction of his daughter.

"One can never tell with Ole Kaelo," Mama Milanoi thought aloud. "He can be the most dreadful spoilsport."

Kaelo, however, did not interfere and Mama Milanoi watched from across the room, smiling a little, as the two young people met. How lovely Taiyo looked that night! She thought she was her very image when she was at her age. She watched the two as they exchanged greetings and their smiles as their eyes met. Then he seemed to ask her a question and she, with downcast eyes, gave him a demure smile. For a moment, Mama Milanoi stood there allowing a ridiculous small blade of envy cut through her heart. She let her heart wander and wondered what might have happened had she met a handsome young man such as the one her daughter was speaking with, fallen in love and got married. If she had had such an opportunity, what might her life have been? May be she would not have been joined at the hip with a bully like…

"Do you know that young man your daughter is talking to?" It was her brother-in-law Simiren standing beside her. "She needs to be informed immediately."

"Is he a bad boy?" Mama Milanoi asked urgently fearing for her daughter.

"Far from it," Simiren answered reassuringly. "In fact he is one of the finest and dependable young men that we have in Nasila."

"What's Taiyo to be informed about him, then?" Mama Milanoi asked, puzzled. "Or is he married and has a vicious wife?"

"You are wrong again," Simiren said smiling broadly. "It is simply this, the young man whose name is Joseph Parmuat is a brother to your daughter. Parmuat, his father is of the clan of *Ilmolelian* of *Iloorasha-kineji* sub-clan, like ourselves. It is therefore not only a great abomination if we were to allow their ignorance to desecrate Nasila cultural values, but their illicit contact would be a taboo that is bound to have untold consequences on us all."

From the corner where she stood watching the noisy events in the living room, Resian saw the meeting of her sister and the lithe young man who she had earlier in the day said was handsome. For some strange reasons, she felt alarmed. Was it jealousy consuming her? But why should she be jealous of her sister? No it was not jealousy. It was fear. It was the fear of losing Taiyo. Taiyo was hers. She was her only sister, her only friend and her only ally. She could not dare lose her or share her love with anybody. Never! When she gave thought to the possibility, her young heart nearly stopped beating. For a brief, almost frightening moment, she allowed the negative emotions take the better of her. She swore – *inkilani-e-papaai* – she would hate anyone, who came between her and her sister.

Taiyo saw her sister come and she thought how timely her arrival was, for she had wanted to share that moment of joy and ecstasy with someone close to her. She smiled dazzlingly as she introduced the two to each other and Resian was rewarded by a twinkle in the young man's eyes as he shook her delicately soft hand. There followed a brief, slightly awkward silence. Around them, the talk and the laughter of the revellers rose and fell like the sound of waves beating upon flooded river banks. Before they had time to say another word, uncle Simiren and their mother stood beside them. It chagrined Taiyo greatly to be told of her clan's relations with the young man she had just met.

Then the time finally came. It was the time to formally receive Parsimei Ole Kaelo and his family back into the *Ilmolelian* fold and into the larger family of the Nasila people and offer blessings for his family's well being.

To conduct the sacred ceremony was an old man who had been sitting in the company of other two old men at a corner of the living room. He was sagging with age and his face was splodged with a maze of wrinkles. His lips had collapsed on his toothless gums while his scalp showed patches of white skin through his thin grey hair.

Earlier in the evening Taiyo had looked at the old man with a piteous face as he sat with his elbows on the table, holding a joint of mutton in both hands and, trying to gnaw on it with his toothless gums. Seeing how much he struggled, obviously with very little success, she had sympathized with him. She had gone into the kitchen fetched a plateful of rice, peas, beans and potatoes and handed it to him. The old man received the food with gratitude, while the other two elders eyed him with envy.

"Thank you very much, my dear child." the old man had said and then asked curiously. "May I know whose daughter you are, my child?"

"I am Ole Kaelo's daughter," answered Taiyo impatiently not wanting to prolong the discussion with the decrepit old man.

Later, Taiyo was surprised to see that the seemingly helpless and toothless old man, was one of the most revered elders in the community. She saw him get up from where he sat with the other two old men, and leaning heavily on his walking stick, moved to the centre of the living room. His pace was dignified as he walked with his chin up and his mouth set in a hard straight line. That was the time that Taiyo observed his heavily wrinkled face. There was a haughty set to his features. For a moment Taiyo felt as if he had fastened his eyes on her and that his gaze was like a physically oppressive force upon her. She suddenly felt much in awe of him.

When he began to speak, his voice boomed and its resonance filled the crowded room. He introduced himself as old Ole Musanka, a member of the *Ilmakesen* clan and of *Ilterito* age-set. He said Nasila was a Maa house and anybody born of Maa, was entitled to its shelter. Maa culture was the blood and marrow that gave sustenance to the body. And the body was the collective masses of Maa. Ole Kaelo, he said, was a tiny strand of hair that had been blown away from its owner's head by a gust of wind. The same wind that had blown it away had blown the strand back onto its owner's head. He said the head could not refuse to receive back the returning strand. But the onus was upon the strand to attach and coil itself back onto the rest of the hair on the head and blend with it. If it did not, he warned, it would drop and get trampled upon the ground. He advised Ole Kaelo to re-assimilate himself into his people's culture.

"Those of us who have been listening to the sound of bells of our cattle," he said quoting the children's song, "know that the cattle of Ole Kaelo are home-bound. They were bound to come, for the founder said when a rat begins to smell, it returns to its mother's home."

"And home is never far from one who is still alive," one of the elders interjected.

"And speaking of home," Ole Musanka said candidly, "Ole Kaelo must be told, home is not this house however magnificent it may be. Home is Maa, home is Nasila, home is family and home is the children. Kill one of the four pillars, and there is no home to speak about. Sever yourself from the culture of your people and you effectively become *olkirikoi*, a man of no fixed abode, your elegant house notwithstanding. Where are the women of Maa? Embrace the wife and children of Kaelo and bring them back into the Nasila fold. Where are the elders of *Ilmolelian?* There is your man. Cut him loose from the snares of alien cultures. I am through."

Then he had a parting shot for Taiyo and Resian. "Do not listen to crusaders of an alien culture that is being perpetrated by a certain *Entangoroi* called *Emakererei*. The wasp advocates that we maintain *intoiye nemengalana* amongst our daughters. *Taba*! May she go down with the setting sun!"

53

After that voluble curse, the old man blessed the Ole Kaelos. He had a special blessing for the daughter of Ole Kaelo who served him with a special dish that evening. He prophesied that she will be a mother of the next leader of Nasila and Maa.

When Parsimei Ole Kaelo later learnt that the daughter mentioned by the seer was Taiyo, he was elated. But Mama Milanoi was troubled. What she feared for her daughters was turning to be real. Taiyo and Resian also felt troubled. They felt squeamish as they stood there, their downcast eyes riveted upon the floor, fear and hopelessness tormenting their young hearts. But who was that person, they wondered, who was referred to as a 'wasp' and who evoked so much virulent hatred amongst the people of Nasila?

Chapter Five

Confusion reigned supreme in the forlorn hearts of the two daughters of Ole Kaelo, immediately after the homecoming ceremony. Feelings of anger, panic, helplessness and hopelessness alternated stressfully in their minds.

Taiyo was the first to be overwhelmingly overcome by lethargic feelings and she sluggishly left the now nearly empty living room for their bedroom. Resian remained behind for a moment helping their mother and other women gather and move utensils to the kitchen and tidy the room.

When she finally got to the bedroom, Resian found it half-lit and quiet. Only one lamp that Taiyo had left for her, still burned. Preparing for bed, she blundered about the darkened bedroom muttering to herself, her movements angrily sharp. Taiyo tensed a little as her sister slid into the bed beside her.

"Taiyo-e-yeiyo," she called huskily, as soon as she settled in bed, a thread of miserable anger discernible in her voice. "Taiyo-e-yeiyo, *doi*."

Taiyo did not answer and kept her breathing normal, feigning sleep. She wondered what her sister's grouse could be at that time, for she always had a grouse about something; if it was not mistreatment by their father, it was her failure to talk to their father to allow them go back to Nakuru to join the Egerton University. But she had no qualms that night about soothing her sister's sour mood.

Her mind felt numb and devoid of feelings. At that very moment she felt utterly confused and wretched.

It was true that she had promised to approach their father about a possibility of their attending the university, but it was equally true that an appropriate opportunity had not availed itself. She knew the importance her sister attached to the subject, and therefore did not want to rush it. She was aware too that, that afternoon, her attention had been drawn away from the narrow confines of her sister's troubles. Yes, even if it was for a brief moment, when she stood with Joseph Parmuat in their living room that evening, she had felt justifiably separated from her sister. But wasn't that natural? After all, they were not children any more, and very soon, she reasoned, they would physically be separated and each would have to fend for herself. Furthermore, that afternoon, when she listened to the children sing and watched them dance, when she later had an opportunity to talk to Joseph Parmuat about music, she became aware of a restlessness that she would have considered totally alien to her nature. It was as if she stood on the threshold of an unknown room, or on a mountain top, excitedly waiting for the sun to rise at dawn to reveal a breathtakingly beautiful scenery which she had not seen before.

Later that night, lying with her back to her sister, her head beneath the blankets, Taiyo allowed her mind to float fleetingly. Like a swift, light cherub, it glided into all directions opening, probing, examining and analysing recent events in their lives that had been most stressful and tormenting. And on her part, lying on her back beside her sister, Resian felt Taiyo's warmth and heard her steady breathing, as she stared grimly into the darkness, feeling unhappy, afraid and utterly alone. She too was troubled.

It was a long night for the two girls. The chirp of the insects, the croaking of the frogs and the mournful calls of the night birds, echoed through the dark house as they lay on their bed, each one of them awake but deep in thought.

"Away with the barbaric culture," cried Taiyo silently and bitterly, "Away with the archaic way of life."

She wept until she had no more tears in her eyes, then she sobbed dryly. Was there no guarantee of justice in life? How could she come across the man who she thought would have filled the void in her heart so fittingly and instantly lose him to the ancient doubtful ancestral links? She was angry with everybody in Nasila, but more so with her uncle Simiren who she infuriatingly blamed for ruining her relationship with Joseph Parmuat. The mere mention of Joseph Parmuat's name evoked delightful feelings that warmly excited her heart. She wondered whether he too could be sleepless at that very hour thinking of her. Did he know before that they were of the same clan and therefore forbidden to have any heterosexual links whatsoever? She thought the gross unfairness of the regressive and outdated culture was definitely a searing torment to her and to all others who were of progressive minds.

But not all was lost though, she reasoned, a flicker of hope lighting up her sorrowful heart. Within the few minutes they had stood there in the living room, Joseph Parmuat had made two promises: to visit her in their home the following day and if her parents agreed, he would coach her in the traditional music and dance she was so much interested in. And her mother who was then present had said, to her delight, that the young man was welcome to visit them the following day. But for the other request about coaching, her mother had categorically refused to be drawn into it, saying that it was Taiyo's father's territory.

Should Joseph Parmuat fulfil those two promises, she thought, she would be utterly satisfied. But all depended on her father.

Resian's situation grew worse. The moment she got beneath the blankets, tears began to run freely down her face. Whether their cause lay in the inescapable loneliness that seemed to stalk her like a lost young leopard, or in the intolerable confusion caused by the ever present insecurity, she could not tell. All she knew was that her world was spinning. Even the bed she was in, seemed to be moving.

The pain in her heart was like the bruising aftermath of a blow. She closed her eyes, took a deep breath, then she exhaled slowly, forcing herself to face the shattering situation that threatened to destroy the world she had known until then. The threat of circumcision was becoming real. Old Ole Musanka had said they should undergo the rite.

She shuddered and squirmed when she recalled the day the *enkamuratani* (circumciser) visited their house in the company of other village women. She was a thin old woman of about sixty years and of average height whose back and shoulders still stood straight. Unlike the other women who were dressed in traditional *shukas*, she wore a tee shirt that was much too large for her spare frame and a heavy, shapeless, skirt-like garment. Her gnarled, calloused feet were bare. When Taiyo shamelessly and burning with curiosity had asked her to show them her tools of trade, she had sprung up with the agility of a young woman and dashed swiftly to where she had left her bag on the table. After rummaging about among her things, she had fished out a dirty oilskin that she held aloft while she triumphantly, like one who had won a match, grinned and stared at them.

The most startling thing about her, was her eyes. They were young, clear, bright and inquisitive. They were, obviously, windows of an exceedingly alert mind.

What horrified Resian and sent shivers right deep into the pit of her stomach, creating a permanent traumatic image in her mind, was the *Olmurunya*. That was a bladelike tool shaped like a smoothing plane blade, that she unwrapped out of the oilskin. She brandished it aloft with her gnarled, withered claw-like hand. She dramatized as she demonstrated to them the dexterity of her fingers and showed the way she went about her profession of transforming young girls into young women through the cut of *Olmurunya*.

Resian did not find it funny. When she thought of the barbaric operation, she felt scared and inched closer to Taiyo who lay there beside her. She thought of the aggressive young man who grinned impudently at them and kept reminding them that they were *intoiye nemengalana*. Would he one day grab them and drag them to *enkamuratani* and let her *olmurunya* transform them into decent women of Nasila? God forbid!

She declared that those withered claw-like hands would only touch her over her dead body! But the only escape route available to them was via her sister who lay there sleeping and breathing quietly. However, she had failed her. She was angry with Taiyo for she had trusted her to persuade their father to allow them return to Nakuru and enroll at the Egerton University, but she had not even tried. Nor had she seemed to listen to her fears on the possibility of being abducted and sent to *enkamuratani*.

She would press her sister even more. And with that promise, dawn came, and she rubbed her irritated swollen red eyes, as the sunlight flooded in and lit all the dark and hidden corners of their bedroom. She stirred and struggled out of bed, grimly set about to begin another day.

Taiyo also stirred. She did not uncover her head, though. She was glad to have a few more minutes under the blankets to collect her thoughts and feelings before facing another day. For after an all but sleepless night in the dark hours, her emotions had alternated alarmingly between an overwhelming and indisputable reckless elation when she thought of Joseph Parmuat and anger, panic and bitterness borne of the disturbing recent events.

It was morning also in the master bedroom and Parsimei was waking up. He lazily turned in his bed, opened his eyes, and yawned: a mighty master's yawn. For a moment he listened to the birds that chirruped away in the trees that surrounded his house and his heart gladdened. He sent a furtive glance at his wife who was still asleep beside him and smiled at her childlike face as she lay there peacefully. Oh, didn't he have a wife there! He was elated. The previous day, she had graced the homecoming ceremony prettily and had played her role of hostess admirably. And that had pleased him greatly. He nudged her lightly and she turned and opened her eyes slightly.

"Are you awake, Lanoo-ai?" he called her affectionately. "It is wake-up time, my dear."

"Already?" she asked drowsily and yawned sleepily. "That was the shortest night I have known in my life."

"It was because we were all very tired," he said listlessly. "Hosting that ceremony greatly sapped our energy."

"And what an exhausting day!" Mama Milanoi exclaimed yawning and stretching. "I am glad it is now behind us."

"You know, as much as I do, the demands of the culture we have now been ushered into," he said.

Mama Milanoi's mind became alert. Her eyes focused and she opened them wide as she paid attention to what her husband was saying. She knew his words could completely change their lives and the lives of their two daughters.

In all those years they were in Nakuru and as they raised the girls to maturity, she had known that her husband was not a strict adherent of the Nasila traditions. He had insisted upon the outward observance of those traditions that he considered to be the hallmark of decency and respectability. But as he had said, she knew as much as he did the demands of the culture into which they had plunged themselves.

She was born and brought up in that culture and therefore, she knew the extent of its tentacles. She knew that as a family, they were already in breach of the tradition, for keeping at home their grown up girls as *intoiye nemengalana* instead of sending for *enkamuratani* to transform them from little girls into young women. That was what happened to her and that was what culture had expected her to do; to prepare her daughters, physically and mentally, to face the challenges of responsible womanhood and motherhood. But there was a dilemma: force the girls to undergo the rituals and lose their faith, love and confidence, or refuse to yield to the tradition and become a pariah in the *Ilmolelian* clan and Nasila society. It was like the legendary unenviable dilemma that faced a man called Ole Nkipida at a deserted hut when he was chased into it by a lion, just to be confronted by a hungry python at the door.

"Yes, I know how much is demanded of us, my husband," she said demurely at last, "but we have to think of the interest of our family first."

"What do you mean?" he asked suddenly sitting up. "I hope you don't imply that our culture comes second. Do you?"

"Not really, my husband," she said ruefully, beating a hasty retreat. "Our culture is everything and it rules our lives."

"Good," he said authoritatively. "Now listen, you must immediately start counselling the girls to understand their roles as potential wives of the men of Nasila. Prepare them to appreciate and accept their future responsibilities as mothers and home builders."

"I'll do that, my husband." she said quietly.

"One other thing," he said evenly. "I'll ask Simiren to request that young teacher called Parmuat, who is of our clan and therefore a brother to the girls, to find time to teach them a few home truths. After that we shall call *enkamuratani* to play her part before we give them away."

Those were the words, whose utterance she so dreaded. And once uttered, she knew, the words instantly became an inviolable edict. Now that he had spoken, the pain was already harrowing and the torment unbearable in her heart. She was already torn between her love for her daughters and her dutiful role of a faithful and obedient wife of Ole Kaelo. But in her culture there was no room for dissent, especially if the subject was in conformity with the culture. Who would side with her if she were to oppose the cultural rituals?

Her only ally would be the woman the elders of Nasila contemptuously called *entangoroi* or the wasp. Those who honoured her called her *Emakererei*, for she was said to have attended Makerere University in Uganda, where she obtained her degree in veterinary science. Mama Milanoi knew her well. Her actual names were *Minik ene Nkoitoi*. Outside Nasila, she was respected and honoured. At thirty, she was already managing an expansive government sheep ranch reputed to hold hundreds of thousands of sheep, about one hundred kilometers away from Nasila. Under her were hundreds of employees who worked at the ranch.

In Nasila however, she was regarded as the devil incarnate. She was hated and reviled for criticising and campaigning vigorously against the traditions that she said abused the rights of the girl child namely girls' circumcision and early marriages. And that had put her in direct collision with the people of Nasila. If she aligned herself with a person who Nasila regarded as having such an obnoxious reputation, where would her marriage stand?

As she lay beside her husband, she gave thought to what they stood for as a family. What did they believe in? Were they traditionalists or were they modernists?

In embracing the retrogressive cultural values, were they now progressing or regressing? Although Ole Kaelo had always been arrogant and impolite in his own way, she had discovered right from the time he married her, he had his own unique chivalrous qualities that neutralised his hubris.

However, ever since they returned to Nasila, a new Ole Kaelo was emerging. He was becoming a Nasilian very fast. And in the Nasilian society, women had no say. It was a patriarchal society where the *Emakererei* and her ilk were fighting to find relevance with little success. But what about herself, what was her position? Did she not support female genital mutilation that was prevalent among her people in Nasila? When she was a girl, girls' circumcision was relevant and she cherished it. It was a rite of passage. In her days there was hardly a girl who got pregnant before marriage. At the same time no girl got married before circumcision. And woe unto her who got pregnant before getting circumcised! She was derogatorily referred to as *entaapai*, and she and her family were always held in derision. She was often circumcised at the time of giving birth and married off to the oldest man in the village. Perhaps that was a deterrent to keep girls chaste in mind and body, she thought to herself.

She wondered what her daughters knew about F.G.M. She had never discussed the subject with them and she blamed herself for her failure to do so. But to be fair to herself she reasoned that before the retrenchment of her husband which caused their return to Nasila, F.G.M was a non-issue in her family. She had regarded the practice as an archaic rite that had been discarded and forgotten. But there it was now, rearing its ugly head and threatening to wreak havoc in the young innocent lives of her daughters.

She would have to broach the subject somehow and get to know what the girls had learned from their peers and other sources. One thing she was aware of was that her daughters did not expect their parents to lead them back through a dark alley, to a retrogressive world of excruciating pain and turmoil. The last thing she would have wished on her daughters was mental torture and torment. Although she knew how difficult it was to change her husband's mind on what he had set to do, the least she could do for them was to prepare a soft landing against what appeared to be an inevitable eventuality.

When they finally got up and went to the living room, Mama Milanoi and her husband found a clean, tidy and well arranged room, far from its appearance the night before. Heavy velvet curtains fluttered lazily in the still fresh air of the morning. Taiyo was busy ferrying breakfast from the kitchen to the table, while Resian, fragile and pretty in her velvet and lace morning gown, her hair piled upon her head, slumped in an armchair, her nose as always buried in a book; reading.

"Look at that daughter of yours," Ole Kaelo told his wife irritably. "While Taiyo works herself to the bone, she lazes about like an over-fed lizard in the hot afternoon sun."

"Resian-ai," her mother called fondly. "Would you please..."

"Would you sit up straight like a respectable girl," her father cut in sharply. "Look at the way you slouch and

65

slump in that chair like a good for nothing lout! I'll not be surprised if you soon become a hunchback!"

"Do sit up straight child," her mother added, with a sudden sharp petulance. "Don't get your father angry early in the morning."

Resian scowled her displeasure for being berated but nevertheless closed her book and scurried back to their bedroom.

Later in the day, Ole Kaelo took his wife and daughters to Nasila stores, to show them their brand new business. They were impressed and instantly liked it. The shop had opened for business two days earlier and it was already full of customers.

It was splendid, large and well stocked. The décor was discreetly and fashionably done while taking into consideration the kind of customers that were expected. The mahogany and brass counters and display cases gleamed. The display boards on the walls carried all kinds of tools, accessories and fittings. The tiled floor was polished to a shiny sheen while bevelled and etched glass and mirrors nailed on strategic pillars and walls reflected every image and glint of light with sparkling clarity. On a large float in the middle of the shop, a range of dairy equipment was exhibited with masterly craftsmanship; their superior quality complementing perfectly the surroundings that had been created to display them. There were milk pails, milk cans, buckets, and cream separators. Beside them were animal feeds and licks of all brands. Also displayed were herbicides, insecticides, alkaricides and fungicides.

Resian, eyeing the splendour with a rather jaundiced eye, nudged her sister and whispered, "All these must have cost *Papaai* a fortune. Need he have done all this? I hope when you finally come round to asking him to send us to the university, he will not say he has spent all his money on this business premises and the stock."

"Surely, Resian, can't you see?" Taiyo whispered back exasperated. "It is important that the shop displays a certain measure of opulence. The customers that *Papaai* wants to attract wouldn't want to shop in a place that resembles a junkyard. Do you remember the shop that *Papaai* took us to in Nakuru when he bought us those dresses and shoes? You loved the grandeur and splendour of the place, didn't you? It made you feel special. Well, that is what *Papaai* is trying to create here. Should he say he has spent all his money here, I will understand. And I dare say, it is well spent!"

Resian looked around her. Satisfying customers, or creating a suitable ambience to attract future profits were, to her, much less important than her burning ambition to go to the university. She cast her eyes to the ceiling and then turned and once more looked around her and said nonchalantly.

"Well, if you say so, big sister."

In one of the stores, they came across, a tall muscular man of about forty-five, bald-headed and amiable, who Kaelo introduced as the manager. His name was Maison. Kaelo left them in his hands and disappeared into yet another store. Maison, conducted them around, introducing them, with unconcealed pride and pleasure to his staff, who reverently bowed on learning that, that was the family of Kaelo.

At last, Maison led them into a neat office where a young beautiful secretary ushered them into a small, comfortable office. One wall was book lined and another entirely taken up by a large metal filing cabinet, its drawers precisely labelled and lettered. The papers on the large oval desk were tidily stacked, as were the magazines on a nearby table upon which stood a framed family colour photograph; taken when the girls were still young. Everything was neat and well-ordered. Without much explanation the girls knew it was their father's office.

It was while they were in Ole Kaelo's comfortable office that Mama Milanoi revealed their father's consent to Taiyo's request to be coached by Joseph Parmuat. Taiyo was enthralled. She hugged her mother and profusely thanked her for putting her case to their father so articulately and successfully.

That evening when they got home, Joseph Parmuat visited them. The moment he appeared at their door, the three Kaelo women instantly liked him: his broad smile, his hearty chuckle, his uproarious rich peals of laughter and his unbridled sense of humour were some of his most endearing qualities.

When Joseph Parmuat entered into their house, she stood back and watched as he was immediately drawn into the small intimate circle of their mother's attention. The girls had always known that their mother had an adroitness that made any man who approached her a part of that charming world of hers. Seeing how their mother monopolized him, for a moment, Taiyo could not suppress a surge of envy. Of course she knew the envy was misplaced, for only recently, since the advent of her own womanhood, had she began to understand her mother and herself. And even Resian, the ever gloomy pessimist of the Kaelo family, was laughing and talking excitedly beside their mother, looking up teasingly into the face of their newly acquired brother. It seemed as if the three Kaelo women had hatched a female conspiracy, of which Joseph Parmuat seemed to be enjoying tremendously, as any man would.

They were about to settle in their seats when they heard a knock. A man they had not seen before entered and greeted them confidently. Without waiting to be invited, he proceeded to find a seat. But that was not queer for it was in line with the Nasilian hospitality where every house was open to all sojourners. The girls looked askance at the man they considered an intruder. He was a quiet, well-built man of thirty or so. He wore a brown pair of trousers and a blue shirt that was not particularly neat. Taiyo thought there was something impersonal about his offhand attitude.

Until he told them what he wanted, or what he was up to, Mama Milanoi and her daughters had to contend with accommodating two incompatible guests in their living room.

Chapter Six

Whether it was by coincidence or by prior arrangement, the girls couldn't tell. But as soon as they had finished serving supper to Joseph Parmuat and the stranger, their father came into the house through the back door. He greeted the two men with little enthusiasm and proceeded to the living room. As was their habit, when their father came into the living room, the girls quickly gathered the dishes, tidied the table and instantly disappeared into the kitchen.

No sooner had they gone into the kitchen than their mother summoned them; their father wanted to speak to them. The girls immediately looked up at their mother enquiringly, apprehensive of the rare summon. Their father usually preferred talking to them through their mother. With trepidation, they trooped back to the living room, steeling themselves to hear whatever he had to say.

The father sat in his armchair facing the fireplace while their mother sat at the end of the sofa. The girls went to sit next to their mother. Joseph Parmuat sat in an armchair not very far from their father and the stranger had not left the dining table where he sat alone.

When he began to speak, their father did not address them directly. Instead he addressed Joseph Parmuat. The girls knew their father well. He liked to address issues and expound on them in order to impress points upon his audience. And he was always impressive when he made his speeches. When they lived in Nakuru, he often took them to official functions or special occasions, and they loved to listen to his pompous speeches.

So after meandering and digressing, in the process telling Parmuat of the difficulties he encountered going to school and how he began to plan for his own future very early in his life, he finally came to the point.

"These children may not know," he said suddenly turning his attention to his daughters. "They may not know and I want to tell them now, that you are their brother. You are no lesser a brother to them than their own mother's son would have been. You are my son as much as their mother's son would have been my son. Perhaps their mother has already told them, and if she has not, she will tell them tonight that Parmuat's family and Kaelo's family are one. We are all of *Ilmolelian* clan, of *Iloorasha-kineji* sub-clan."

He told Joseph Parmuat that he had brought up his daughters well. They were well behaved and that he was proud of them. However, having been away from Nasila all their lives, they had missed out on the the basic cultural values that harmonized the lives of Nasila people.

In addition to what they learnt at school or in addition to what they were yet to learn through books, he stressed, it was imperative that they learned habits, traditions and their culture that would make their parents and the Nasila people proud of them. He added that although he considered the girls intelligent, there was need for them to develop into responsible mature women of the future. That was necessary, he said emphatically, because there was nothing better that parents looked forward to, than to see their children settle in their own homes.

He had hastened to add that although, at their age

they might consider what he was saying as ridiculously irrelevant, he knew by experience that there was nothing better than beginning to plan for one's future early. He warned the girls that they might find a few cultural demands obnoxious but they would have to be stoic and accept them with the understanding that it was those not-too-pleasant traditions that nurtured and bound their people together. "And those families that had refused to rejoin their people," he added thoughtfully," "had been blasted into smithereens by alien cultures."

"It should never happen to us," he concluded dramatically.

When their mother spoke to them later, emphasizing what their father had told them, they wore blank faces and deliberately concealed their reaction. She therefore, did not realize that they held extremely divergent views.

That was the most exciting news that Taiyo had received ever since they came to Nasila. She was exultant. Although their father never for once mentioned that Joseph Parmuat was to coach her in traditional music and dance, the fact that he had allowed them to interact with him filled her heart with pride and joy. And she could hardly hide her elation. Even the repeated assertion that Joseph Parmuat was their brother by virtue of their cultural links, failed to daunt her spirit. Was she simply infatuated with him? If she was, she hoped the feeling would soon simmer down. What pleased her most however, was that she now had a confidant whom she could ask some of those embarrassing questions that she could not dare ask her mother or anybody else.

It was however different for Resian. She was furious.

Deep right into her heart she was seething with ire. And it irked her terribly to have had to sit there listening to their father as he prepared them for a journey that she thought was to lead them back to the stone-age era. She scornfully dismissed the cultural coaching that Joseph Parmuat was to undertake as worthless, waste of time and an act of imbecility. She likened the whole saga to a grown-up person whose mind degenerated into an idiot and had to content with playing with mud. It was utter foolishness!

"It may not be as bad as you imagine, little sister," Taiyo said, trying to mollify her angry sister, "maybe by the time brother Parmuat is through with us, we shall be the wiser."

"Wiser indeed!" jeered Resian, "Yes, by the time he shall be through with us, we shall have been taught a great lesson in stoicism. We won't blink or wince even as *enkamuratani* mutilates our sexuality into smithereens!"

After they got to their bedroom, Taiyo poured tea from a flask that she carried from the kitchen, into two cups. She handed one to Resian who took it without raising her eyes. Taiyo was already aware of the tension between them. In all their lives, only twice had they had a serious quarrel. On each of those occasions, Taiyo recalled, the hurt had been exacerbated by the breaking of a bond that had always been so firm as to be unquestioned. But the two had a resilient character and no sooner had they quarrelled than they were reconciled and were cheerful again. The problem that time round was that they did not see things in the same light. Whereas she was also happy that they now had Joseph Parmuat as a brother who they would interact

73

with and discuss some of the perplexing questions that bedevilled them, Resian suspected that Taiyo would use her newly acquired acquaintance with him to marginalize her. And she was not ready to be abandoned by her sister.

Resian lay, much later in the night, fully clothed except for shoes and a jacket, listening to her sister's slight and delicate snores next to her underneath the blankets. She turned and took her by the shoulder and rocked her slightly.

"Taiyo-e-yeiyo, are you asleep?"

She heard Taiyo move and turn to face her. Then she dimly saw her as she lifted herself upon her elbow to level herself with her. And on her part, Resian leaned forward, speaking very softly.

"I am disturbed," she said. "I am beginning to think it is disadvantageous being a woman in this society."

"For heaven's sake, Resian," exclaimed Taiyo, making a small sound, affectionate and exasperate. "Is it worth staying awake the whole night thinking of such mundane things?"

"Call them mundane," Resian pursued relentlessly. "But I keep wondering what would have happened had we been sons rather than daughters. Do you think father would have looked for a clan sister to coach us and take us through the dim cultural paths of Nasila?"

"Resian, honestly, I don't know any better than you. But, little sister, your guess is just as good as mine. Most likely we would have been let loose to romp about in the village and gather our experiences as we go along."

"Exactly!" Resian said bitterly. "Yes, because we are females, a male in the name of a clan brother is sought to come along and teach us the A B C D of a good Nasilian wife so that we shall please our future husbands. No, I refuse to be taught. I will either be taught at the university what is universally beneficial to all mankind or be taught nothing!"

The following afternoon, when Joseph Parmuat came to visit them, the mysterious stranger also came. He wore a shabby, old, black, woollen suit and a clean but wrinkled white shirt. He had had a haircut and his previously bushy moustache had been trimmed. Even his muddy shoes had been cleaned and polished to a bright black sheen. He came carrying on his shoulder, a hindquarter of mutton wrapped up in a khaki brown paper. Mama Milanoi received the meat gratefully.

That had become the man's habit. He would disappear only to saunter in like the owner of the house two days later, bringing with him either a bag of flour, a bag of sugar, a quarter of mutton or a large bundle of lamb chops. He would hand over his gifts to Mama Milanoi quietly and because the house was always frequented by visitors, any additional food stuff was always welcome.

Later the girls came to know that the stranger was known as Olarinkoi. Whether their father had known him before, they couldn't tell. What they came to acknowledge was that their father had accepted the strange man's presence in his home graciously. And soon the man made his stay useful and his services invaluable and indispensable. He would often come very early in the morning to tend the flower gardens and slash the grass on the lawn. By the time they gathered for breakfast, he would be sitting silently ready to eat with them as if he was a member of the family. And although the girls hardly ever spoke to him, they had nevertheless become completely accustomed to his presence and strangely counted him as one of them when preparing meals.

On his part, Olarinkoi acted almost indifferently towards Taiyo and Resian. He directed his attention to their father and mother. What perplexed the girls was his ever silent presence in their house. He was always there, sitting quietly and staring unblinkingly, like a leopard would while stealthily stalking an antelope.

Joseph Parmuat did not like Olarinkoi. The two hardly acknowledged one another's presence and most of the time they did not even exchange greetings. But when Joseph Parmuat discussed a subject with the girls, Olarinkoi would listen keenly to what he was telling them. Once in a while he would butt in and give his unsolicited advice or his own version of a story.

The following day at about eleven o'clock in the morning, Taiyo, Resian and their mother were in the kitchen peeling potatoes in preparation for lunch. They were joined by the girls' aunt, *yeiyo-botorr,* who, after greetings, also took a knife and began peeling the potatoes with them. Even as they peeled potatoes, each girl had her own other assignment that went along simultaneously with what they were doing. Taiyo was cooking a meat stew. She took great care in its preparation, ensuring that all the necessary ingredients were in proper proportions, and that each was added to the mixture at the right time. The heat was also regulated so that the meat fried gently in its own fat until it was deliciously golden brown, before adding chopped coriander, tomatoes, onions and a little bit of curry powder to make a tasty rich thick gravy. Any time she added a little water, she threw in a pinch of salt and tasted the gravy to make sure that the taste was just right.

Resian had already cooked the rice that was now simmering slowly at one corner of the kitchen. She had already placed live charcoal on the lid of the *sufuria* so that the heat equally emanated from the top as well as from its bottom.

"What a diligent pair of workers you have here my *enkaini*," said *yeiyo-botorr* cheerfully in genuine praise of the girls. "And they are wonderful cooks too!"

"Whom would they take after if they are not good workers?" Mama Milanoi asked equally cheerful. "Their father is a diligent worker and so am I. When they eventually get married and are accused of laziness, or when their husbands complain that they can't prepare tasty meals, they will not blame us."

"No one can accuse us of laziness," cut in Taiyo happily, her spirit buoyed up by her aunt's praise. "And *yeiyo* here has been our best and ever resourceful teacher."

"That is as it should be," *Yeiyo-botorr* enthused, "We were taught by our mothers who were also taught by their mothers, and so on and on back to the time we ascended the Kerio Valley."

"I have no problem acquiring more and more knowledge, skills and even specialized experience," Resian said in a flat defiant tone that had Taiyo squirming with apprehension. "I have no problem at all and I thank *Yeiyo* for her untiring effort in teaching us. But my question is: do we go to all these lengths to please some lazy bunch of busybodies who do nothing but lounge about in the living rooms, yawning and stretching, waiting for tasty food to land on the table before them? No, I refuse to be taught to solely please male counterparts. They can also cook, and they can, and should also learn to please us females. Period!"

Yeiyo-botorr was shocked. Mama Milanoi was dumbfounded and was at a complete loss for words. Taiyo stared at her sister in consternation.

"Resian-*siake*-!" pleaded Taiyo "Please give respect to *Yeiyoo bottor* and stop your uncalled for tirade.

"But surely, Resian," her mother said, regaining her composure. "Have you no respect for your father who is also male? What have gotten into you, child, lately?" And turning to her "*enkaini, Yeiyo-botorr,* this child was not like this before we came here. I don't know what has gone wrong."

"Nothing is wrong with me," Resian retorted furiously. And pointing at the living room with her finger, she fiercely charged, "I have no quarrel with my father for whom I have tremendous respect. It is the likes of *Olarinkoi* I am mad at, and all those other males who come here ordering us to do that or the other for them, simply because they are males. When women visit us, they give us the leeway to respond to their requests. But as we burn our fingers here, Mr. Olarinkoi is dozing off comfortably in our living room waiting for his lunch and possibly a little angry and impatient with us for delaying it."

"It is enough," cried *Yeyo—botorr* viciously. She instantly abandoned the peeling of potatoes and threw the knife into the pails that held the peeled potatoes and supporting herself by holding onto a nearby wall, she slowly and painfully lifted her large, heavy body and struggled to stand up. "My *enkaini*, I agree with you that something is wrong with our child. And I think I know what ails her. Come along with me and I will tell you what I think ails her."

"I am not sick…" Resian was saying when she was cut short by Taiyo.

"Even if you are not sick, you cannot argue with *Yeiyo-botorr*," Taiyo told her sternly as soon as they were out of earshot of their mother and *Yeiyo-botorr*, "there are things one has to learn on their own. One of them is that you cannot antagonize the older people by arguing with them however untenable their argument may be. That goes without saying, my dear little sister."

"I know what is wrong with your daughter," yeiyo-botorr told Mama Milanoi harshly as they walked out of the house, "Your daughter has *Olkuenyi*. You know what that is! It is a bad spirit. And it is in her blood. You can now see the danger of keeping *intoiye nemengalana* at home. It is not healthy and it is neither in the interest of the children nor their parents. To hide a boil that is under the armpit is unwise, for sooner or later it will burst and emit a foul smell. It is time to circumcise your daughters and get rid of *Olkuenyi*. It is that simple." And she was gone.

Resian outburst troubled both her mother and her sister Taiyo. Mama Milanoi considered what her *enkaini* had said about the bad spirit called *olkuenyi* and she shuddered with apprehension. She knew what *olkuenyi* was.

In Nakuru, where she had been, the town people would have called it *kisirani*. It was always regarded as an ominous harbinger to a terrible thing. It was said to be contagious, and therefore one with *olkuenyi* was shunned and avoided like the plague. The suggestion that by spilling blood through circumcision the ill-spirit could be purged away once and for all, was not new to her.

When she was young, a lot of diseases and especially those which could not be properly diagnosed were dealt with through a blood-letting treatment known as *angam*. In that practice, the part of the body where the ailment was supposed to originate from was identified and several nicks were made on the skin and the blood sucked out.

She wondered whether she should tell her husband about her *enkaini's* diagnosis of their daughter's ailment. She would not be surprised if he summoned the *enkamuratani* the first thing the following morning with her *olmurunya*, and have the job done forthwith. If that happened, she knew it would terribly hurt the girls.

Although Taiyo did not like *Olarinkoi*, she did not hate him. She just did not care a hoot whether he ate or slept hungry. She wondered why her sister Resian hated him with such passion. And thinking of the man, she wondered who he was. Their father did not tell them that he was of their clan *Ilmolelian*, the way he told them about Joseph Parmuat. Who was he then? What was his background? And what was he doing in their home day in day out? Although he did odd jobs in their compound, Taiyo knew he was not an employee, and in fact when their father wanted a thorough job done at the compound, he always hired a man to do it. And obviously the occasional foodstuffs that he brought into the house could not be the reason that made their father tolerate him. She knew their father was well-off and therefore did not depend on the miserly bundles of food that he occasionally brought into their house. What was his mission in their home?

So when Joseph Parmuat came in that afternoon, Taiyo enquired about *Olarinkoi*. In his usual jocular manner, he first roared with hearty laughter. Then he asked her whether any of them had fallen in love with him and whether that was the reason why they were digging out his history. Taiyo joined in the cheerful laughter interjecting to say it was much easier to fall in love with a creepy cold serpent than it was possible to fall in love with the likes of Olarinkoi. Seriously, Joseph Parmuat said he knew two people who went by the name of Olarinkoi. He knew the person who sat in their sitting room and knew of another who went by that name who lived more than one hundred and fifty years before.

"Which of the two do you want to know about?" he asked in his usually humorous way. "Don't ask me if they are related, for I have no idea."

"Tell me about the two," said Taiyo cheerfully, curiosity taking the better of her. "Hope the one who lived more than one hundred and fifty years ago did not have a tail and lived on trees like a monkey!"

"To the contrary, my dear sister," Joseph Parmuat chuckled, tickled by Taiyo's comic description. "The older fellow is more defined than the one we know physically."

"Tell me about the one we know physically," she said excitedly, her anticipation of an exciting story firing her curiosity. "And then you may tell me about the legendary one later."

He told her the much he knew about Olarinkoi. The man was a mystery. Nobody seemed to know him well. A man who thought he knew something about him said he was of *Ilukumae* clan and came from a place called *Polonga,* about two hundred kilometers from Nasila. Another who thought he knew him better disagreed. He said he thought the man belonged to the *Iltaro-sero* clan and that he came from a place called *Enooloitikoishi,* not far from where that woman who Nasila people demonized and called her a wasp, managed a government sheep ranch. A third person said he knew him very well and that he was of *Ilmolelian* clan but an *Olkirikoi,* a good for nothing wanderer who survived by ingratiating himself with the rich, offering to do odd jobs for them. A fourth person dismissed all the rest and described Olarinkoi as a useless sycophant who changed allegiance to clans as often as a chameleon changed its colour.

"Who do you think Olarinkoi, is then?" he asked Taiyo in jest amidst aproarious laughter. "Tell me, girl who is he?"

"He is the typical Nasilian gentleman," she said shaking with laughter. "Yes, a little of him is sprinkled upon the lives of all of you, Nasilian men!"

"I hope you are joking," he said seriously. "It is tragic if that is the way you judge all of us."

"More or less," she answered jokingly." "But that is beside the point. Now that we have failed to place the present day Olarinkoi, tell me about the old Olarinkoi. Maybe by understanding the old we may come to know the present and possibly know the one who will emerge in future."

Taiyo sat quietly as Joseph Parmuat narrated the moving story of the legendary Olarinkoi.

The saga of the extremely brutal and despotic rule of Olarinkoi and his tyrannical warriors that were known as *Ilarinkon*, remained permanently etched in the collective psyche of the Maa people. Although it was estimated that the infamous invasion took place between a hundred and fifty and two hundred years earlier, the Maa people were brutalized in such bestial cruelty that, after so many years men still burned with fury, while women cried with shame when they were reminded of what befell their ancestors. And to ensure that the tragic history of that dark period was never forgotten, the oppression that was visited upon them by the tyrants was always vividly described, so that the struggle to free themselves from the yoke of that tyranny became a painful reminder of what can become of a people caught napping by the enemy.

The despot was said to have belonged to a splinter group of the Maa people that were left down Kerio Valley, when the ladder that they had used to scale the edge of the precipice broke halfway, sending those who had not ascended hurtling down the cliffs. It was not known when the *Ilarinkon* re-ascended, but it was thought to be not less than fifty years after the first ascension. They were said to have been so frustrated by their inability to ascend that when they finally managed to climb over the precipice, they were so stressed that they looked for anyone upon whom to download their frustration. By that time, their language had slightly changed and their warriors were heavily built on account of the daily exercises their bodies were subjected to as they built a new ladder, and scaled the edges of the cliff to put it in place.

The spies that Olarinkoi had dispatched to gather intelligence on the Maa people immediately reported back to him that they found expansive land, lush with green grass, luscious fruits of all kinds that hang down fruit-trees ready to be plucked. Wild animals roamed the lands freely and thousands upon thousands of Maa people's cattle and sheep grazed lazily upon green pastures that stretched to the horizon. But of the people, only old men, women and children were in the villages. No single moran was sighted.

They learnt that the Maa *morans* had gone to an *enjore* – a major raid that *morans* undertook from time to time, as an escapade meant to keep themselves fit for battle and at the same time to intimidate the neighbouring people so that they were constantly in awe of them. In such raids, they did not spare any young men they met and they brought in all the cattle they could drive back.

It was after getting the report, that *Olarinkoi* and his men struck. Although they were met with little resistance, that did not deter them from visiting their frustration upon the people of Maa. The raid was executed with such lightning speed that within days they had subdued the entire countryside and caused such mayhem and destruction as had never been witnessed by the people of Maa; it was simply a blood bath. They slaughtered any male in their path, brutalized women and children and burnt down homesteads. Remnants of the male survivors were so intimidated that, nudged by survival *instincts*, they had to quickly lay strategies in order to save their lives. They discarded their male clothings and ornaments and put on women's wrap-ons called *Olokesena* and hang on their extended earlobes, ornamental coils of copper wire known as *isurutia* that were normally worn by old women or by circumcision initiates who were recuperating. That they did to disguise their identities and pass as women instead of men in order to escape death.

Luck was not with the Maa warriors. For once, their *Oloiboni* who had always prophesied their success during the *enjore*, had guessed wrongly this time round. They were shocked to find the people they had gone to raid armed to the teeth and well prepared. They were waiting for them in the hills away from their villages. They engaged them in a fierce battle that turned out to be a fiasco. Many of them were killed and others injured. And those who returned did not drive back any cattle.

The Maa *morans* who returned home were immediately confronted by the hostile, battle-hardened warriors of Olarinkoi. As they descended Iltepes hills, they could see column after column of the tall muscular Ilarinkon *morans,* resplendent in their red ochre-soaked *shukas*. Tall monkey-skin headgear swayed on their heads as they walked. They carried their heavy decorated shields, while their long spears gleamed in the shimmering hot afternoon sun. The jingles fastened onto their thighs made a terrifying clanging sound that heightened the fearful and dangerous foreboding that hung in the air.

It was obvious that the Maa warriors were disadvantaged. They had been demoralized by the recent defeat and weakened by the long trek back home. Some of them were nursing injuries, while all of them were hungry and thirsty. From where they were, they could see that they were terribly outnumbered by their adversaries. So when the two sides finally locked horns, the battle was brutal, brief and conclusive. The Maa warriors were predictably defeated and resoundingly vanquished.

Buoyed up by their victory, the *Ilarinkon* warriors rounded up all the Maa people and assembled them on a hill so as to intimidate them and thereafter introduce them to their new ruler. It was then that *Olarinkoi* suddenly emerged from a nearby thicket. If his dramatic appearance was meant to shock the Maa people, then it more than did it! They were not only shocked by the towering giant that sauntered swaggeringly towards them, but his terrifying appearance sent shivers right down into their hearts.

The man was more of a monster than human. He was about eight feet tall and his entire body, save for the face, was hairy. The hair on his head, that was known as *oltaika*, that shimmered with oily red ochre, was thick and long and flowed flawlessly down to his shoulders. And his frame was so thick that three men standing behind him could not be visible to a person standing in front of him.

He demonstrated the strength of his large hands by grabbing two Maa men who stood shivering before him, and holding them by their necks, he forcibly squeezed their throats, instantly choking them. He then threw down their lifeless bodies onto the ground. He grinned with glee and glanced around him, his fierce, piercing, large unsmiling eyes sending even more shivers and consternation to those he directed the beam. The women squirmed and gasped while the men ground their teeth with impotent fury.

The people were gripped by more fear when his spear, carried for him by two men, each holding it by one end, was brought to him. It was about ten feet high and its blade was as wide as a machete. Its handle was as thick as the arm of an average man. He pointed it at the men and the women screamed with terror, pleading that he be merciful and spare their men. He relented. But it was his shield that was most scary. It was so huge that it was carried by four men. In the background thousands upon thousands of red *shuka*-clad and strong-bodied *Ilarinkon* warriors stood holding their weapons menacingly. Their sight alone, subdued the entire Maa population.

It was then that the man spoke. Making his demands, he emphatically told them he would brook no nonsense. He would wreak more havoc if they failed to fulfill and carry out his orders in full. From that day on, he ordered in a booming thunderous voice, his men would be handed fifty bulls to slaughter every day. Ten cows out of every hundred that each family owned were to be brought to him immediately. Thereafter, one calf out of ten born, must be surrendered to him. All women who were of child bearing age were to make themselves available to entertain the *Ilarinkon* warriors when called upon to do so.

All the Maa were dumbfounded and at the same time bitter. They held meeting after meeting to find ways to resist the perplexing demands but they did not find any workable solution to counter them.

The women were most perturbed. They were forced to compose lewd songs which they had to perform in the most outrageous and indecent postures and styles. But what angered them most was that mothers had to perform the offensive dances with their daughters.

On their part, the *Ilarinkon* warriors exploited their unassailable position to abuse the women. In their terribly obnoxious manners, they made bawdy jokes that demeaned the women. And they extremely perplexed them when they teasingly provoked them knowing that they were not able to resist their natural instinctive desires, aroused by their immoral and repugnant suggestive moves made before them. And the women hated themselves for their apparent inability to refuse to give in to those desires that the ill-mannered *Ilarinkon* exploited with malicious hilarity.

The women held meetings all over the country searching for answers. After years of searching, one woman declared that she had located within herself, the source of that salacity that caused the involuntary gravitation towards men when provoked. After debating for long, the Maa women finally said they had found the answer to their perplexity. And when the solution was tried it worked perfectly. They then made a lasting resolution and celebrated its birth with song and dance. And it was from that resolution collectively made by women of Maa, that gave birth to *enkamuratani*. And her *olmurunya* was shaped, sharpened and handed to her.

Many years later, after being subjected to all kinds of barbarities by the *Ilarinkon*, the Maa people eventually revolted and overthrew the *Olarinkoi* despotic rule. They killed *Olarinkoi* and liberated themselves, taking back the leadership of their country.

And long after the *Olarinkoi* and his warriors were gone, the institution that their misrule forced upon the Maa women was still strong and kicking." Joseph Parmuat said triumphantly and ended his story.

"Oh God!" exclaimed Taiyo flabbergasted, "is that a true story?"

"It is a true story," Joseph Parmuat confirmed seriously. "And it has been handed down from generation to generation with very little added to it. If you want to know, that was the origin of the so called Female Genital Mutilation that the likes of *Emakererei* have devoted their lives to fight."

"Resian and I are soon joining her to fight the repugnant ritual," Taiyo said equally serious.

"I'll join you too," he said roaring with laughter. "But direct your fire at the right target. It is the women and not men who founded what eventually became a tradition. And it is only women who would end it if they so desired: Period."

Chapter Seven

Resian was still waiting for her sister Taiyo to speak to their father over their enrolment at the Egerton University. It had been a frustrating long wait, but she was still optimistic that sooner or later, her sister would catch their father in an agreeable mood. She had given up on her mother who, after several attempts to draw her into their scheme, had proved to be cleverly evasive.

On that particular day, Resian was overly optimistic. That morning, Taiyo had left for the shop in the company of their father. She had excitedly promised Resian that if all went well, she would definitely bring up the subject of their enrolment into Egerton university. So, as she worked with her mother in the kitchen, Resian's heart warmed up and glowed with pleasant expectations. She let her spirit float fleetingly into the fanciful world of beautiful things. That was the world of *yote yawezekana,* a popular song of the day that cooed to say, all things were possible. In her mind she saw herself already admitted into the university and walking majestically with other students into one of those awesome lecture theatres, while donning her academic regalia. Her reverie was however suddenly cut short by her mother's introduction of a subject she least expected her to broach.

"My daughter," she called unexpectedly, while stirring her pot of ugali. "Have you ever heard of something called F.G.M?"

"Female Genital Mutilation? Why, yes, not only have I heard of it," Resian replied her eyes wide open with surprise. "I know about it. Why do you ask?"

"I know in Nakuru, this was not a subject that concerned us much. But in Nasila, it is on every lip."

"Yes, that is very true," Resian said trying to entice her mother to say more. "The other day Taiyo learnt from Joseph Parmuat that Female circumcision was initiated by women themselves about two hundred years earlier. And that it was as a result of sexual abuse and harassment by an invading despot called *Olarinkoi* and his warriors. Is that true *Yeiyo*? I thought it was one of those myths that were created by men to blame women for everything that works against them."

"What Joseph Parmuat told Taiyo is factually correct," her mother told her confidently. "It was the shame and anger that was provoked by *Ilarinkon* taunts, lewd teasing and provocative posturing that made the women do what they did to curtail those desires the worthless predators exploited to prey upon them."

"That may have been true then," Resian said looking directly into her mother's eyes. "But what is the reason for doing it today? *Ilarinkon* are no longer with us, or are they,?"

"The original *Ilarinkon* may have gone," her mother said unconvincingly, "but other *Ilarinkon* are still with us."

"Exactly!" said Resian triumphantly. "Yes, it is the latter day *Ilarinkon* who are wreaking havoc on us women. Surely *Yeiyo*, if one discovered a nasty but potent medicine that once taken cured an ailment, must they continue to swallow it everyday – ten years down the line. I find that not only ridiculous but also absurd. The sensible thing would be to discard the bitter medicine once they are cured. Period! Tell me *Yeiyo,* what use is F.G.M to today's woman?"

"Are you suggesting that it is men who continue to perpetuate this cultural rite?" her mother asked perplexed by her daughter's argument.

"Yes, they are creators of the labyrinth that the women continue to meander around," she said philosophically. "Even if I am reluctantly convinced that it was women and not men who initiated that obnoxious ritual, who provoked the women to do so? The *Ilarinkon* who were purported to have pushed women into mutilating their sexuality were men. And the ancient *Ilarinkon* were no different from today's *Ilarinkon*. The ancient Ilarikon were sadists and despotic. Today's Ilarinkon are worse. In addition to being despotic, they are oppressive tyrants; and one of their ways of oppressing us is to demand that F.G.M be perpetuated against us forever!"

A loud knock at the door disrupted their conversation. Before they could respond, there was another knock. Only this time, short urgent raps made in insistent quick succession followed.

"See who it is," her mother told her, happy to get rid of her. She rued the moment she introduced that explosive subject.

Although she had got used to people knocking at any time, that particular knock nearly angered Resian. Why should anybody butt in when she and her mother were carrying out a fruitful discussion? It was rare for her mother to open up to that extent and she would have wished to bring up other issues that required such frankness. Muttering under her breath, she quickly walked from the kitchen through the living room to the outer hall and opened the front door.

A man stood at the doorway, briefcase in hand. He was tall, broad-shouldered and he wore a blue business suit, white shirt and a light blue tie. The muscles of his arms bulged under the sleeves of his coat. His face, above his closely trimmed beard and moustache, was brown and leathery; possibly from exposure to the sun and wind. He had a wide mouth from which protruded two long upper teeth that had a wide gap between them, making him look like a warthog. She didn't like his long slanting eyes. His pierced and extended earlobes hang comically down his neck, each loop seeming to beg for something to be hooked over it.

"Is this the home of Parsimei Ole Kaelo?" the man asked in a cold, sharp and precise voice.

"Yes it is," answered Resian in a subdued voice, an alarmingly ominous feeling creeping into her heart. "What can I do for you?"

"I have come to see him." he said authoritatively and took a step into the house. In an arrogantly confident manner, he asked, "is he in?"

"No he's not in at the moment," Resian answered also taking a step forward to block him; she hoped he would go away. She added impatiently. "He's probably at the shop in town."

"He is not there," the man said emphatically, shaking his head, "I have just come from there."

He peered at Resian. Those slanting black eyes had slid from her face and were now openly and with a slow deliberation, appreciatively scanning her body. A creepy sensation sent cold shivers down her spine.

"Would you want to come back later when my father

is back?" Resian asked hoping that the detestable man would not stay. "No one knows what time he might come back."

"No, I'll rather wait," he said confidently. "I am very sure your father would be very happy to find me here." As if he had just remembered what he should have informed her the moment he arrived, he cleared his throat and told her importantly, "By the way, my name is Oloisudori. Yes Mr. Edward Oloisudori Loonkiyaa." He waited for a moment, obviously expecting that she would recognize those important names. Seeing that she did not react to the mention of the names, he said again insistently, "just wait until you see how happy Ole Kaelo will be when he finds me waiting for him in his house." Suddenly, his voice becoming softer and almost intimate, he whispered, "I'll be happy to tell him what a hospitable daughter he has." "Who else is here in the house?"

"My mother," Resian answered nonchalantly.

"Perhaps you will tell her that I am here to see your father."

"I'll do…" Resian said impatiently as she stepped back. But before she could complete her statement, he had brushed past her in one swift movement that nearly caught her off-balance. In a flash he had pushed his way into the living room and as he passed by her, she certainly felt the fingers of his lifted hand graze the fullness of her breast. With a surge of outraged embarrassment and rigid indignation, she glared at him viciously. She muttered inaudibly, "what an ill-mannered devil this man is!" And as she fled to the kitchen she felt those black eyes, sharp and probing, moving like creepy fingers upon her back.

Her mother was stirring a vegetable stew when Resian entered, and she glanced abstractedly at her.

"Who was that?" she asked.

"A man who says he is called Oloisudori," she said acidly. "He says he has come to see *Papaai*."

"Oloisudori? Let me see... Oloisudori?" her mother said repeatedly, rolling her eyes to the ceiling as she tried to place the name. Failing to remember where she had heard that name, she shook her head, "No, I don't think I know a man by that name."

"Whoever he is, Yeiyo," said Resian angrily, "he is a mannerless dirty old man!"

"Check your tongue, child!" her mother rebuked her harshly. "Soon you are going to disgrace your father by the way you speak. Didn't you see the way you horrified your *Yeiyo-botorr* the other day when you spoke like one with a demented spirit? You must bridle your tongue and be careful of what you say, otherwise you will soon be called *enadua-kutuk*."

"I am sorry, *Yeiyo*," said Resian remorsefully. "But surely, *Yeiyo,* mustn't one mention the despicable character of an old man who behaves badly before a girl young enough to be his daughter?"

"However disreputable the man may be," her mother warned her, "be careful Resian. We don't know what connection the man has with your father and it would be catastrophic if your tongue would be the one to sever his relations with other men. Go to the sitting room and tell him I am busy preparing lunch. Get him a cup of tea or something else to drink and make him comfortable before your father comes. I am sure he will be here soon."

Reluctantly, Resian took a flask that contained tea and a cup and slowly walked back to the sitting room. The moment she reappeared, Resian saw Oloisudori crane his neck, watching her. She quickly placed the flask and cup on the table and her hands automatically flew to the buttons of her blouse, that she suddenly felt, from the look in his eyes, must have been unbuttoned. But she found them buttoned.

"It must have taken long for you to decide whether to give or not give me a cup of tea?" he said sarcastically, and he laughed.

The man's words shocked Resian and she backed away from him. In the process she collided with a nearby coffee table and nearly lost her balance.

"Sorry," she said regaining her balance and composure. "But we always serve tea to our visitors even when our mother has not told us to do so."

"In that case, I must apologise for my mistaken thought," Oloisudori said as he took the cup of tea she was handing him. He let a small suggestive silence grow between them before saying, "I am indeed sorry, pretty lady." Then he smiled at her, a demonic and intrusive smile, gracing his face.

For the very few minutes she stood there before him, she felt his intent black languorous eyes moving up and down her face and body with a relentless intimacy that nearly immobilized her with embarrassment. She felt as if his hands were all over her body caressing her against her will. She even felt angry with herself, when she reasoned that by standing there she was encouraging him to humiliate her. But somehow, it was as if he had hypnotized

96

her, for as much as she had wanted to flee, she found her feet rooted to the spot. Even inexperienced as she was in the way men behaved, she saw from his smile his pleasure in her obvious fear and confusion. And instinctively, she sensed cruelty in him. Sweat trickled down her stomach, broke out on her face, before becoming clammy on her cheeks. She shook her head as if to check whether she was really awake.

"*Yeiyo* told me to tell you," she said, like one who was awakening from sleep, "she is busy preparing lunch. She asks that you make yourself comfortable and wait for *Papaai*. He is about to come."

"Very well," he said authoritatively and then added quickly in a changed soft voice." "By the way, you haven't told me your name."

"Resian," she whispered.

"What a beautiful name," he said once more in his intimate voice, his huge, slanting eyes probing her, stripping her naked, assessing her, shaming her and judging her. "Resian *ene* Kaelo," he added.

Just then, Resian heard her father talking to someone outside. She all but ran to the kitchen to announce to her mother that her *Papaai* had come then she rushed back across the sitting room, down along the corridor that led to the small hall, to the door. She clumsily threw the door open and collided head on with her father.

"Have you run amok, child?" her father asked irritably aghast at Resian's queer behaviour. "Why do you run like one who has seen an apparition?"

"I'm sorry, *Papaai*," she said with utter embarrassment and remorse. "There is a man in our sitting room who has come to see you."

"Is he a cannibal that you have to run away from him so recklessly?" he asked sarcastically and then added acidly, "sometimes your behaviour borders on imbecility. Who is he?"

"He says his name is Oloisudori," she said in a subdued voice, her eyes downcast.

"Oh, my God!" her father exclaimed under his breath, straightening up, his eyes suddenly dilating widely. "Oloisudori of all people! Oh my God! I wonder what has gone wrong for him to come looking for me!"

"I don't know, *Papaai*," Resian said concernedly, worried at the turn of events. "He was saying..."

Her father ignored her. Brushing past her, he strode briskly into the living room with both his arms outstretched in front of him, ready to embrace his visitor.

"Oloisudori Loonkiyaa!" he called out loudly, laughing in feigned excitement. "What an unexpected pleasure to have you in my house. I hope all is well, my dear brother."

"The pleasure is mutual, brother Kaelo," Oloisudori said importantly, struggling to stand in order to receive Kaelo's hug. "I assure you all things are under control."

It was then that Resian, who had followed her father to the living room noted that the two men were of the same height and possibly of the same age. But what amazed and greatly perturbed her, was to hear a slight tremor in her father's voice as he addressed Oloisudori. She certainly detected a measure of desperation and fear in him. She noticed a faint sheen of perspiration on his face and Oloisudori took advantage of her father's discomfiture to grin at her, as if to gleefully tell her "you see, what did I tell you?"

"Where is your mother?" Kaelo suddenly asked turning to Resian. But before she could answer, he was already calling her out loudly using her formal maternal name, "*Ngoto* Taiyo."

"Yes," answered Resian's mother from the kitchen.

"Come here at once," he ordered in a panic-stricken voice. Turning to Resian once more he snapped irritably. "Resian, for heaven's sake, what are you still doing here? Go to the kitchen at once and make yourself useful!"

"Yes, *Papaai*," Resian answered demurely.

But before she disappeared, Oloisudori detained her for a moment with a wave of his hand to say, "Brother Kaelo, you have a wonderful daughter here. In your absence, she received and entertained me in the most delightful manner." Kaelo snorted and grunted but said nothing.

When Mama Milanoi appeared, her husband introduced her to Oloisudori. He then became quite lyrical about Oloisudori's pivotal role that gave them the financial stability they were now enjoying in Nasila. He mentioned the contracts that he had assisted him to win and others that were still in the pipeline. "This man is more than a brother to me," he said emotionally "There is nothing, and I repeat, nothing that he ought to be denied in this home."

Resian shut the door behind her and effectively cut off her father's effusive praise of the man she loathed. She walked through the kitchen to the back door. Opening it slowly she got out, shut it behind her, and leaned against it; grateful for the clean cool air. She shuddered when she thought of those slanting shamelessly questing eyes.

Was there no better man that her father could find to do business with? Then she remembered her sister Taiyo and the promise to speak to their father. "Oh, my God," she exclaimed to herself excitedly "I am standing here foolishly thinking of Oloisudori's stupid antics, while I could actually be on my way to the university!" She felt sure Taiyo had spoken to their father and possibly he had already consented. She stood quite still for a moment. She was enthralled. Then she quickly walked round the house and got back to the front.

As she walked to the gate, she saw her sister sitting on a log next to Joseph Parmuat. One look into her sister's face, and Resian was sure things did not click. For fear of losing the chance to go to the university, she found herself hoping that Taiyo had not spoken to their father and that he hadn't refused and therefore there was still hope. What she feared most was to have the door shut permanently on them.

Taiyo knew her sister's expectation. As soon as Resian got to where they were seated with Joseph Parmuat, she quickly explained to her in the most persuasive language possible, how she tried, without success, to talk to their father. She had hoped to find him alone and in an agreeable mood, but all that had proved difficult.

Strangely, for the first time, she found Resian understanding. Instead of getting sulky, as she often did, she quickly said she appreciated her sister's effort and that she was happy the door was still open. She was sure an opportune time would offer itself, and at that time, she believed, divine powers would have prevailed upon their father. She was that optimistic. She completely closed her mind to the possibility that their father could reject their request: that was an extremity too horrible to be contemplated. She chose to remain hopeful.

"*Papaai* has a monster for a visitor this afternoon," Resian said, effectively changing the subject. "You should see him to believe me when I say he is ugly and mean. And he is an absolutely horrible man with extremely deplorable manners. I can't imagine what business *Papaai* would be transacting with such a person! He is simply *Olbitirr*."

Taiyo exploded into an uproarious laughter at the man's description, while Joseph Parmuat's dark eyebrows shot up almost to his hairline, eyes gleaming with surprised amusement.

"Honestly, Resian, what a thing to say about a human being!" Taiyo said still in stitches. "Only a man out of this world would look that horrible!"

"And for some reasons that I don't understand, *Papaai* seems terrified of him."

"*Papaai*, of all people, terrified?" Taiyo said wide-eyed with incredulity. "I have never seen him terrified."

"Did you get to know the name of the monster?" Joseph Parmuat asked perceiving that the girls were overly amazed rather than being over anxious about their father's discomfiture.

"He announced importantly that his name is Mr. Edward Oloisudori Loonkiyaa," Resian said mimicking him while roaring with laughter.

"Did you say Oloisudori? Of all people!" Joseph Parmuat exclaimed to the consternation of the girls. "That man is bad news! He is a monster in the true sense of the word."

"Who is he?" the girls asked simultaneously. "What kind of person is he?"

Oloisudori was a feared man not only in Nasila but far and wide. He said if there was anything obnoxious that Nasila had ever exported to other parts of the country, apart from the ancient infamous cattle raids and the services of the *enkamuratani,* it was the notorious criminality of Oloisudori. Just as his name implied, he was a shadowy figure. Nobody seemed to know his exact business. He liked to refer to himself as a jack-of-all-trade, which was true because he had his fingers on agriculture, finance, tourism, import and export, mining and motor trade. He was also known to be a poacher, smuggler and robber. But what he perfected skillfully was being an extortionist. That went hand in hand with his other specialised role of a hired assassin. He did not play all those roles alone as his gang of collaborators and agents worked under his direct supervision.

Little was known of Oloisudori's background. Those older than him said he came to Nasila when he was a boy of ten. It was said he was adopted by the family of *Loonkiyaa* who brought him up alongside their other sons. He was circumcised with the rest of the sons and became a valorous *moran*. But after his stint as a *moran*, he turned into a hardcore criminal who had been jailed on numerous occasions. He was now said to be incorrigible and the fact that he was often successful in his criminal forays, however devious they were, often portrayed a wrong image to the youth who thought he offered an alternative route to wealth and riches.

It was as an extortionist that Oloisudori excelled. In most cases he enticed his victims by loaning them large sums of money or organising for them to clinch and sign lucrative contracts with big organisations or win attractive contracts to supply agricultural inputs to large parastatals. Once his victims were deeply involved in the business, he would turn up to make ridiculous demands and threaten to withdraw the contracts. In many cases, his victims were left with little options but to play to his own rules. The consequences of not playing the game as he wished, were always brutal and unpalatable.

By the time Joseph Parmuat was through with the monster's history, the girls were near tears. They feared for their father and for themselves. They wondered why their father had got himself involved with that monster's murky business. Was the house they were living in and the business that their father had founded, financed by the monster? Resian was even more fearful when she recalled the anxiety that was evident in their father's face when he found Oloisudori in their house. When she recalled the arrogance and condescension that Oloisudori had displayed while in their living room, she was in no doubt that their father had fallen victim of the demonic extortionist.

But Taiyo looked at things from a brighter perspective. She was convinced that their father could not be that naive as to get involved with such an evil man. She reasoned that there must have been another explanation for the monster's visit to their home. But the three agreed on one thing: Oloisudori was a bad, bad man.

After sitting on the log chatting for a while, Joseph Parmuat departed. The girls then proceeded slowly to their house, talking.

"Guess what Taiyo-eyeiyo," Resian said excitedly. "Yeiyo, this afternoon shocked me by voluntarily talking about F.G.M."

"No, Resian, that's not true," Taiyo answered, her eyes dilating with surprise, and stopping so as to give serious attention to what her sister was saying. *Yeiyo* talking about F.G. M on her own accord? Unless she was preparing ground for shocking news. By the way, I hope she did not tell you that there are plans to drag and take us soon to *enkamuratani?*"

"No, not at all," Resian said vehemently. "You know if she did, we would not be here saying what we are now saying."

"Anyway, tell me," Taiyo pursued the subject relentlessly. "What did she say about F.G.M.?"

"She asked me what I knew about it," Resian said gesticulating wildly to emphasize her words. "And I told her not only what I knew about F.G.M but I added that it was certainly a tool of oppression used by men to put women down. I also told her that, that story about F.G.M having been introduced by women who had been harassed and sexually abused by Ilarinkon invaders centuries earlier, was not convincing. Had the practice been introduced by the women of the time, to stem the Ilarinkon lewd excesses, I argued, then it should have become extinct with their departure."

"Did you ask her whether she supported F.G.M.?" Taiyo asked tongue in her cheek. "And did you find out whether there was a plan being hatched to have us conform with the obnoxious Nasila ritual?"

"That was what I was going to find out when the monster came knocking." Resian said as they resumed their walk towards the house.

"We must find out that this evening," Taiyo said seriously. "To be forewarned is to be forearmed."

They climbed the steps slowly and as they reached the front door, it opened to reveal Kaelo and his visitor. Taiyo and Resian stepped back to allow Oloisudori through. He greeted Taiyo politely and smiled at Resian confidently as if to suggest that a bond between them had been established and their familiarity was now a matter of mutual understanding. Resian dropped her gaze to the floor.

"There goes the monster," Resian hissed angrily through clenched teeth, as her father and Oloisudori walked down the steps. "He is the devil incarnate!" Bearing in mind what Joseph Parmuat told us about him, Taiyo said nonchalantly. "Olosudori could very easily pass as just another innocent Nasila elder."

"God forbid," Resian hissed, her lips tightening dangerously. Just the sight of Oloisudori had revived the loathing she had for him. "I pray that God will never give him a chance to pass as an innocent Nasila elder."

Just then, their father returned. Resian looked at him and perceived something queer about him. She was alarmed. Did she imagine it or was there something unnatural about him? She wondered. And what was it? Her father looked at her and quickly averted his eyes and looked elsewhere. She noticed that something was amiss. She felt very certain there was something awful in the air.

"Resian, go to the kitchen and help your mother prepare supper," her father said sharply. "And make it snappy!"

The look on her father's face immobilized her. She glanced at him curiously. He was watching her too, his wrinkled face unsmiling. She then regained her composure and was about to go when once again something in his face made her hesitate for a moment, thinking he was about to say something more to her.

"What are you waiting for?" he thundered angrily. "Go to the kitchen this instant."

Taiyo was by then busy closing windows and drawing curtains. Standing by one window that faced the west, she looked through it for a long moment, lost in thought. Then she walked into the living room where her father sat rigidly on an armchair, his right elbow planted on his right knee while his right cupped hand supported his chin. He was staring without blinking at the fireplace, his thoughts obviously not in that house.

"*Papaai*," Taiyo called her father, looking at him with reverence. "Is something wrong?"

"What? Oh no," her father said confusedly turning unfocused eyes upon her. "Nothing is wrong my dear daughter."

"Brother Joseph Parmuat told us," she said taking utmost care not to upset him, "that the gentleman who has just left is a reputable financier and that wherever you see him, great business transactions are in the offing, is that right, *Papaai*?"

"Yes, yes, that's right," he stammered fidgeting uncomfortably in his seat. "Yes, he is certainly a reputable businessman and truly a great business transaction is in the offing."

"And all is well, *Papaai*?" Taiyo insisted relentlessly.

"Yes, yes, I have said." he said smiling sheepishly, while avoiding her eyes, "everything is fine. It is just…" he hesitated for a moment, and then scratched his head absent-mindedly. "…just that we are going to do a few things here at home a little bit differently. A few changes here and there affecting all of us. Other than those little changes, everything else is just fine."

"What are those little things, *Papaai*?" asked Taiyo inquisitively, her eyes staring at him fixedly.

"Nothing serious," he said getting impatient. "And whatever they are, know that your father is in control. Now join your mother and Resian in the kitchen and make sure food is ready soon. I would like to retire to bed early today."

When the girls went to the kitchen they were surprised by their mother's aloofness. Her absent-mindedness that evening had already made her burn and ruin the rice that was to be their evening meal. Her daughters tried to charm her, tease her, prod her, provoke her without much success. Had her taciturnity anything to do with Oloisudori's visit? If that was the case, they reasoned, then the demonic extortionist's visit was outrageously ruinous.

Chapter Eight

It was the turn of Parsimei Ole Kaelo and Mama Milanoi ene Kaelo, to have a long, troubled and dark night. Husband and wife had gone to bed early. They were now agonizing about the same matter but lamenting separately in their minds and in their forlorn hearts. They turned and turned again on their bed repeatedly, like *ilmintilis* being roasted in the fire.

Parsimei's head spun incessantly. He rued the day he met Oloisudori. Seeing what befell him that afternoon, he wondered what devil had convinced him to carry out business dealings with such an evil man. Judging from the queer demand Oloisudori had made on him, he wondered whether he wasn't a member of a shadowy cult that he had heard mentioned for a long time, and which was known as *Ilmasonik*.

It was said that the cult thrived on blackmail and extortion. One of the ways it operated was to approach an ambitious businessman and lure him into their ensnaring schemes. A lucrative money making business proposal would be hatched and handed to the unsuspecting businessman by a member of the cult. Once enticed and convinced that he would make millions of shillings within a short period of time, the businessman would be loaned large sums of money to plough into his business. Within a short time, the business would boom and the businessman would prosper. Then the woes would begin. It was then that absurd demands were made. Often, it was demanded that the indebted businessman should sacrifice his beloved ones to the gods of the cult. And the beloved ones included wife, sons or daughters. The consequences of failing to fulfill the demands it was said, were always catastrophic and fatal.

He had never believed those stories, but that night, as he lay on his bed, he began to wonder whether Oloisudori was not a member of such a cult. What, in the name of God, had he done to deserve such torment? He cried silently and bitterly. Although he was an experienced businessman, he lamented sorrowfully, he had acted so perilously as to risk the lives of the members of his family.

He certainly had known Oloisudori's criminal records for a long time. But he could not tell why he had turned a blind eye to his enticement. He had even been warned of his wickedness and his villainous behaviour but he declined to heed the warning. Ole Supeyo, his friend and mentor, had told him bluntly that doing business with Oloisudori was like toying with a live electrified wire. He had even warned him about Oloisudori's rotten immoral behaviors that he likened to that of a randy he-goat and warned him to keep him away from his daughters.

Oloisudori's notoriety as a lethal extortionist was not unknown to him. He knew many people who had become victims to his blackmail tactics after failing to meet his demonic demands. And it was not once or twice that he had heard of his arrest and detention on suspicion that he had been involved in bank robberies, assassinations or disappearance of certain individuals. But being adroit in the manner in which he executed his criminal activities, in addition to having a knack in covering his tracks, he always bounced back after such incarcerations to continue with his nefarious activities.

He knew it was the pursuit of success that made him interact with Oloisudori. And men who mattered in society–men of property–were the successful. Success was attainment, fortune and prosperity; it was triumph and it gave one happiness. It did not matter how it was obtained. No, the end product justified the means, however horrible.

Oloisudori was successful, he thought angrily. Yes, he was successful and was reverently bestowed respectful titles such as *Mzee* and *Mheshimiwa*. He often rubbed shoulders with the mighty of the land and all doors swung open automatically when he approached. And who did not want to be referred to as a successful businessman, just like Oloisudori was? Who did not want to have a blooming import and export business, a flourishing transport business or a thriving farming inputs supply business? What could be better than when one reached that state of affluence, as Oloisudori did, when one was able to live in six ostentatious houses in six different towns, with a woman and servants in each one of them?

Yes, that was how Oloisudori defined success, Parsimei thought bitterly. And he and many others desired to define it in the same way. The archaic adage that exhorted young and upcoming businessmen to take care of cents and let shillings take care of themselves was regarded by the likes of Oloisudori to be not only nonsensical but tortuous and untenable. Instant riches, just as instant tea or instant coffee were the in thing. And the instantaneous bliss brought in an on-the-spot feeling of well being, felicity and happiness. That was what everyone wanted, Kaelo reasoned, and that was what he himself had always wanted. And that was the reason, like a stinking rotten carcass would draw a torrent of flies to itself, people like him and many others got drawn to the murky business of Oloisudori.

"But now, had the chicken had come home to roost," Ole Kaelo lamented ruefully. Oloisudori was now demanding his pound of flesh. He recalled the events of that afternoon when Oloisudori came calling. Seeing him in his house unexpectedly, had signalled trouble with his contracts. But Oloisudori had allayed his fears, saying all was well in that direction. That had restored his peace and calmed his frayed nerves. The success of the shop depended entirely on those contracts. Even the large stocks that he held in those godowns were secured on the strength of those contracts. It was therefore gratifying to hear him confirm that all was well. What did he want then? He had wondered. But he did not have to wonder for long for Oloisudori did not believe in niceties. He had lifted his head, and letting a small silence draw out between them, he told him, "There is a small matter that I would like to discuss."

"Yes," Ole Kaelo had said, terrified.

Oloisudori had reached into his pocket, pulled out a packet of cigarettes, extracted one and lit it. He inhaled and exhaled the smoke unhurriedly, and then added, "that daughter of yours, Resian," he said condescendingly, "she interests me."

"Pardon me?" Ole Kaelo had asked, shocked and in disbelief. The man's reputation was truly barbarous, he thought angrily.

"I am interested in your daughter Resian," Oloisudori

said evenly, as if he was talking of a sheep or goat. "And I have a friend who will also be interested in your other daughter. Simply put, I would like to relieve you of your two daughters!"

"Oloisudori Lonkiyaa, please," Ole Kaelo had pleaded desperately. "Ask me of anything else, but spare my daughters."

"Didn't you tell your wife just now that there is nothing I should be denied in your home?" Oloisudori had asked smiling unpleasantly, "or were you just pulling my leg?"

Regrettably and predictably, Oloisudori had got his way, even if partially. Ole Kaelo's shut eyes rolled in their sockets as he painfully bit his lips that were caught between his tightly clenched teeth. Since the time he heard them, Oloisudori demands had not ceased to anger him. Even then, as he lay on his bed, he was still seething with impotent fury. When he first heard Oloisudori say that his daughter Resian had interested him, he did not understand what he had meant. But when he said he had a friend who he thought would be interested in Taiyo, and he therefore intended to take them both, he was shocked.

He had then given thought to the girls. As a father, it was his responsibility to bring them up, care for them, educate them and guarantee their safety at all times. He could see them in his mind as they played around when they were helpless babies; skipping up and down as toddlers and thereafter as they walked around proudly and carefree as grown-up happy daughters that they were.

It excruciatingly pained him to think that circumstances would force him to hand any of them to a man who was not their choice. He thought of Taiyo, his favourite daughter and the apple of his eye. How terrible it would be, he thought sorrowfully, to see her cry forlornly, while questioning the sincerity of his love for her, and asking him the reason for his betrayal. Even Resian, with her sullenness and gracelessness that he disliked, he had found out surprisingly that he had a soft spot for her. He cried and his heart bled for her, when after an intense hard-tackling haggle amid Oloisudori's threats of fleecing him and ensuring that he did not have a penny in his name, they had eventually agreed that she was to be the sacrificial lamb.

For him to save his business, to save his home and to save his daughter Taiyo, he had agreed, she had to go.

Her mother was inconsolable, but what could they do? Even his other demand that the girls' status of being *intoiye nemengalana* should be terminated infuriated him. Although it was true that his daughters were late in undergoing the cultural rite, he had argued vehemently, it was his prerogative as a father to decide when to call the *enkamuratani*, and nobody had the right to push him to do it against his will. Oloisudori had then decided that he would take her in, and have the ritual performed on her at his home for; he had said, he did not trust *intoiye nemengalana* at his home. Kaelo had felt sick and nauseated by the whole affair. Such talks were abnormal between a father-in-law and a would-be son-in-law. But could Oloisudori, a man of his own age, be his son-in-law? The world had come to an end, he decried sadly. Did he even know Oloisudori's clan? Had he been of *Ilmolelian* clan as he was, would that have deterred him from marrying Resian?

Little did he know that Oloisudori strange demand

was made on the spur of the moment. He had intended to come and make a monetary demand on Kaelo based on his blackmail tactics, but all of that was forgotten the moment he saw Resian. He had instantly fallen in love with her.

For some strange reasons he did not understand, her instinctive terror had awakened in him an excitement he had thought was long lost to him. It had delightfully invigorated and sharpened his tired senses and reminded him of his youthful moments of ecstasy and vivacity. He admired her physical and sensual attraction, especially those of her full breasts, her strong and supple waist, the curve of her wide hips and her shapely long legs. Long after he had left Kaelo's house, the thought of Resian's young, lush, heavy body, not only brought moisture to the palms of his hands, but a stirring in his loins.

Like all other things that he had desired in life, he told himself happily, Resian was his for the taking. There was nothing that Oloisudori Lonkiyaa desired and did not get.

Mama Milanoi also turned in her bed. She tossed and tossed. As a woman with child and about to give birth would writhe and cry with pain, she writhed and cried with pain. Her silent anguished cry burned deep in her heart and in the pit of her stomach like an inferno in the bowels of the earth. Yes, she was inconsolable. Was that what she set out to achieve in Nasila? She lamented bitterly. No, certainly not.

She had thought Nasila was beckoning them back into her fold the way a mother would beckon back her wayward children. She had thought Nasila was calling them back to

114

give them a chance to share in its good fortunes and have a chance to be associated with the great and powerful culture of its people. Above all, she had thought that Nasila was going to offer them a golden chance to marry off their two daughters to its respectable sons and usher them to greater prospects than they would have ever dreamed to get in Nakuru.

A voice in the dark night told her, in a husky whisper, that they had received their just reward. They had wanted prosperous sons-in-law, and Oloisudori was one such son-in-law, for he was stinking rich, and he had already offered them the chance to share Nasila's good fortunes. The magnificent house they lived in was built with finances secured by the guarantee Oloisudori gave by way of those invaluable contracts. Similarly, the business they ran in Nasila was financed through the banks by guarantees that he offered, and they therefore depended on his goodwill.

She learnt all that from her husband that afternoon after Oloisudori had left. But the timing was immaterial for had she known earlier it would not have made any difference. Just as it was during her time, it was the man who made decisions as to which direction their lives took. When he took a wrong decision, the family was the one to bear the brunt of its unpalatable consequences.

'Could Oloisudori be her son-in-law? God forbid! How could a man who was the age of her husband be her son-in-law? Where was the Nasila culture?'

In the past, she recalled, such a thing would have never happened. Culture would not have allowed it to happen. In those old good days, had her husband tried to enforce such an abomination, she would have appealed to the elders court which certainly would have ruled him out of order and possibly fined him together with his purported son-in-law. A public rebuke and an ensuing cleansing ceremony conducted by the fearsome *Oloiboni* would have shamed the culture-abusers and their collaborators and that would have acted as a deterrent to future attempts.

Culture also allowed her to call for mass action. That was a women court. It was swift, vindictive and decisive. And it was most feared by men. It was rarely activated, but when it was, it paralysed all activities in the homesteads. Men instinctively knew its battle cry and when they heard it, all of them, even the old and infirm took to the hills. Yes, it was a 'tsunami' that did not discriminate. It swept away all the men.

She recalled one incident when she was about ten years old. A mannerless old man got infatuated with a fourteen-year-old daughter of his agemate and who also happened to be a clansmate. The randy old man followed the girl everywhere she went. He followed her to the river when she went to draw water, and to the bushes, when she went to fetch firewood. He would get up very early in the morning just to have a glimpse of her when she was milking. One day, he became bold enough and seduced her as she milked her mother's cows. The girl was infuriated and reported the incident to her mother.

The girl's mother appealed to the women's court. Immediately, the 'village wireless' was activated and it spread the news like a bush-fire during a drought. Within hours, all women had been informed and a plan of action was hatched. The girl was called and instructed on how to act.

The following morning at dawn, women from all homesteads except the one where the offending old man resided, let out the calves. They allowed them to suckle their mothers freely. No cow was milked that morning and no fire was lit in the hearths. Then all the women proceeded to the homestead of the accused, armed with all kinds of weapons that included firewood, *ilkurteta*, *ilkipiren*, *isosiani* and their husbands' knobkerries.

The girl had been instructed to act normally and carry out her milking duties in the manner she always did. As usual the old man was there trying to seduce her. The poor fellow did not know what was in store for him. He was ensnared!

Then all hell broke loose! Women poured into the homestead in their hundreds. They descended upon the poor old man beating him thoroughly and stripping him naked. They teased him and taunted him, offering themselves to him en masse. They pulled his ears, slapped him and kicked him. They then bound his hands and the girl was given the rope to hold as a leash. She was instructed to lead him as the women prodded him with their sticks, pushing him along the path. He was paraded naked, and led to all the homesteads. Woe to any man that was found on the way! He was beaten and shamed. Any time they came across a group of people, the girl was told to ask the old man, "*Papaai*, did you really intend to do this to me?" and the old man was forced to reply shamefully, "Yes, my dear daughter!"

So, when the men heard the women battle cry, they knew the 'tsunami' had come and they ran out of their homesteads as fast as their legs could carry them. They fled to the hills. And it was only in the evening, after sending a peace delegation made up of the very old and infirm men, were they allowed back into the village. By that time, the accused had gasped the last gulp of air, and was no more.

After getting to their homes, the women did not give their men any food. There was no milk because they had not milked the cows that day, and the houses were cold for no fire had been lit. The men did not ask any questions for that was the punishment that the culture meted out to the menfolk collectively when one of them offended the sensibilities of Maa. The following day, the hungry old men called the fearsome *Oloiboni* to cleanse the homesteads and restore peace, love and unity.

Mama Milanoi wondered where that culture had fled to. Was there no one to tame the likes of Oloisudori? Had the culture become moribund, useless and impotent? Another husky whisper told her the Maa culture had gone nowhere. It was still there and it was intact. It was like the waters of Nasila and all other rivers of Maa.

Nasila river had been there as far back as Nasila people could remember. It had sustained the life of man and beast from time immemorial. But Nasila water was no longer the water she drew when she was a little girl. It was no longer the water she and her friends scooped up with their hands and drank happily to quench their thirst after a long hot day in the fields. No, the water was no longer the same. The water had been polluted. In those days the water was so clean and clear that the pebbles on the riverbed were visible. Even the mudfish and the crab-like creatures called *enkileleo* were so clearly visible in the water one would have thought they were in a clear glass container.

That was no more. Upstream, people were washing vehicles, they were washing smelling hides and skins, they were emptying sacks of agricultural chemicals and other offending and poisonous pollutants into Nasila river. It would not be long, Mama Milanoi reasoned sorrowfully, before the life-giving water of Nasila began to sicken and kill.

And so was Nasila culture. The founder had intended that the culture would regulate the lives of the people, and indeed it did. It charted out the way for everyone, from cradle to the grave. It defined relationships, it created laws that governed the ownership of property and settled disputes. It did not discriminate, it did not favour anyone over the others, it gave everyone a chance to live a full life; it protected everyone within its confines and provided cleansing procedures for those who defiled it. It was simply a cherished way of life for all the Maa people, including those in Nasila. It was no more. It was now defiled and polluted by the likes of Oloisudori. Yes, the old Nasila culture had become mutable and it now contained defiant mutants that it could not regulate and which were above Nasila laws.

She thought of her own house. Yes, change was creeping in. Her daughters were different. They had gone through a school system that intermingled them with children from other cultures. They knew very little of Nasila culture. They were children of a new undefined culture. Theirs was a mutant of another kind.

Her daughter Resian, Mama Milanoi thought sadly, as

she turned once more on her bed, was a hard nut to crack. She was obstinate and defiant. She certainly epitomized the new undefined culture. She knew she had an independent mind and she was not easy to handle. If her father thought she was docile and that he would just call her and hand her over to Oloisudori, he was in for a rude shock. No amount of intimidation or threats could easily break her. She always said she knew her rights and would not allow anyone to trample them.

She did not know how they would have handled the question of her circumcision hadn't her father turned down Oloisudori's demand that it be done before he took her to his home.

She wondered how Oloisudori would react when Resian rebuffed him. From what he saw of the monster that afternoon, he feared for her daughter's life. The monster could do anything including snuffing out the life of an innocent child like Resian. What in the name of God did her family do to deserve the anguish they were going through? She cried out silently and passionately.

Next to her, her husband turned. He growled and gritted his teeth like an animal that was unable to free itself from a snare. He yawned and shook his head vigorously the way a bull would do to expel water from its ears after a rainy night. He then rubbed his nose violently and sighed.

"Are you awake, *Ngoto* Resian?" he asked, calling her unusually as Resian's mother rather than Taiyo's mother as he normally did.

"I never slept a wink, *menye* Resian," she answered in the same manner.

"Have you thought of any other thing we can do about Resian?" He asked in a heavy sorrowful voice.

"About Resian?" she asked puzzled. "Were we contemplating any other action other than the one we agreed upon with Oloisudori?"

"No, not any other action," he said sadly. "I have been thinking of how to break the news to her."

"Since Oloisudori said he will be back in a month's time," Mama Milanoi said equally sorrowful, "let us not rush it, my husband.
This is a delicate matter that requires careful handling."

"I agree with you, my wife," Kaelo said groping for her hand. When he got hold of it, he squeezed it gently as he said soothingly, "I did not plan this to happen to our daughter."

"I know."

"Who knows?" he said a flicker of hope lighting his troubled heart, "something positive might come out of this."

"Who knows?" she repeated resignedly.

A beautiful sunrise of yet another morning that was dominated by flights of birds that flashed between the trees in the compound, seemed to bring back sanity and serenity into the home of Ole Kaelo. Tiny *intinyoit* and brilliant *ilekishu* birds twittered and chirped, making the air alive with their constant motion and their cheerful calls.

Kaelo was the first to come out of their bedroom. His morning greetings were unusually cheerful. Resian was however quick to detect something artificial in that cheerfulness. She thought their father was being somehow insincere. Where was his usual insensate anger that she had come to expect whenever he found her in a room? Why were his eyes shifty and withdrawn into their sockets like one who had had little or no sleep at all?

Taiyo on the other hand, was very happy to see their father cheerful. He had appeared gloomy the previous night. Their father could be high-handed and tyrannical but the central position he occupied in their home and the pivotal role he played in stabilizing their sometimes turbulent lives could not be underrated. Any sign of instability in him, was the worst threat to their lives and it sent untold shivers right down to the bedrock of the family's foundation.

Their mother's sweet smile when she entered the living room bewitched the girls and brought in a ray of sunshine that seemed to cheer up Resian's mood.

So when they sat for breakfast that morning the Kaelos were a happy family again. And Taiyo took advantage of that regained happiness to announce that their brother Joseph Parmuat had accepted to coach them in traditional music and dance. Their father readily and eagerly consented to it and even went further to give them a room outside the main house, that he intended to use as an office as the practising room. Seeing their father's enthusiasm, Resian nearly got tempted to put her request to him to be allowed to go back to Nakuru and enroll as a student at Egerton University. But she had a premonition that all was not well. She also feared that should he reject it, it would be impossible to bring it up again. At the end, she opted to be patient.

Even the entrance of Olarinkoi into the house and his rude intrusion onto the breakfast table, did little to dampen the high spirits that embraced the Kaelo family.

It was surprising that, of all people, it was Resian who fetched him a cup, poured tea into it and handed it to him cheerfully. He acknowledged her with a throaty grunt.

Mama Milanoi knew in her heart that all that was a meaningless charade. It excruciatingly pained her to see Resian smile cheerfully, oblivious of the impending disaster that loomed large like ominous heavy black clouds.

Chapter Nine

Joseph Parmuat began to coach Resian and Taiyo in traditional song and dance. He did it every evening after school. But soon, Resian's interest in the coaching quickly fizzled out and waned. She knew her unquenchable thirst was in the university education and that could not be substituted for anything else. She eventually stopped attending and left Taiyo to be coached alone.

Soon, Taiyo found her happiness. She looked forward to seeing Joseph Parmuat in the evening, and when at the end of the practice session, time came for them to part, she was reluctant to leave. Over the past weeks, she had unexpectedly discovered a haven, a place of song, dance and laughter in that room. It was truly a place of relaxed companionship and mutual understanding. She found a place where she could enjoy song and dance with someone who through ties of Nasila kinship, and shared interest, related with her on one to one basis and without any condescension.

Joseph Parmuat also enjoyed Taiyo's company. He found it a joy to coach her, and dancing with her elicited an elation from his heart that he did not know ever existed. He was however cautious in the way he expressed that elation. Ever since he knew that the Kaelos were from the *Ilmolelian* clan and of the *Iloorasha-kineji* sub-clan, like his family, he considered Kaelo to be his father according to their culture and he therefore tried to internalise the fact that Taiyo and Resian were his sisters. He also knew the profound respect and trust with which he was regarded by the girls' parents. He did not therefore want any untoward behaviour on his part to raise any doubt or taint his hitherto untainted character.

But it had not been easy for the two of them. Even that very evening as they stood close heaving their chests to and fro, it was still not easy. Joseph Parmuat glanced around her; his smile warm. He loved the way she swung her earrings that glinted in the soft evening sunlight, emphasizing the graceful length of her neck. That particular evening, she wore a tight green woollen dress that accentuated her narrow shoulders and bulging hips. The effect was striking. She danced with abandon. Her eyes gleamed beneath her eyelashes and she moved her head haughtily and gracefully. Her body made a certain movement of the hips that was seductive and enticing. And as she did so, mischief was written all over her pretty face, eyes downcast in a modesty that was so false as to be a challenge to him. He noticed it and smiled again appreciatively.

At the sight of that smile, Taiyo's heart lifted with tender happiness. Her excitement showed on her face. It shone with innocent serenity from her eyes and softened the line of her mouth. They looked at one another and their eyes held, for the briefest of moments, and then Joseph Parmuat abruptly turned away.

Joseph Parmuat was determined not to let shame and scandal besmirch his name and that of the Kaelos. He also did not want Taiyo to be hurt, for he knew the end result of an illicit and clandestine relationship, as theirs, if allowed to develop would be catastrophic to her and her future. He himself would not escape castigation and the punishment that was meted out to offenders by Nasila culture. Such punishment would include payment of compensation in the form of cattle, in addition to suffering a public rebuke and undergoing a demeaning cleansing ceremony.

In order to avoid a situation where he would find himself alone with Taiyo, he enlisted Resian's help by ensuring that she was always with them when he taught Taiyo song and dance. To achieve that, he introduced and taught an interesting lesson about Nasila culture after each coaching session. He selected aspects of culture that touched on the lives of young people and to his delight, he found Resian ardently interested to know more. Her constant presence irked and chagrined Taiyo greatly, but she could not raise any complaint, for it was her sister's right also to be taught.

He taught them about love. He told them the kinds of love that young people in Nasila were involved in. There was the conventional kind where a young man and a girl would fall in love. Since nearly all the girls were always booked for marriage, sometimes even before they were born, those involved in the conventional kind of love were regarded as betrothed, and therefore any other love, other than to the betrothed was regarded illicit and clandestine. That did not however deter young people from loving one another passionately.

The *elangatare* which was what that kind of love was called was competitive, but abstinence was strictly observed. Winning the admiration of the girls was adored by young men and they did anything including engaging in dangerous stunts to win the girls' hearts. And there was nothing that filled the girls with admiration more than the mention of valorous feats such as killing of marauding lions or defending the people and their cattle from enemies, that the young men often engaged themselves in. Those who excelled in those feats and were known to be of good behaviour and discipline were always the darlings of the girls.

A song of praise composed by a girlfriend in praise of the valorous deeds of her boyfriend, and which was adopted by the rest of the women, was the highest accolade that a young man could get. And the song of praise was only adopted by all the women when there was an agreement and consensus by all the young people that the deeds mentioned in the song were indeed valorously achieved by him. When that happened, the young man would bask in that glory until another young man broke that record by achieving even better results.

Should the betrothed misbehave or do anything to offend the sensibilities of the Nasila culture and therefore lost the favour of the girl's parents, he would forfeit the right to marry the girl. And if the *Olangata* (boyfriend) was ready to marry his *elangata* (girlfriend) the young man's parents would approach the girl's parents seeking marriage. When that *enkaputi* was sealed and the marriage ceremony performed, the young people regarded that as the greatest achievement; that was always the most blissful marriage in Nasila.

The other kind of love was called *patureishi*. It ran simultaneously with the conventional kind of love, in that a young man and a girl were individually allowed by culture to have a *patureishi* love alongside the conventional type of love. *Patureishi* was a platonic love that each young person was allowed to engage in. And the way it operated was that, a young man looked for a girl who was not related to him in any way, and who was known to be of good behaviour and discipline. He would approach her with the assistance of his sisters, and request her to be his *patureishi*. If the girl accepted the proposal, the young man would be asked to swear that he would strictly adhere to the stringent regulations that must be observed in that kind of relationship. If the young man vowed to observe the rules, there was an exchange of ornaments and *esongoyo*, an aromatic herb, was given to the girl by the young man. Then the relationship was sealed.

The news of the sealed relationship was circulated and spread among the young people. It also reached their families and the young man's girlfriend and the girl's boyfriend. It was made sure that there was no rivalry whatsoever between the two sets of friendship. In all cases, it was made clear that *patureishi* took priority over the conventional love. When a young man came to visit his *patureishi* the girl made sure that she informed her boyfriend who would then keep his distance. And all other people, young and old, respected the relationship.

The *patureishi* institution was meant to check the conduct and behaviour of the young people and keep them disciplined. Parents of the young man would give him a young bull to sell to buy beads ornaments for his *patureishi*. Later when the relationship had matured, they would give him an ewe to give to the girl as a mark of respect that would continue between them for the rest of their lives. When the young man swore in the name of his *patureishi,* the swearing would be taken as serious and solemn, and he would not be expected to negate it.

Woe to the young man if he reneged on that deal. The *patureishi* would investigate the matter and if she confirmed that her young man had engaged himself in a disgraceful act of misconduct, such as molestation of children, petty thievery, disrespect of women, or an act of cowardice; she would act swiftly to shame him. She would remove all the beads ornaments that he had given her and carry them to the pastures where the calves were grazing. She would look for a calf that belonged to his mother and would adorn its neck with the ornaments. When the calves streamed home in the evening, there would be the decorated calf that belonged to the mother of the estranged and shamed *patureishi!* All the people in that village and in all other villages would know that he had been abandoned by his *patureishi* because of his misbehaviour and indiscipline. And the young man would have to run away from home for sometime, to escape the burning shame. In a case like that, he would have to work extra hard and for a long time to win back the confidence of the girls and build his reputation anew.

But a young man who balanced his two relationships appropriately and behaved in accordance with the norms given by the culture of the Nasila people, was accorded respect and regarded as a potential leader and elder of the future of Maa.

"Let me be your *patureishi* if it really exists," Resian said jokingly.

"No way," Joseph Parmuat answered happily." "Since you are my sister, you don't qualify to be my *patureishi*."

"To speak the truth, brother Parmuat," Resian said seriously, "I have never heard of patureishi. Does it really exist?" "It is a recent casualty of the changing trends in Nasila," Joseph Parmuat said, his face-wrinkled with concern. "Individualism, petty jealousy and lack of trust killed that once important aspect of Nasila culture."

"I believe culture and traditions are never static," said Taiyo pointedly. "By being dynamic, culture shades off aspects that become irrelevant with time. Two examples of such moribund aspects of culture are Female Genital Mutilation and the clan system that forces people who have no blood relations whatsoever not to have relationship contrary to their wishes. These should have disappeared at the turn of the last century. But, alas, they are not disappearing soon, thanks to those who continue to have a stranglehold on the culture for the sole purpose of perpetuating their rule."

"Oh, my! I didn't know that you hold such strong views on the Nasila culture," Joseph Parmuat said chuckling. "In any case, you cannot say our culture has been static. It has already shed off many negative aspects some of which were obnoxious, such as the tradition of throwing the dead and the dying to the hyenas, or the inhuman tradition of abandoning the very old and terminally ill people in deserted homestead to be disembowelled by wild animals. That was ghastly, wasn't it?"

"Yes, those traditions were certainly ghastly." Resian said vehemently. "They were as obnoxious as F.G.M is obnoxious today. If I had power, I would constitute a committee that would go through all the known culture with a fine tooth comb and consign all the bad and negative ones to the dustbin of history."

"If one did that," said Joseph Parmuat knotting his

brows to show the seriousness in which he considered the matter, "that person would be as tyrannical and despotic as the old Olarinkoi was."

"Okay, okay! Let us agree that Nasila culture will soon shed itself of F.G.M," Resian said uncompromisingly. "There are no two ways about it. But, by the way, why is that there is always a scramble for girls to marry in Nasila, to the extent that men are forced to book unborn baby girls, and then they still have to wait for thirteen to fourteen years for them to mature?"

"It is simply because demand outstrips supply," Joseph Parmuat said roaring with laughter. "You see, when one man marries seven women, he deprives another six of potential wives. It is that simple. Soon you will see Nasila men coming to your father's home to book the two of you for marriage!"

"Not us!" Taiyo and Resian said simultaneously. "We shall never allow it!" Taiyo added jokingly, "but why go fishing in shallow waters while the blue sea is teeming with fish? Advise Nasila men to go to Nakuru and other towns where girls are a dozen for a shilling! There is an inordinate demand for men there."

Joseph Parmuat glanced at her enquiringly. He knew Taiyo had been trying to put a message across to him all the time during that evening, but he deliberately declined to take the cue. Any time she tried to look directly into his eyes, he slyly averted his and either turned and looked at Resian or looked across the distant plains and to the hill beyond.

His elusiveness did not however deter the indefatigable Taiyo. She had fallen in love with him and she knew without doubt that he too had. The only thing that stood between them was the archaic Nasila culture. And she didn't give a hoot about it. She therefore did not feel guilty whatsoever in pursuing the desire of her heart. The apparent chasm that separated them did not matter to her. Moreover, she told herself decidedly, if she visited him in his house and convinced him that they belonged to one another, they could always leave Nasila for another destination and life would continue out there without the bothersome Nasila culture.

Once she made up her mind, she set out to go and visit him in his house in the evening of the following day. She had never been to his house before, but he had pointed out to her where it was. She had observed his routine. He would go to his house first after school to change into evening clothes, before coaching them in song and dance.

Joseph Parmuat two roomed house was the first one in a row of blocks that had four such houses each. When she got to the door, she found it unlocked and pushed the door open; she peeped in.

"Joseph, are you in?" she called and hesitated for a moment before walking into the living room. "Joseph, where are you?"

Joseph Parmuat was not in the living room. She stood silently observing a room she had not seen before. Considering that the house belonged to a bachelor, she appreciatively thought it elegant and well arranged. In one corner stood a round table covered with a long fringed cloth and upon it was a tray on which a water jug and neatly arranged glasses stood. There was another table at the centre of the room with four armchairs around it. In another corner, stood a sideboard upon which several framed photographs were set. Nearby, upon a coffee table, was a stove and a few spotlessly clean pots and other utensils. She thought the entire room was as tidy as the most virtuous housewife could ever have wished to find.

Curiosity and an inquisitive impulse made her slip into the next room, that was Joseph Parmuat's bedroom. That too, she found it neat and tidy. His bed was wide and was neatly made. It was covered in an exquisite blue bed cover and a pillow in a matching colour pillow case, lay at the headboard of the bed. The wall behind the bed was lined with shelves neatly packed with books. More books were stacked beside an armchair set comfortably beside the bed. Another sideboard stood at the corner of the bedroom. Upon its shiny surface, several large silver framed photographs of school children either singing or dancing, stood.

Then she picked the only photograph that was different. It was a picture of a tall, handsome, distinguished looking young man in a black suit and tie, looking out upon the world with faint quizzical amusement. There was a hint of humour about the eyes on the wide face she had come to love. She was still scrutinizing the picture when the soft closing of the door behind her made her jump. Joseph Parmuat stood with a surprised look in his eyes.

"I am so sorry for intruding into your house," Taiyo said her face with its usually brown complexion becoming ashamed with embarrassment.

"It is okay," Joseph Parmuat replied, an inscrutable

smile on his face. " This is your brother's house and you are welcome any time."

There was a fleeting moment of silence that drew her eyes to his face. He too lifted his eyes to hers, and for the briefest of seconds, the two pairs of eyes met and held.

"I felt a bit bored and I thought I could call on you so that we can walk back to our house…" she stopped, swamped in confusion. Then she added quietly, "I am sorry. I suppose I really should not have come."

"Don't be ridiculous," he said still smiling. He dropped the bag he had carried onto the bed. "I have just been to the shops to purchase a few items before coming to your place."

There was another moment of silence in which neither of them moved.

"Joseph," she began eloquently. "There is need for us to talk about us."

"No, Taiyo, my dear sister," he protested vehemently. "There is no need for us to discuss matters we know are hurtful to us."

In silence she watched him as he took his velvet jacket hung behind the door and shrugged it onto his shoulders. "We may now go," he said and turned abruptly from her and began to walk quickly towards the door to the living room.

"Joseph!" The tone of her voice stopped him in his tracks. He stood for a moment, quite still, his back to her, his hand on the door handle, his wide shoulders slightly and defensively hunched before he slowly turned back to face her.

"Joseph," she called again her eyes searching his face.

"Let us not pretend that the two of us are not hurting in the same way."

"What are we going to do?" he asked his heart in terrible agony from which, for that one moment he did not attempt to shield. "It is for you I fear my dear lady. Nasila culture is violently dangerous when its sensibilities are violated."

"I don't care," she shouted and lifted her chin sharply, feeling the rise of such a conflict of emotion in her heart, that for a moment she feared she might scream. "No, I don't care about the oppressive Nasila culture. Why should I care about violating the backward culture when it does not care when it violates my own rights? I know you are in love with me the way I am in love with you." She looked up at him and his tall figure blurred before her eyes. "Joseph, deny before me right now that you love me. Do it right now!" sShe said hysterically, her voice too loud and out of control. The tears spilled hot down her cheeks. She did not bother to hide them or to brush them away.

Suddenly, Joseph Parmuat's heart was touched and he moved swiftly towards her. A single step took him to where she stood and he passionately took her into his arms. All control lost, she sobbed furiously, her body shaking, her head buried in his shoulder. His arm tightened about her while she felt his hand gentle in her hair. He was murmuring quiet soothing words that through the storm of her emotions meant nothing. The only thing that mattered and which she was aware of at that moment was the feel of his body against hers; its warmth and the brush of his crisp thick woolly hair against her cheek. She could not move. She pressed so close to him that she could hear the beating of his heart as if it were in her own body.

"No, Joseph," she said in an infantile whimper. "I can't bear that we can't express the love that we have for one another because of some primitive culture. If by loving you, I offend the sensibilities of Nasila then let me offend them and face the consequences of doing so!"

"I also love you, very much," Joseph Parmuat responded finally. "I loved you the moment I saw you during your father's homecoming ceremony. But then the clan matter came to separate us. It is true we have no blood relation. But Nasila culture dictates who are related and who are not. We are slotted among those who cannot marry."

"No, it can't be, I cannot accept its verdict," she said petulantly her words agonized. "No way, never!" She stopped, confused and angry with herself at her inarticulate outburst. She took several long steadying breaths and then said, "I cannot accept that a culture that does not feed me, clothe me, or house me comes to control my life. Our lives belong to us Joseph. The destiny of our lives is in our own hands. We should guard it jealously."

At last they drew a little apart. His eyes were open, honest and steady upon her face.

"I have also made up my mind, here and then," he said with exhilaration. He closed his eyes, took a deep slow breath and said with a trembling emotional voice. "I am too, ready to face any eventuality that may arise out of our love for one another."

"Thank you," she whispered and her tears began to overflow again. Her warm delicate fingers gripped his firmly as she said excitedly, "I knew all along that, you couldn't too throw away something so special and so precious. I don't care what others might think. We knew it right from the beginning and we know it now that something so wonderful can't be wrong. We must however initially be careful not to hurt others, especially *Papaai*, but eventually it will be inevitable that we reveal our love to everyone. After all, we can't love in darkness for ever, can we?" He said nothing to that.

When they later walked into the practice room they found Resian waiting for them, sitting as she always did hunched up in a chair, her nose determinedly buried in a book, reading. If she detected anything strange with her sister and their adopted brother, she did not show.

Taiyo was exhilarated beyond words. She was ecstatic; She was simply in a seventh heaven. From the first day she saw Joseph Parmuat, during her father's home-coming ceremony, she had fallen in love with him instantly: She thought he was the incarnation, the very picture of her dreams. She recalled the way it happened. She had been standing there with her sister Resian, their eyes glued to the handsome, arrogantly athletic *morans* who cut such a dash, as they danced and shrieked boisterously. She was greatly attracted by the way they moved to the centre of the circle, and one by one or in pairs, jumped high up in the air in step with the guttural chants of the other *morans* as they heaved their chests forwards and backwards excitedly. One *moran* in particular caught her eye. He was unique among the rest in that he was dark-haired while the rest had smeared greasy red ochre into their hair. He was a tall lithe young man, who, when he got his chance to jump, leapt higher and with more grace than any of the others. She was immediately attracted to him and her gaze henceforth riveted upon him. The attraction translated into love. And from that day, she was besotted with that love.

Taiyo had won over Joseph Parmuat or so she thought. She felt as if she was now on her way to win a major battle. Ever since they relocated to Nasila, she considered herself to be in a war zone against the debilitating Nasila culture. It was a war of liberation of the Nasila woman. She knew there were many battle fronts in a war. Other combatants had come out to fight and all that was needed to win was strong leadership. She thought they already had that in the indefatigable Minik ene Nkoitoi, *the Emakererei*. She was in one of the fronts. How she burned with an ardent desire to join her one day. She was their role model. She was their inspiration.

Taiyo knew that the day her secret love to Joseph Parmuat became public knowledge, there would be strong angry reactions from the elders of Nasila. But she intended to defiantly stand her ground, asserting that their lives with Joseph Parmuat belonged to them and them alone. But if the heat became unbearable, she concluded, they would always relocate to town and join what their mother, the other day, called people of an undefined culture, or what the Nasila people would call *ilmeekure-kishulare*.

Joseph Parmuat felt differently. When he went back to his house that evening after coaching the girls something, seemed to have changed dramatically and drastically. He recalled Taiyo's dazzling smile and the way her beauty filled him with enchantment. But the enchanting feeling seemed to have evaporated fast and in its place, his heart was now filled with a devastating feeling of hopelessness. There was a strange emptiness in him, a sort of hollowness he had never experienced before. His heart was desolate like a deserted house.

He couldn't place the problem. He had won the heart of the girl he ardently admired. That should have filled his heart with exhilaration. Instead it was filled with a frightening premonition.

Yes, he now knew. He was like a fish that had just jumped out of water in pursuit of one morsel, but was now finding itself unable to breath and was on the verge of death. Yes, it had swallowed the morsel, but what good was it to its body if it died? It was now desperately trying to wriggle back into the water. Was the morsel worth the risk the fish had taken and nearly lost its dear life? The morsel was enticing, succulent and luscious, but was it worth dying for? Other morsels that did not require one to die for, were available in the water. They were equally succulent and luscious, although they may not be equally attractive and enticing. Did he have to abandon Nasila culture in exchange of a woman who sneered at its tenets? Was she one who could be tamed or was she like a wild donkey? Even if she could, how would he ever jump the huddle of her status that negatively described her as being among *intoiye nemengalana*?

How about the complication brought about by the fact that she was a daughter of an *Ilmolelian* elder who was of *Iloorasha-kineji* like his own father and which made her his own sister? How would he ever go round that? He considered running away from Nasila and its culture but

139

that left a sour taste in his mouth. No, Nasila culture was too valuable to be abandoned. It gave him values. It gave him his identity. It gave him the latitudes within which to check his excesses and warned him when he went out of its confines. Yes, Nasila culture was the father and mother that brought up and nurtured its children to maturity. Nasila culture was too valuable and too important to be abandoned in exchange of a woman's love. But was Taiyo just another woman? He searched and searched his heart again. At the end, it was the wisdom of Maa that prevailed. Its founder had said a man could never run away from his clan and his age-set. He declined her love.

Chapter Ten

Apprehension set in the hearts of Ole Kaelo and Mama Milanoi. The awaited day was here; Oloisudori was about to claim his prize. Since the day Oloisudori left, they had had sleepless nights. They turned the subject over and over, but they were yet to find a way out of the impending disaster. Ole Kaelo had therefore continued to bury his head in the sand like the proverbial ostrich with a hope that time might provide a solution. He hoped against hope that the Nasilian adage that said bad days receded while good days approached, would come true.

Although they had decided to conceal the information regarding Oloisudori's evil intention, Resian continued to be apprehensive. She had a premonition. She had become hyper sensitive about her future and the possibility of her enrolling as a student at the Egerton University. Fear had crept into her life and a small voice seemed to warn her of impending danger. She wondered at times whether she was hallucinating or she was seeing strange faceless persons lurking at every dark corner of their house, especially at night. Before they went to bed, she made sure she had double-checked the doors. Although she was not superstitious, a recent incident where a bird called *Olmultut* came to coo sorrowfully at their gate, worried her. Joseph Parmuat had told them that when the bird cooed sorrowfully, it was always a harbinger of bad news. Its cry was always ominous.

It was different with Taiyo. Her mood was upbeat. Even her mother had noticed that in the last few days she had become extremely happy. She carried out her housekeeping duties while humming, whistling or singing loudly. What a wonderful daughter she had in Taiyo, her mother repeatedly thought happily, while observing the way she satisfactorily played her multiple roles as first-born daughter of the Kaelo family, sister to Resian, capable organizer in the home, ever present help as a housekeeper and a most cherished companion to her mother. Her mother thought her daughter's new found happiness was a welcome ray of sunshine in a home where gloom, cheerlessness and despondency had become a hallmark.

After procrastinating for quite sometime, Ole Kaelo and his wife decided to seek help. Kaelo would consult his friend and mentor, Ole Supeyo, while his wife would consult her *inkainito*, the wives of Simiren, Ole Kaelo's brother.

That morning's breakfast was taken in a sombre mood. Olarinkoi was the only one who did not seem to be preoccupied. His ubiquitous presence at every meal had now been accepted by everyone in the home. His silence and withdrawn nature nearly made him invisible, which was the opposite of Kaelo whose presence dominated the room.

"Yeiyo, shall we prepare a meat stew or a vegetable stew to go with the rice for lunch?" asked Taiyo as they neared the end of the breakfast.

"No, don't prepare anything." We have asked Maison to organise lunch for you at the shop. Your father and I are going out for some business and we shall not be back until this evening."

Kaelo shot a significant glance at his wife who, impervious, worked with neat dexterity at her crochet.

He then turned and looked at Resian with a thoughtful and piteous mien. Resian observed that her father was troubled but she did not know the reason. She wondered if his troubles had anything to do with the business taking him away for the day.

Taiyo's happiness insulated her from any feelings. Her mind was preoccupied by a pleasurable expectation that seemed to drag the hours of the day. She eagerly looked forward to meeting Joseph Parmuat in the evening so that she could express to him the ecstatic feeling borne of their newly found love.

The girls went to the shop where they were kept busy by Maison, the manager, who gave them stock bin cards, the records of which they were to reconcile with the physical stocks. They were delighted to find that he had prepared them a delicious lunch of *nyama choma* served with *ugali*.

At about three, they took their leave and set to go home. It was a hot afternoon and the heat was oppressive. They therefore walked slowly, occasionally stopping under a shady tree to take a rest. They had just resumed their walk and were passing though a bushy area when Resian spotted two men eyeing them from behind a tree. She pointed them out to Taiyo who suggested that they walk on as probably they were harmless herdsmen.

After getting closer, they immediately recognized one of the men who accosted them on their first day in Nasila and later jeered at them on that occasion of the homecoming ceremony. They were alarmed, afraid, and they trembled as the two men stood there grinninng down at them.

The men came out to the road and blocked the girls' way. The bravery which might have enabled them to face the two vagabonds, fizzled out quickly when they saw the bulging muscles of their arms and the demonic determination in their eyes to harm them. Their fear was heightened by the heavy knobkerries that the two men brandished menacingly. One of them, got hold of Taiyo and tried to drag her into the bush while the other wrestled with Resian. The girls screamed and screamed as they scratched the men's faces with their sharp fingernails.

But that was the farthest they could go. What happened next, happened so fast that the assailants and the victims were dumbfounded. It was like a bolt of thunder in a clear cloudless day.

Suddenly and unexpectedly, a third man sprang out of the bushes like a ghost. He first went for the man who was struggling with Resian on the ground. He seized the front of his shirt and coat and jerked him to his feet. He brought his right fist down in a powerful blow, lifting himself to his toes and putting the strength from his legs, back and arm behind his knuckles as they crushed into the man's nose and mouth. Blood exploded from the man's nose and mouth. He reeled across the road and slammed into a tree trunk with a force that shook the whole tree. He lay there motionless.

The stranger then took three quick steps and caught up with the man who had been dragging Taiyo into the bushes. The man tried to flee, but the stranger caught him by the collar of his coat and yanked him back. As he bounced back, the stranger drove his fist into the man's stomach and he doubled over. He then brought down his right fist and hit him on the side of his head. Blood splattered onto the ground. He too slumped on the ground writing in pain.

It was then that the girls recognized their hero. It was Olarinkoi. He did not talk or look at them. He stood there trembling with anger, breathing heavily, with his fists clenched and looking down at the men who lay in a heap. One of the men moved his limbs weakly and moaned hoarsely as thick, heavy streams of blood trickled from his nose and lips to the soil. Olarinkoi stepped forward, lifted his foot and kicked him viciously on the ribs. The man let out a loud yell and fell silent.

"That will teach them a lesson," Olarinkoi said. He majestically and pompously straightened the collar and the cuffs of his shirt and dusted its sleeves with his hand. "Now, go home girls."

Taiyo and Resian looked up at Olarinkoi gratefully. They could not find words to express their gratitude. It was only when he told them to go home that they collected themselves and began to walk. Although not injured, they were terribly shaken. They sobbed with rage and shame. The incident left a feeling of invasion and degradation. Their dresses were soiled and torn and one of Resian's breast ached from the vicious squeeze by one of the vagabonds.

When they got home, their parents had not returned. They still felt soiled and greasy. The stench of the men's sweaty filthy clothes and bodies still lingered in their nostrils and the feel of their rough hard hands still burned on their delicate skins. They took a bath and washed the dirty clothes.

They could never thank Olarinkoi adequately. They were lucky he had come at the nick of time. They could not imagine what would have happened to them had he not come at the very moment. One thing was certain: they would have been raped!

Later that night as they lay on their bed, each one of them was contemplative. Resian thought how hazardous it was to live in a society where men thought they had a right to every woman's body. The sooner she left Nasila, she thought angrily, the better it would be for her.

Taiyo also seethed with fury. She thought the two vagabonds that accosted them were part of the tyrannical Nasila culture that did not respect women. The incident strengthened her resolve that she was a combatant in a war zone. She hoped she would one day team up with the *Emakererei* to fight for women and girl child rights.

Chapter Eleven

Taiyo and Resian tearfully and eagerly waited for the arrival of their parents. They burned to tell them of the traumatizing incident. They also wanted to tell them of Olarinkoi's unexpected arrival and his quick valorous action which had rescued them from rape. Indeed the two were humbled by Olarinkoi's bravery and concern for their safely, especially when they recalled the way they had always ignored him and regarded him as good for nothing baggage.

Resian impressed upon her sister to use that incident to push their father to accept to let them go back to Nakuru and enroll at the Egerton University. Although the incident was unfortunate, she reasoned, it could convince him that Nasila was not a safe place. It was teeming with wolves, hyenas and crazy vagabonds. Had they been raped, his worry now would be whether his daughters had been infected with the H.I.V and A.I.D.S. The fact that they were lucky that time round, she told her sister emphatically, did not mean the incident could not recur with disastrous consequences. The alternative, she concluded in jest, was for their father to engage Olarinkoi's services to guard them twenty-four hours a day.

Taiyo did not require a lot of persuasion that evening. She was equally, traumatized. She was still dazed and she had not stopped seeing the blurred figure of that big-bodied hooligan zooming before her eyes as he tried to drag her into the bushes. She was determined to take the first available opportunity to persuade their father to let them return to Nakuru and enroll at the university. After all, she reasoned, both of them had attained the required qualifications and all they needed was the enrolment at the university and a sponsor.

Their parents looked tired, harassed and aloof when they arrived home. Their father immediately removed his shoes, slumped into a chair and stared at the ceiling unblinkingly. Their mother went straight into their bedroom and did not come out. For reasons they did not know, Olarinkoi did not return after that afternoon's incident. Joseph Parmuat too did not turn up. The girls had therefore to keep their horrific story, however urgent, to themselves until their parents had recovered from whatever was troubling them.

And they were truly troubled. Ole Kaelo's mission to Ole Supeyo had backfired. He had hoped, being his friend and mentor, to persuade him to take over all those stocks in his godowns that he had secured on the strength of those contracts that Oloisudori had enabled him sign with the parastatals. Had he accepted the arrangement and paid off all his liabilities to the banks, Ole Kaelo would have sneered at Oloisudori and told him to keep his hands off his daughter Resian. But Ole Supeyo had declined the offer effectively throwing him back to the hyena.

Mama Milanoi's mission did not fare any better. When she sought advice from her *inkainito*, regarding Oloisudori, they candidly responded that she and her husband were behaving like the proverbial greedy hyena that straddled two parallel paths with the ridiculous intention of reaching two destinations simultaneously so as not to miss the meals in either places. It however, died miserably without reaching any of the places. They accused them of being

148

aloof and selective on the aspects of Nasila culture they chose to interact with.

They had challenged her to persuade Ole Kaelo to let the girls stay with them for a period of time and let them bond with the other children. If they did that, they told her, they would see the difference. The senior most wife of Simiren, *Yeiyoo-botorr,* said Mama Milanoi might be surprised to find the girls asking to be circumcised without any coercion.

She had said she would take the challenge. But when Mama Milanoi found her husband devastated by whatever he was told by Ole Supeyo, she was not able to broach the subject.

When the girls got up the following morning their hearts were still heavy and the gloomy atmosphere of the previous night still hung in the air like a dark cloud. Nature seemed to be in agreement with the depressing atmosphere, as a thick mist clouded the distant hills to the east, blocking the usually radiant sunshine from pouring into their living room. But their mother's mood was completely different. Her previous night's taciturnity had turned into loquacity.

When their father later turned up for breakfast, he was edgy and his eyes were shifty. It was only when they told him what had befallen them the previous day that he was shocked back to his senses. He got agitated and angrily gnashed his teeth. He hit the table top with his clenched fist, rattling the crockery on it. He shouted in a thunderous booming voice saying an assault on his daughters was not only an affront to him personally that he could not tolerate but a threat to the security of his children and home that he could never ever allow to surface as long as he lived. Getting up suddenly, he briskly walked back to their bedroom. Their mother who was equally shocked and angered by the depressing news, followed her husband. The girls were left there crestfallen. Despondency and downheartedness alternated in their young hearts wreaking untold havoc in their already troubled lives.

Melancholy turned into fear when the girls saw their father re-emerge from the bedroom armed with a sword and knobkerrie. His eyes glittered with fury and his face turned ashen with combat. His mouth frothed and trembled as he murmured expletives. With long angry strides, he walked out of the house in a huff banging the door behind him. The girls were left wringing their hands and biting their fingernails with grief and apprehension.

When their mother eventually told them what she wanted them to do, the girls found that the quick succession of events that culminated in their father angrily storming out of the house, had mellowed their hearts and taken away their fighting spirit. They readily accepted that they needed a change of scene, if only temporarily. With their mother promising that in their absence she would try to convince their father to allow them to go back to Nakuru and enroll as students at the Egerton University, she nipped in the bud any opposition that Resian might have raised. She told them she wanted them to move into their uncle Simiren's home and live with them for sometime so that they could get to know them well, as well as know other people who lived in the neighbourhood. She repeatedly assured them that there was nothing sinister in the offing. As their loving mother, she told them reassuringly, she only wanted the best for them.

By noon, Taiyo and Resian had packed their suitcases and they were on their way to their uncle's home. They were most surprised by the warm reception that they received and when neighbours heard that Ole Kaelo's daughters had come to live with their aunts, cousins and their other relatives, they streamed into Simiren's homestead, and like that first day when they arrived into Nasila, there was a celebration mood in the air. They were greeted by so many cheerful people who shouted and hooted excitedly that they nearly got confused. This sharply contrasted with the gloomy atmosphere that they left behind in their home and for that they were appreciative.

Seeing the hearty welcome, the girls wholeheartedly plunged into that life with adventure in their hearts. With renewed interests and fresh feeling of affinity and without any condescension whatsoever, they observed the life at Simiren Ole Kaelo's home.

Life and work in that home was communal. Although each mother had her house and cooked her own food, all grown up daughters helped each one of them, to bring in water, firewood, and assisted in the actual cooking. Those mothers who were incapacitated by pregnancy, as two of them were at that time, received most help as the grown-up daughters were posted to their houses nearly permanently.

The most senior mother of the house, *Yeiyo-botorr,* could be said to have had patriarchal authority that neared that of Simiren, because she deputised him in the home. Whereas Simiren took care of weightier matters of the family such as the animal husbandry, trade and the sources

151

of food, *Yeiyo-botorr* took off his shoulders all matters of administration in the homestead. Hardly were there any disagreements on that front. When disputes arose they were speedily and amicably settled.

The girls were housed by *Yeiyo-kiti*. It was in there that they slept on that first day when they arrived from Nakuru and they occupied the same bedroom and slept in the same comfortable and warm bed.

They quickly bonded with her, for they found her closer to them both in age and thinking. She was modern, judging by the standard of that home. They also found her amicable, kind-hearted and understanding. It was a joy staying in her house.

It did not take long before Taiyo and Resian got used to the tempo of life in their uncle's home. Within that short period, they had learnt quite a lot. They could now tell how easy it was to stereotype the Nasila culture by highlighting the negative aspects while ignoring the positive ones. In their uncle's home, they learnt basic truths of Nasila culture and the day to day life that they would have never been taught by anybody anywhere.

They learnt with a lot of interest and excitement that to be able to fit into their uncle's home, one had to be selfless. That was inevitably so because in that home, everything was shared. In no time, the girls found themselves sharing with everyone else in that home, love, news, happiness, sorrows, experiences, time, lotion, combs, work and anything else that could be shared. They gave and they received in equal measure. They experienced children being taught, right from infancy, to be mindful of others and be respectful to seniors. They were taught to shun such negative attributes as selfishness.

Other than the old women, like *Kokoo-o-Sein*, who lived in a hut adjacent to Simiren's homestead, and who told riveting stories to children in her hut every evening, there was no formal learning of Nasila culture. *Olkuak* was the way of life. *Olkuak* was culture the young learnt from the old. If one wanted to belong, he or she had to take all its aspects in stride.

In school, the girls recalled learning that culture was the advance development of the human mind and body by training and experience. What they were now learning in that home was that Nasila culture was part of the larger Maa culture. And that elders defined it as the way of life of Maa people. It was *Olkuak le* Maa. It comprised their beliefs, their social institutions, and all their characteristics as a people. Any new way that went contrary to that established norm was considered to be against the Maa culture.

With the introduction of formal education, Resian thought, she could now understand the origin of a contradiction that existed in the minds of Nasila people. She could now see that although parents in Nasila wanted their children educated, they also feared the influence of that education, and rightly so. They must have found soon that the brightest of their sons, such as their own father, who pursued education out of Nasila, soon got alienated and hardly came back home.

Yes, it was the value systems that the new education introduced, that violently shook the foundation of Nasila culture. The quest for the new education was however, irrepressible, and its gains invaluable so much that it was now Nasila culture that was grappling with the changes it brought. And the changes were not only subtle but insidious, threatening an explosion in the not too distant future.

Their *Yeiyo-kiti* told them that she had been observing a new trend that other people might have ignored. A few of those Nasila sons and daughters who had emigrated to towns, were now slowly returning back to come to settle in the rural areas. She gave the example of their own father, Minik ene Nkoitoi the *Emakererei*, Reteti Korema, Setek Tumbes and a few others. Depending on how successful their return would be, she said, they might influence other people in towns to follow suit on finding that life in the rural areas could be meaningful and bearable.

The girls were excited to learn that their *Yeiyo-kiti* was known to their role model, Minik-ene Nkoitoi, the *Emakerereei*. She told them they originated from the same village called Mbenek Dapashi and they went to the same primary school. But being four years older, Minik left her behind when she passed her examination and was called to join high school away from their village. Years later after she was married, she learnt that Minik had gone to Makerere University where she studied veterinary medicine and acquired the name of *Emakererei*.

They were very interested in *Emakererei's* story for in her story, they saw themselves. "Was she circumcised?" they asked their *Yeiyo-kiti* mischievously. *Yeiyo-kiti* dodged the question a little by busying herself with some tasks in her kitchen where they sat. The crackling of the fire had stopped and only the smouldering log called *Ologol* still glowed, with the charcoal on it winking and twinkling weakly in the darkening room.

"I am not certain about that," she said smilingly at last.

"I must say I admire *Emakererei*," Resian said happily. "She seems to be a courageous woman who firmly opposes what she considers wrong without caring whether she rubs the men of culture the wrong way. Many women would not dare go against the grain. I would definitely want to be like her."

"So would I," Taiyo said. "We hope to join her soon. And when we do, Nasila will have the Kaelo's daughters to reckon with!"

Later in the afternoon as they walked down to Nasila river to draw water, Taiyo and Resian revisited their discussion with Yeiyo-Kiti. They also gave thought to Minik ene Nkoitoi, the *Emakererei*. They admired her gallant fight intransigent positions held by men against women. The fight she was spearheading would inevitably eradicate all those oppressive edicts and still leave the Nasila culture intact.

"Can you imagine the fury of the fathers whose five hundred girls she has snatched?" Resian asked excitedly. "I can see them grudgingly returning the bride-price that they had received."

"It is no wonder they hate her with a passion." said Taiyo equally excited.

They were silent as they climbed the hill on their way back from Nasila river to draw water. The water containers that they carried on their backs were now heavy. The straps that supported the containers pressed down their heads with a painful exhaustion.

As they walked, each one of them allowed her mind to fleetingly roam the fanciful land of wishful thinking. Resian thought how wonderful it would be, had she had a chance to enroll at the Egerton University and after graduation had a chance to work with her role model, Minik ene Nkoitoi, the *Emakererei* at the sheep ranch that she managed. She imagined herself already there driving a large flock of sheep. And when she thought of sheep, her mind flew back to fifteen years or so earlier and reminisced the first time she saw a sheep. It was a childhood memory, a memorable picture from the swirling scene around her which had been captured and preserved by her mind when she and Taiyo accompanied their father to the Nakuru Agricultural Show. She could still see in her mind a group of big, docile, tawny woolly animals that stood panting drowsily in a green pasture, with the sun beaming down brightly from a clear blue sky. She had then admired the white long overcoats that the handlers wore.

Taiyo also thought of *Emakererei*. She would ask Joseph Parmuat, to assist her compose a song in her praise. She had already put words to a tune she had composed to ridicule the three women who she thought collaborated with men to oppress the women folk. They were Nasila's three blind mice who, she thought, did not seem to know that the world was changing. Those were the witches (*enkasakutoni*), who threatened to curse *intoiye nemengalana* and ensured they did not get husbands nor children; the midwife (*enkaitoyoni*) who threatened to spy on the young women as they gave birth to ensure that any who was still among *intoiye-nemengalana* had her status altered there and then; and the dreaded circumciser (*Enkamuratani*), who would never tire of wielding her *Olmurunya* menacingly. She sang the song silently in her heart and a smile lighted her face.

Ndero uni modok	Three blind mice,
Tenidol eipirri	If you see the way they run,
Nemirr entasat naata olalem.	One chasing a woman with a knife
Olalem okordiloki enchashurr	A knife that was crooked in its sheath,
Eitu aikata adol ina kingasia	I have never seen such wonder
Naijo Ndero uni modok.	Like those displayed by the three blind mice.

After breakfast, on one of the days, Taiyo and Resian received a message from their parents, asking them to go back home. Their stay in that homestead had been so enjoyable and refreshing that they were reluctant to end it. However, they could not defy their parents' order and they began to prepare for their departure.

The following day was a special day. Directed by *Yeiyo-botorr,* the entire family ate together. On such days, food was prepared, cooked and rare delicacies served in her house. No child, under whatever circumstance, would have wanted to be absent from *Yeiyo-botorr's* house on such a day, they loved the special meals.

In uncle Simeren's home favouritism was never allowed. It was an offence to pretend to be a favourite child. If that was detected, the child was always shunned by the others. It was only *Yeiyo-botorr,* who occupied a special position in the home, who received favour from her husband without anyone frowning.

If an animal was to be slaughtered, it was done in *Yeiyo-botorr's* house where the first share of meat was cooked or roasted and eaten by the whole family together, and the rest was shared out equally to all the houses. Similarly, when shopping was done in bulk, it was first brought to *'Yeiyo-botorr's* house from where it was shared equally to the rest of the houses.

On that particular day, two he-goats had been slaughtered and *Yeiyo-botorr* gave instructions as to which pieces of meat were to be fried, which ones were to be stewed and which ones were to be reserved for roasting. *Yeiyo-kiti* was a specialist in making sausages out of the tripe and the small intestines. She was already busy cleaning them and making them ready to be stuffed with the already chopped cooked meat.

It was when Taiyo and Resian went into *Yeiyo-botorr's* house, where all the children were seated together with their mothers and uncle Simiren, that they were surprised to find their parents present. Apart from being totally unexpected, their visit was an anticlimax of some sort, coming at the time when they were really enjoying themselves.

Later in the evening when the children of the four houses learnt that their sisters whom they had come to love so much had to go back to their home, they all cried without restraint.

But what awaited them at their home, only their parents knew. However, Resian felt apprehensive when on more than one occasions, her father glanced at her furtively.

In the past she had got used to her father glaring at her with disapproval but she thought the sheepish look in his eyes was frightening and only time would tell what it portended.

Chapter Twelve

When Ole Kaelo heard of his daughters near-rape incident, he was so incensed that he was hopping mad. He was raving mad like a buffalo that had been infected with the east coast fever that was known as *Olmilo*. He was aggressively spoiling for a fight. Every now and then he groaned loudly like one in pain and clicked his tongue. Like a madman, he muttered to himself, making nasty waspish remarks.

He stopped any man he met on the way and gave a harangue on the corruption of Nasila morals, to an extent that his innocent defenceless daughters could be beastly attacked by deranged morons in broad daylight. The bitter and emotional invectives, he angrily uttered, had provoked and incited so many young men, especially of *Ilmolelian* clan, that by the time he reached his destination, the school where Joseph Parmuat taught, twenty or so young men armed to the teeth had joined him and were now furiously baying for the blood of whoever attacked his children.

"What are you doing here?" Ole Kaelo charged angrily and thunderously at Joseph Parmuat.
"Must you teach other people's children when your own sisters have been devoured by hyenas?"

"Oh, my God!" gasped Joseph Parmuat with shock. "What has happened, my dear father?

Tremblingly, Ole Kaelo gave him a brief explanation of what had happened to his daughters. He said by sheer mercy of God, Olarinkoi happened by coincidence to have been passing by, and saved the girls from molestation and possible sexual abuse. By the time he finished explaining,

160

Joseph Parmuat was so agitated that he too was trembling with anger like *Olourrurr* tree under a turbulent gale. He considered the disturbing news to be an emergency.

Striding swiftly to where a gong hung from a frame, he took a metal rod beside it and repeatedly struck it, forcefully giving it a deep ringing sound. The deep sorrowful sound sent panic-stricken children streaming out of their classes to the assembly line. The teachers had taught them over the years that the ordinary school bell was for announcing the commencement and the ending of classes. But the sounding of the gong either meant that the matter to be announced was too dangerous and therefore required prompt evacuation, or too urgent that it could not wait to be announced at the end of the day. They had been taught that on hearing the gong they were to instantly abandon everything they were doing and immediately run to the assembly line. And when they came out running, they were struck by fear when they saw many young armed men suggesting that danger was looming dangerously in the air. Their eyes dilated and they squirmed with fear when they saw the tall muscular man, whom they had known to own the biggest shop in Nasila, trembling and with froth oozing from the corners of his mouth. His razor-sharp weapon glittered dangerously in the morning sunshine.

Joseph Parmuat loudly called out the names of the boys from the *Ilmolelian* clan and told the rest to go back into their classes. He then instructed the *Ilmolelian* boys to immediately go home and tell their elder brothers and their fathers that there was an urgent meeting of the clan that they were required to attend immediately and without

161

fail at *Oerata* plain.

As soon as the boys were dispatched, those present immediately put their heads together and made enquiries amongst themselves as to who could be the possible suspected culprits. Olarinkoi, who would have told them who the vagabonds were, was nowhere to be found. He had vanished into thin air immediately after rescuing the girls. At the end of their deliberation, they had come up with a list of suspects.

When the larger group arrived, the meeting began in earnest. Speaker after speaker spoke, each one of them whipping up the emotions for the others. When after a long deliberation it was eventually concluded that the culprits were none other than Lante son of Kanyira of *Ilukumae* clan, and Ntara son of Muyo, also of *Ilukumae* clan, the die was cast. It was said that the *Ilukumae* clan had a grudge against *Ilmolelian*, and the action of the two vagabonds was nothing but a smoke screen that hid the real intention of the *Ilukumae*. They said, all recent provocations showed the disrespect and contempt in which they regarded the *Ilmolelian*. They even thought the provocative and scornful action of the two vagabonds was a gauntlet that was thrown at their feet by the *Ilukumae* men who were daring them to pick it. Instances in the past, were given, when the same *Ilukumae* had provoked them but when they had ignored them, the *ilukumae* had construed that to be a sign of weakness or cowardice.

After enumerating all the evil that was purportedly visited upon *Ilmolelian* by the *Ilukumae*, it was decided there and then that a decisive action be taken at once to stem out further provocation by the *Ilukumae*. It was imperative, they declared, that they retaliated with such vindictive force, so as to show the *Ilnkumae*, that *Ilmolelian* were not their whipping boys. And the beginning point, they declared angrily, was the hunting down of the two men who accosted the daughters of Ole Kaelo.

Later that evening a battle cry was sounded. The *Ilmolelian* young and old men who were still strong enough to fight and their sympathizers from *Ilmakesen* clan who were their distant cousins, came out fully armed and formed *enkitungat*, which was an *ad hoc* group of warriors that was specifically formed to hunt down the two vagabonds. It was an abrasive group that was instructed to be deliberately aggressive and corrosively provocative when dealing with any member of *Ilukumae* clan so as to annoy them and provoke them to engage them in battle.

The search for the two vagabonds was intense and thorough. There were thirty angry men thoroughly combing the bushes. They remained constantly on the alert as they proceeded swiftly but with caution, their eyes on the ground looking for the two men's footprints. Ole Kaelo panted with exhaustion, but he soldiered on, the anger that still burned in his heart energizing his legs. Joseph Parmuat followed him closely, to ensure the old man's was safe, for he knew he was not used to walking in the harsh terrain.

Now and again, the footprints of the two men would be spotted on the ground, sending the hunters wild with renewed vigour and vindictive determination to find the evil men and avenge the atrocities visited upon the *Ilmolelian* clan by the *Ilukumae* clan in general, and the evil and immoral act that the two villains had visited upon the two daughters of Ole Kaelo in particular.

They soon reached an area of rolling hills and wide open stretches of low *Olosiro* undergrowth. To avoid being seen by the two fleeing vagabonds, the men had to stay under the cover of trees and skirt around the open space.

The men had just topped a low hilly rise and had started trotting down the other side, when two old men walking along a path from the direction they were facing became visible in the distance. One was tall and heavyset, with his blanket roll hanging from his shoulder, his knobkerry and spear held in one hand while the other held a walking stick. The shorter one wore a long overcoat over a red *shuka* that protruded below it at the knee. Large blue beads hung down his extended earlobes and danced and swayed in constant motion as he walked. They conversed animatedly as they walked slowly and leisurely.

Ole Kaelo was looking at the approaching old men when three or four green-breasted birds called *ilkasero* flashed through the air and perched in a bush further back in the trees. Then they fluttered their wings rapidly and flared away from the bush. Ole Kaelo turned his head slightly and looked absently at the bush. There seemed to be something strange. He suddenly stiffened and his eyes widened. He thought he saw a shadowy figure in the trees. He peered once again, and confirmed that it was a man on a tree. He was completely motionless and invisible against the mottled pattern of the ground and foliage. Then there was a slight flowing movement and a couple of leaves on the lower branch of the bush stirred slightly as though a breath of wind had touched them, then the man was gone, disappearing instantly behind a tree.

Ole Kaelo's eyes were riveted on the tree and he almost missed another movement. A dusky shadow flicked from another tree to an adjacent one in the space of time it took his eyes to blink. He looked from the first tree to the second, still not very sure he had seen people and not monkeys. Then there was a sinuous movement along the ground by the second tree as the man there disappeared into another bush.

The other men also saw what Kaelo was seeing and they stealthily began to encircle the trees where the men hid. By then, there was an open space of about fifteen or so metres between the trees in which the two men hid and the two old men who were approaching.

Suddenly and without warning, the two men darted from the bushes in a lightning speed across the open space. The thirty men together with Ole Kaelo and Joseph Parmuat sprinted murderously from the bushes and hotly pursued the two with their weapons high up in the air ready to strike deadly blows.

The two approaching old men saw the thirty armed men running towards them with swords and knobkerries, and got alarmed. They stopped and stared confusedly. The happenings dawned on them when the young men, who seemed to be fleeing from mortal danger, fell at their feet and hugged their legs pleading for intercession. When the old men hesitated, the two cried more, pushing themselves underneath the old men's clothing between their legs. But before any pleading could take place, they had been clobbered thoroughly and were bleeding profusely from various parts of their bodies.

"*Aatulutoiye, Papaai*!" one young man fearfully pleaded.

"*Aatasaiyia tomituoki siake*!" the other cried out passionately.

The men were eventually spared. According to Nasila culture, a man who pleaded for mercy and fearfully hid his head between the legs of an old man, no matter what crime he had committed, always had his life spared. They were however roughed up and made to undergo intense interrogation.

Joseph Parmuat slapped and kicked them several times before they involuntarily gave all the details that were demanded from them. Parmuat thought he owed it to the two girls to avenge their torment and the embarrassment they had received from the shameless would-be-rapists and vagabonds. Ole Kaelo too, slapped and kicked the two men to avenge the shameful act that the two brutes had visited upon his daughters.

It was during the interrogation that a queer revelation surfaced. One of the vagabonds, although he was of *Ilukumae* clan, was related to Taiyo and Resian. Ntara Muyo was their first cousin. He was a son of Mama Milanoi's sister who was married to Muyo, an elder of *Ilukumae*. On learning that, Joseph Parmuat was most embarrassed. Although he was of *Ilmolelian* clan of *Iloorasha*-Kineji sub clan, he was not as closely related to the girls as that vagabond was. Ole Kaelo too was flabbergasted. He was however grateful that a major disaster had been averted, for had he caused the death of that young man, he would have brought upon himself a curse that could not be easily cleansed.

And that revelation spared the Nasila people a blood-bath. The anticipated battle between *Ilmolelian* and the *Ilukumae* clans was averted by the shameful revelation. An elaborate cleansing ceremony was planned and the *Ilukumae* clan were to compensate Ole Kaelo for the trauma he had undergone. Ntara Muyo was to give a heifer each to Taiyo and Resian and an extra heifer to erase the shame that was brought about by the offence and restore the respect for which a brother and his sisters regarded one another. Lante son of Kanyira was to pay two heifers.

Mama Milanoi thought that the offence her nephew committed was too ignominious and inexcusable, especially now that it had introduced tripartite complications that involved her father's clan of *Ilmakesen,* her husband's clan of *Ilmolelian,* and now the young man's father, Ole Muyo's clan of *Ilukumae.*

Although she did not consider herself irascible, the offence the young man had committed against his cousins incensed her so much that at times she thought she was becoming irrational. At one extreme point of her irrationality, she had found herself wishing that the rascal had been clobbered to death on that day he was cornered. But when reason prevailed upon her, she discarded her intransigent view that the young man was an incorrigible criminal who could not be corrected and whose only remedy was elimination.

Mama Milanoi began to see the wisdom of the Maa founder who ensured that justice was always tempered with mercy. It was that tenet of Nasila culture, she thought, that gave that villain son of her sister and his criminal friend a second chance to live when they tucked their heads between the protective legs of the two old men. Like chicks that tucked their heads under the protective wing of their mother when a hawk appeared in the sky, so did they find protection in the indispensable Nasila culture. And who could tell? The young men, now that they had been given a second chance, could develop virtues such as loyalty and truthfulness and live to be respected elders of Maa.

When her husband joined her, she was surprised to find his mind more liberal. He said he regretted his earlier views that an offence committed by an individual was committed on behalf of the clan the individual belonged to, and therefore, the entire clan became culpable and collectively punishable.

When calm returned and there was a conducive atmosphere for discussion, Ole Kaelo thought it was time they revisited several pertinent issues pertaining to Oloisudori's impending visit. He knew how relentless and pertinacious the demonic man was. No amount of persuasion would change his mind about Resian. Two days earlier he had received a message from him saying he was delaying the visit for another month to allow him time to put finishing touches to the house where his bride would be accomodated.

Before discussing Oloisudori's issue, Ole Kaelo thought it better to touch on a matter that was less controversial. He told his wife about the meeting and the verdict of the council of elders that met to deliberate upon the case. The two boys had been fined two heifers each with Mama Milanoi's nephew Ntara Muyo, being fined an extra heifer to cover the shame that he had occasioned by accosting his own sister. In addition, Ntara Muyo had been banished from ever stepping into Ole Kaelo's home or having anything to do with his daughters for the rest of his life. To mollify his wife's feeling, knowing the attack was carried out by her nephew, Ole Kaelo said he would give back the three heifers Ole Muyo was to pay on behalf of his son, as a peace offering – to cement their families relations. That done, peace returned in earnest.

But Oloisudori's impending visit continued to gnaw at them. The mere thought of the visit brought a nasty twinge of conscience in his heart. What Oloisudori saw in their daughter Resian, he simply could not understand. Truly, even as a father, he could see that his daughter's body was blossoming like the body of any other girl at her age but, he thought there was nothing spectacular in her body that was so much at odds with her plain and unremarkable face. He had to admit that if it were not for his reputation and the age factor, Oloisudori would have been the perfect match for that sullen and hardheaded daughter of his. After all, Oloisudori was not just any other suitor. He was a man of substance and a man of property. Ole Kaelo began to warm up to the idea that Oloisudori could, after all, be a son-in-law. Where else would he ever get such a business offer as the one Oloisudori had offered him, and for what a price? When all but one road was closed to a protagonist, however narrow that one road was, the protagonist had to squeeze through it especially if that road was a matter of life and death. To lose his business premises, lose all those stocks and possibly lose his only dwelling, was to him a matter of life and death. To survive, he realised with finality, he had to change his attitude towards Oloisudori;

he had to embrace him.

He began to rationalise all matters pertaining to Oloisudori. He thought of the disquieting matter of his reputation. He thought it was all hearsay. It was some vague gossip and possibly pure nonsense. He concluded that those lies about Oloisudori were being bandied about by enemies of his development. The six wives the man was said to be married to, were daughters of men like him. There was, therefore, nothing wrong with his daughter being the wife of Oloisudori. Who else could have made it possible for him to sign those lucrative contracts other than Oloisudori who, as it now transpired, did it purely to win his daughter's hand? If his daughter Resian abandoned her *Olkuenyi* and accepted to be married to Oloisudori, he told himself, she would soon have her own establishment and a wealthy husband who had much ambition. However, even with all those pleasurable convictions, the mention of Oloisudori's name brought a wry twist to Ole Kaelo's lips.

Once convinced, Ole Kaelo also persuaded his wife that all what remained for them to do was find an agreeable and amicable way of handing Resian to Oloisudori.

The return of Taiyo and Resian brought back life to the nearly desolate home. Excited laughter and exchange of bantering remarks returned in earnest. They were elated at having visited their uncle's home and they hoped to continue and maintain the established relationship.

Their mother told them of the vagabond saga; one of the apprehended villains Ntara Muyo, was their cousin. He was a son to one of her sisters, married to an'*Ilukumae* man called Muyo. When she told them of the council of elders' verdict and the number of cattle each villain had to pay as a fine, Resian hit the roof with indignation.

"No, never!" she thundered angrily, "*Yeiyo*, that can't be. The thugs must be arrested and taken to court so that they go to jail. The least they should get is twenty-years jail term."

"I agree entirely with Resian," Taiyo said emphatically. "Our trauma cannot be appeased by a mere two heifers while the villains are walking freely. Who knows, they could even right now be stalking another pair of young innocent girls. Surely, *Yeiyo*?"

The angry girls complained tearfully. Their mother thought they were being petulant and she did everything she could to allay their fears and calm their nerves.

The surface ripples caused by the incident passed away within the next few days. Mama Milanoi had her say in the matter and expressed her gratification for having been able to stem the tide of rebellion within the girls hearts. She did not doubt that Resian was capable of carrying out the threat, and she feared if that happened, new deadly battle fronts would be opened. For one, the fragile truce that had been established between *Ilmolelian* and *Ilukumae* clans would flare up afresh. Two, the Kaelos and the Kuyos would battle afresh, while she would be seen to wrestle her own sister to the ground as the entire new conflict pitted them against one another.

Although the ripples had calmed down, below the surface was a deeper and longer lasting effect from the incident, and the way it had been resolved. There was another subtle shift in the relationship between the girls and their mother. The girls ties and the bonding with their uncle's family could not be concealed. The result was a strengthening of their independence and a diminishing of their parents authority over them. The change in the relationship between Resian and her father was less subtle. It appeared that her father became aware of the possibility of a serious rift between him and his daughter, and apparently went to greater pains to make himself more congenial. She was still moody and sullen at times but ever since they began interacting with their uncle's family, she was consistently more amicable. However, their mother still found Resian's attitude to life unpredictable and her daughter's grasp of her personality remained vague.

One pleasant thing the girls noticed when they began interacting freely with Nasila people, was that men began to treat them differently. There were no more impudent stares and grins when they walked past them. One or two surreptitiously stared or watched from the distance, but when they passed near them, they were greeted with respect. Some of the younger men grinned and spoke in a friendly manner mixed with admiration. But the older men regarded them with a friendly and almost fatherly attitude. The girls had never been happier. A feeling of involvement developed as they came to know more people in Nasila.

Little did they know it was a lull before a turbulent storm.

Chapter Thirteen

Edward Oloisudori Loonkiyaa had ambushed them again. He had earlier promised to go for Resian in two weeks but he abruptly changed his mind; he would pick her up the following day. He was going to be accompanied by his three important friends and he specifically wanted Resian to cook for them.

The message sent panic into the hearts of Ole Kaelo and his wife. They had been dilly dallying for a long time unable to find the best way to approach Resian and break the news to her. At last, their procrastination had caught up with them.

Taiyo and Resian had been to the practice room where Joseph Parmuat had been coaching Taiyo in song and dance. Resian had sat there reading. At the end of the coaching, Taiyo had gone straight to the bathroom to take a shower and change. Resian sauntered into the living room where their mother and father sat comfortably in the overstuffed armchairs set in the corner near a warm charcoal brazier. Her father was reading an old newspaper which he set aside when she entered.

"*Ne-yeiyo-ai nanyorr*," he called her pleasantly, his voice warm and cordial.

"*Yeoo*," she answered, greatly surprised and made wary by her father's use of the pleasant diminutive reserved only for the person one loved very much. The determinedly pleasant tone raised an eyebrow.

"How was your day, my dear child?" he asked a broad smile lighting his face.

"It was fine, *Papaai*," she answered a little confused.

"Taiyo and I went to *Yeiyo-botorr's* garden and helped her weed her potatoes."

"Wonderful," he roared with a warm friendly laughter, "so you can now weed, eh?"

"Of course yes, *Papaai*," Resian answered apprehensively. She pushed her hands into the pockets of her skirt and hunched her shoulders defensively. As long as she could remember, her father had never taken the slightest interest in anything she had said or done, except to criticise or rebuke her. That conversation was making her suspicious and uneasy.

"I know you are a wonderful cook and an efficient housekeeper," her father said unexpectedly, his eyes glittering in unexplained excitement. "Now that you are able to take care of a farm, I am proud to say I have got a daughter who is an all rounder, who is able to take care of her own establishment."

"Thank you, *Papaai*, for the compliment," said Resian sheepishly, too embarrassed at being the focus of attention. Absent-mindedly she added, "Tomorrow we shall be assisting *Yeiyo-kiti* to plaster her kitchen."

"No, not tomorrow, Resian," her father answered emphatically, his tone suddenly hardening. He withdrew behind the wings of his chair the way a tortoise withdraws into its shell. "Tomorrow, I would like you to remain here at home and help your mother prepare lunch for some visitors."

"Visitors?" Resian asked, surprised.

"Yes, Oloisudori is coming for lunch," her father said evenly as if to show there was nothing special about him, "I was going to ask Taiyo to stay and help your mother, but it seems as if you had impressed Oloisudori so much the last time he was here, that he particularly asked that you be here to receive him and his party. It is good to be impressive, isn't it, eh?"

Resian did not respond. The long moment of appalled silence was so dense that it was suffocating. It was ominously pregnant with sudden terror, and Resian was amazed to see her mother sit quietly as if nothing was happening.

"Must I be there, *Papaai*?" Resian asked desperately. "Surely, *Yeiyo* can manage on her own. Isn't it *Yeiyo*?"

"You have to be there, Resian!" her father thundered with finality. "It is important to me that you be there."

"But, *Papaai*, please...."

"I have said you have to stay at home tomorrow and help your mother with the preparation of the lunch," he growled, the familiar edge of ill-temper showing in his voice, but his eyes avoided hers. "There is an end to all this nonsense!"

"I have never served such important people, *Papaai*," she once again said pleadingly. "And you know I get nervous when I am forced into such a situation."

"You must learn to get used to such situations!" he shouted angrily and glared at her with such distaste that Resian stepped back from him, biting her lip. His voice was cold as he added acidly. "What kind of a wife will you make if you don't take time to learn the social graces?"

"*Papaai, siake,*" she made a last attempt to plead to her father's inner feelings. She hesitated for a while and then plunged headlong. "I can't just stand Oloisudori. He is like a monster and he frightens me...."

175

"Enough of that," her father ordered angrily. "And now get out of my sight. But remember to be there tomorrow. And you must stem out that argumentative attitude that is creeping into you. Now go!"

With a clenched right fist, he forcefully hit his open left palm, his eyes fierce with anger. But right inside his heart he knew his anger was coupled with something else. It had some edge of guilt on his part. It was also bewildering and frightening. Even more frightening was to hear her call Oloisudori a monster. It was simply dreadful!

As she hurriedly left the living room, Resian staggered and caught her foot under the leg of a chair. Her father's lips tightened, and he glared at her, saying nothing. Blindly, she walked out into the outer hall, through the front door, down the steps, and right to the garden. Her jaw was clenched, her lower lip caught painfully between her teeth. Why, in God's name, she asked herself vehemently did Oloisudori have to insist that she must be there when he and his friends ate their lunch? She shook her head fiercely. She couldn't do it, she wouldn't do it, she declared.

She walked to an *Oloponi* tree at the centre of the garden. Finding a log underneath it, she sank down on it her shoulders drooping, her knees drawn to her breasts and her arms folded upon them. She sat so for a long time, shivering in the gnawing cold, staring into the darkness barely blinking. In a helpless gesture of unhappiness she bowed her head, resting her forehead on her arms, and went into serious reflection on what her father was trying to force her to do.

She did not believe him when he said Oloisudori had chosen her over Taiyo, to prepare lunch for him. She did not believe that. She knew her father despised her and hated her ever since she was young. She wondered what he disliked so much about her. Was it her fault? Her father would never provoke Taiyo the way he constantly provoked her. He would never rebuke, scold or ridicule Taiyo the way he repeatedly rebuked, scolded and ridiculed her. She thought he was now going a step further to make her an adjunct to his enterprise whose only purpose was to entertain his business associates, such as Oloisudori and his friends. Had her father respected her feelings, he would have listened to her when she said she did not like Oloisudori. She wondered why he was still insistent that she must be there, even after giving her reasons.

It was Taiyo who went to fetch her sister in the garden.

"Resian, for heaven's sake, what are you doing here?" she rebuked her sternly when she found her hunched up in the dark. "It is so cold out here. Look at you, you are shivering!"

"I was about to come in," Resian said demurely.

"Stupid thing!" Taiyo snapped. "Imagine coming out here without a pullover. Honestly, Resian, haven't you the slightest common sense? Come on now, let's go!"

They went into the house and Resian angrily told her sister, about her father's demand. Taiyo, however, thought her sister was being frivolous. Although she had always known that their father disliked Resian, she thought she was now giving him reason to hate her even more. And truly, she had seen that their father was growing more and more disappointed with her. His continued reprimand to Resian had become very embarrassing to Taiyo as he kept on giving her as an example of a well behaved and well disciplined girl to the chagrin of Resian. Even their mother had said several times that Taiyo was a paragon of virtue; a true model of Maa feminine decorum. And that was because she hardly ever talked to her father unless he spoke to her, and then only to answer him with utmost respect whatever question he had asked her. Their mother thought Taiyo had learnt from her not to question things or ask why they were done one way and not the other, unless it was really her business to do so.

And because of Taiyo's behaviour which their father perceived to be exemplary, he never lost an opportunity to impress upon Resian, to emulate her sister. However, the comparison had always upset Resian and remained a constant reminder of her perceived failures. Obviously, she could not have known how disillusioned her father had been right from the day she was born. Perhaps had she known how deeply he felt the misfortune of having her as a daughter rather than the son he had wanted, she could have reacted differently to his constant and unceasing rebuke and ridicule.

Resian blamed her father for the tension that continued to grip their home ever since they came to Nasila. And she did not hide that fact from their mother. She blamed the new development on what she called a newborn *mongrel*; a new culture that was partly Maa and partly a combination of a myriads of cultures found in Nakuru town. And that was the animal he had introduced into his home in Nasila which was now threatening to devour her first and thereafter everyone else, one by one.

When they recently stayed in their uncle's home, she had come face to face with some of the best tenets of Nasila culture that was also the Maa culture. She found out that the girl child was always protected and shielded from males who ogled and stared at them with not so good intentions. Whenever there were male visitors in the home the girls were shepherded away, into one of the aunts houses. And their aunts served the visitors. The girls only came out after the guests had gone. Some of the elders, were courteous enough to ask, before they entered into a house, whether there were children in there. And in Maa, the term children always referred to girls. If they were in, elders would either move to another house or if they must enter, the mother of the girls would tell her daughters to move to one of her aunts' houses and in such a case, the elders would politely stand outside the house until the girls had left. During their stay in their uncle's home, they hardly came face to face with him. There was hardly any interaction between the fathers and their daughters. And the fathers jealously guarded the privacy of their daughters and ensured their security.

It took a lot of persuasion to have Resian agree to serve Oloisudori and his friends the following day. And she was only convinced when she was told her father's business depended on her decision.

By morning, stubborn Resian had gotten her way. She had demanded that her sister Taiyo also be enlisted among those who would serve the distinguished guests. When her mother resisted, saying the guest's wish should be respected, Resian had put up a spirited fight, arguing that it was wrong for them as a family to allow a visitor, whoever

179

he was, to dictate as to who amongst the members of the family should attend to him. She rejected Taiyo's argument that since they had promised *Yeiyo-kiti* that they would go and help her plaster her kitchen; she would better be there to represent her. Resian said their *Yeiyo-kiti* would surely understand when they explained to her that the cause of their inability to avail themselves to assist her, was the arrival of their father's visitors. In lowered tones, she had told Taiyo she needed her presence to fortify her spirit for she said, Oloisudori really terrified her.

It was after their mother consulted their father that it was settled. Taiyo was to assist in serving the visitors alongside her sister Resian.

Taiyo found her sister's fear of Oloisudori's presence justified. He arrived in a procession of four imposing chauffeur-driven four-wheel drive vehicles. Behind the four vehicles trailed a pick-up whose back was covered in a tarpaulin. At the back left of each of the four vehicles sat a man of stature.

Taiyo and Resian craned their necks to watch through their kitchen window as the four great men arrived in style. They were driven slowly to the front of the house, with their amber parking lights flickering in unison. The girls thought their father looked harassed as he stood alone, hands clasped in front of him as if in prayer. He kept shuffling his feet nervously as he waited. Resian compared her father to a man she had read in a book called *a major domo*, who was incharge of servants in a large house. Although Taiyo did not share the snideness of her sister, she too thought their father cut a sorry figure as he stood alone with an ingratiating smile on his face. His faded beige suit was unimpressive.

When the first big car stopped before him, the girls saw their father's tongue flick out like that of a chameleon as he nervously licked his dry lips. His eyes glittered as he stooped to carefully open the door of the shiny limousine.

"Oloisudori Lonkiyaa, Sir," the girls heard the tremor in their father's voice, excited and stammering. "Welcome to the humble abode of your friend and bro...er er.fa... er..."

The man who came out of the car was a sight to remember. It was evident that he meant to be ostentatious. Right from the designer shoe thrust out of the high-sided vehicle; the blue pin-striped designer business suit; the golden watch that dangled from his hand; the golden bracelet matching cuff links; and the golden chain that adorned his neck, all were flaunted in a show of opulence. That was Edward Oloisudori Lonkiyaa.

And when his three friends alighted, Taiyo and Resian shuddered at their sight. Even Taiyo who was usually not interested in discerning appearances, got alarmed and wondered what the men's mission was. All the men looked alike; they were of the same height and possibly weighed nearly the same. Like a bridegroom and his escorts, they wore matching suits and adorned expensive golden ornaments like those of Oloisudori. Only one of the men had an extra adornment: a golden tooth that shone brilliantly when he smiled.

Resian's words in a way were prophetic, Taiyo thought; not only did she dislike Oloisudori the moment he walked through the door to their house, but she also immensely hated the pomposity that he and his friends displayed. The tall, muscular and distinguished looking Oloisudori, was indeed exactly as Resian had described him. He was bad mannered, discourteous and certainly overbearing. With sure feminine instincts, Taiyo sensed that the man's mission in their home was more than a business excursion.

She was alarmed, even fearful when it dawned on her that the evil looking man was possibly targeting her sister Resian, and hence his demand that she be there to serve him on that day. His pretended kindness, warmth and charm as he greeted them, were nothing but an empty facade, she concluded. Taiyo thought the man's obvious disdainful regard for their father was enough to make her contemptuously consign him to the dustbin. Even the very many gifts he brought for every member of the family did not impress Taiyo. They all paled in her eyes and looked worthless. And like the demon that she thought he was, Oloisudori doled out the gift gleefully.

To their father, he gave suiting materials that would make four suits of different colours; six lengths of beautifully embroidered materials to make the coveted *vitenge* to the mother; silk materials of different colours to Taiyo and a pretty golden brooch and twelve lengths of different kinds of material to Resian. In addition, there was a golden pendant, a golden bracelet and a cutely designed golden ring. And finally, to their father came another gift: a briefcase whose content was not immediately disclosed.

The lunch was a great success. At first Resian was reluctant to perform the special task that had been assigned to her. But after being nudged by Taiyo, she consented. She carried the water dish in which people would wash their hands though she did not like doing that because it entailed moving from one person to the other, and she had to stand before each person and allow them to stare at her face or engage in some ridiculous discussion as they washed. And true to her thoughts, when she stood before each one of the three friends of Oloisudori, they detained and peered at her as if to try to pry and know her worth. When she got to Oloisudori, he took a long time washing his hands as he gloatingly peered at her.

Mama Milanoi outdid herself in honour of her husband's visitor and his friends. She presented before them a fitting delicious meal. First there was the tasty appetizers which included chopped little pieces of roast liver, heart, and *ilimintilis* that were followed by a selection of cold boiled mutton. Then there followed Mama Milanoi's speciality of delicious *nyama choma* eaten with *kachumbari* and vegetables. The men ate ravenously and with great appetite. Although she had not made any desserts ever since she left Nakuru, Mama Milanoi thought Oloisudori and his friends deserved special treatment. She therefore presented to them very tasty thinly sliced oranges sprinkled with sugar. And the men loved them.

The conversation at the table was entertaining but reserved. Ole Kaelo was tense and kept on throwing furtive glances at his daughters as if to make sure that they did not do anything to spoil the party. The girls however did not disappoint him. And the men told Mama Milanoi and her daughters that they had a beautiful home and that they had enjoyed their visit. Oloisudori's friends were loquacious, especially after the fifth bottle of hot spirits was emptied.

When the party broke up at three in the afternoon, amidst warm appreciation from the friends of Oloisudori, Ole Kaelo was all smiles. He thought he had been rated a worthy companion of the likes of Oloisudori. He had 'arrived'.

And when Oloisudori asked his friends what they thought of the girl, it was thumbs up by all the three. "She is the catch of the year," they declared.

Later in the evening after Taiyo and Resian had cleared the table, washed all utensils and cleaned the kitchen, Taiyo came back to the living room. She found her father sitting alone enjoying a last glass of the hot drink the visitors had been drinking. He was reading a newspaper, his reading glasses perched upon the tip of his nose. On hearing his daughter enter, he looked up, pushed back the reading glasses and briefly stared at her. Taiyo was careful in the way she approached her father for she knew he was edgy and sensitive. She however wanted to find out from him what he thought of the luncheon and in the process see whether she would get a hint on what it was all about. The body language of the four men and the lavish gifts they gave had disturbed her and got her suspicious. She had a lot of trust and confidence in her father, but she feared unscrupulous people like Oloisudori could, like Joseph Parmuat had told them, lead him into a murky alley and then turn round to extort the impossible from him.

"I came to see whether you are comfortable, *Papaai*," Taiyo said pleasantly.

"Yes, indeed, I am," he answered and nodded a little absently. "I am comfortable, my dear child."

"It was a lovely day, wasn't it, *Papaai*?" she asked as she plumped up a cushion on a sofa. "And I hope Resian and I did everything you expected us to do to make the visitors comfortable and happy."

"Indeed you did everything," he said curtly. "Yes, I must say the visitors were happy."

"And Mr. Oloisudori is becoming a very close business associate of yours, isn't he *Papaai*?" she asked eyeing him slyly as she moved a chair back to its accustomed place. "He can really be generous, eh?"

"Most certainly he is."

"Did he take part in funding our shop?" she continued and rued it immediately for she noticed he was getting irritated.

"Yes, but why do you ask?" he snapped showing signs of a rising temper.

"Nothing, *Papaai*," Taiyo answered quickly trying to avert an oncoming clash. "I just thought we should know so that we can in future treat him with the respect he deserves."

"Good!" he said with finality and picked up his glass, tipped and drained off its content in one quick gulp.

Taiyo hesitated. Now that she had failed to get any information from her father, she thought she could try another line. From the day they came back from their uncle's home, she and Resian had been waiting for their mother to tell them what their father's response had been regarding their request to be allowed to go back to Nakuru to enroll as students at the Egerton University. Over the past few weeks, Resian irritating sulks notwithstanding, Taiyo knew her conscience had not been entirely clear.

She had on several occasions promised her sister that she would speak to their father, but she had never come round to doing so.

"*Papaai*," she called him pleasantly.

By then, her father had folded his newspaper and was now busy folding his glasses – putting them into their leather case. That done, he placed the leather case neatly upon the folded newspaper. "Yes, my dear child."

From the kitchen came the loud voices of Resian and their mother as they argued about something. Taiyo saw her father turn his head and cock it to that direction, listening. She knew she had lost his attention. "I am sorry my child, what were you saying?"

"I was just saying," Taiyo hesitated and noting that her father's thoughts were no longer with her, gave up the idea of speaking to him that night about the university. She hoped there would be another chance soon.
"I was just wishing you a good night."

"Yes, of course," he said absent-mindedly. "Good night my dear."
And as she left the room, her father called back and said. "Please call Resian for me."

That alarmed Resian but strangely, the alarm turned into optimism. As she quickly walked to the living room where their father was still seated, she felt optimistic: glad tidings had finally come. Either their mother had successfully argued their case before their father and he had finally consented to their request to enroll at Egerton University, or her sister Taiyo had at last done it. Oh, wonderful sister Taiyo! She was still replaying those pleasurable words when she reached where her father was seated.

"Yes, *Papaai*," Resian said apprehensively. "I am here. Taiyo tells me you are calling me?"

"Yes, yes," her father replied. "Please take a seat."

"Yes, *Papaai*," Resian repeated as she sat on a chair far away from her father.

"Come nearer ... child," her father said pleasantly. "Why do you sit a mile away? Come nearer."

Resian moved her chair hardly an inch from where it was and then she looked up into her father's face with eager expectation.

"If I do remember well," her father began in a low even tone, "you will be nineteen in September this year, am I right?"

"You are quite right, *Papaai*." Resian answered eyeing him curiously. His face was unusually kind. His eyes held hers as he smiled broadly. 'That's it!' she thought triumphantly. 'That must be it!'

"You and I have not discussed important issues for a long time," he said with a friendly chuckle that was intended to bring her closer to him. "I thought today would be the best day to break the news. Your future is very important to me, my dear child."

Resian thought the concern in her father's voice, rang false. She hesitated, but could not hold herself any more. The anxiety was too great.

"*Papaai*, is it *Yeiyo* or Taiyo who spoke to you?" she asked sensationally, thinking she was stating the obvious. But seeing her father's face cloud, she added quickly. "Who between them spoke to you about our enrollment at the Egerton University?"

"What are you talking about, child?" her father who

seemed perplexed and dumbfounded, asked after a long and uncomfortable silence.

"Both *Yeiyo* and Taiyo promised to talk to you about it, and I thought she had."

"What, in the name of God are you talking about, child?" he repeated this time agitated and shaking his head vigorously. "No, I have never spoken to anybody about any of you enrolling at the university. Never! When I said I wanted us to discuss your future, that isn't what I meant at all. Of course not!" Resian looked at her father's face enquiringly.

"I was going to tell you ..." he hesitated and then stopped. His usual irritation and short temper reasserted themselves. "Never mind what I was going to say. For heavens sake, Resian, go back to the kitchen. I'll talk to you another day. Ask your mother to come here immediately!"

The sound of his tone carried a definite finality.

Chapter Fourteen

Ole Kaelo visit to Oloisudori's home greatly changed him. He felt rejuvenated like a man who had just returned from the mountain top where he had inhaled and exhaled the thin, fresh and invigorating mountain air. The scales it seemed had fallen from his eyes and suddenly he was able to see what he had failed to see all the years he was working in Nakuru.

Oloisudori had invited him and his wife to visit one of his six homes ostensibly as a gesture of appreciation for the hospitality he had accorded him and his friends when they visited his home. However, he had wanted them to see and appreciate in the proximity of his kingdom; the kind of peson he was. During the visit, he had hoped they would savour the pleasures and the kind of life their daughter Resian was going to enjoy. He was sure if they had a glimpse of the palatial home that was nearing completion and which he had particularly built for Resian, his struggles to entice and lure her to accept to move in and live with him would come to an end. He was sure they would immediately take over the struggle to persuade her to agree to marry him.

Ole Kaelo had felt greatly flattered when Oloisudori compared Resian with the legendary beautiful brown girl who dominated the songs of four generations of *morans* in the past fifty years. Her beauty had set new standards upon which the Maa beauty queens were judged, and were up to then still appreciated. The legend described the girl as so charmingly beautiful that she caused the *morans* to traverse the vast, dry and hot plains of Susua all the way

189

to Mosiro, where the girl lived with her parents, just to have a glimpse of her beauty. It was said that the *morans* on seeing her, would stand in a daze staring fixedly at her. They would drink in the subtlety of her beauty: her baby face with those bewitching dimples on her cheeks, her white pearl-like teeth planted on black gums, and that captivating natural gap called *enchilaloi* that prettily sat conspicuously between her upper front teeth. She was said to be petite, had a narrow waist and long shapely legs. Her large languorous eyes were said to sap energy from the knees of those to whom she directed her glance, incapacitating them at once. All those besotted with her love could not help but sing in unison:

Entito nanyokie naitudungo	Brown Girl who caused
Ilmurran Susua	*Morans* to traverse *Susua.*

Oloisudori thought Resian was like that girl and more. She was also like the famous English lady whose love besotted a great legendary gentleman called Lord Ngata. In fact Oloisudori thought he and Lord Ngata could have been birds of the same feather. What he learned of the great settler, he thought, put him shoulder to shoulder with him.

When the two of them settled on what they wanted to do, Oloisudori thought pleasantly, nothing would hold them back. The great settler went to England, met a lady and fell in love with her so much that, he was prepared to bring heaven down to earth to please her. Similarly, when Oloisudori went to Nasila and met Resian, he thought he felt what the legendary settler felt. Like him, he was also ready to undertake everything to have her installed in his palatial home as his wife. His only hope was that the chivalry he felt was not going to end up in disappointment like it happened with Lord Ngata. It was said after building a stately castle for his beloved bride to be, the lady was said to have come the whole way from England, looked askance at the majestic castle, turned and looked another way, never to look at it again. From then on, the love of the Lord to the much admired and esteemed lady was unrequited and that pained him a great deal. And that had triggered such virulent hatred for women in the heart of the old gentleman, that for the rest of his life, he never allowed a woman to come anywhere near him.

To avoid that kind of disappointment and great pain, Oloisudori thought he would beautify the palatial home that he was building for Resian so much that on seeing it, she would have no option but to fall in love with it. And when he had had her as his wife, he would do everything possible to win her love. Even when Ole Kaelo had told him that his daughter yearned to go to the university to study, he had said he would readily consent to the request and would let her enroll as a student as soon as she settled. The only little delay anticipated, he had thought triumphantly, was the period required for her to undergo the little ritual of removing her from the list of *intoiye nemengalana,* a process that he thought would hardly take more than three months. How wonderful it would be, he mused delightfully, to have a graduate among his wives. It was certainly going to be an added feather to his cap.

How unfortunate it was that he did not have his daughters with him when he and his wife visited Oloisudori? Ole Kaelo reminisced as he sat in his living room musing quietly. Had they been with them and had they seen what he and his wife saw during that conducted tour, the story would have been different.

He imagined his stubborn daughter Resian would by now be thanking her God for creating her a woman and endowing her with the kind of beauty that would enchant a wealthy man like Oloisudori. And it was only a stupid woman, like his daughter Resian would probably be, who would turn down the offer to own the riches they saw in Oloisudori's home.

It was true, he thought as he recalled what his grandfather used to say, only a woman went to bed poor and woke up stinking rich the following morning. Even his beloved daughter Taiyo could also be lucky soon. Didn't Oloisudori say on that first day when he visited them that he had a friend who would be interested in Taiyo? He hoped he would come soon and he would be like Oloisudori, who would quietly hand over to him a briefcase stuffed with notes worth a cool half a million shillings without as much as a glance or a mention of what he had given.

He reclined on his sofa and allowed his mind to enjoy the pleasures of reminiscence. And with a reminiscent smile on his lips, he travelled back with Oloisudori to his palatial home in Naivasha.

They had sat on the back seat in the imposing vehicle, while his wife had sat next to the driver. Body guards rode the vehicles closely behind them. It was not until they got to the first gate that opened to his compound that they came to know who Oloisudori was. It was unbelievable that one man would employ so many people to do nothing but indulge his every whim. To man his numerous gates that opened to the lawn, were fierce looking guards who searched visitors so thoroughly that one would have thought they were unwanted criminals. By the time they got to the last gate, Ole Kaelo felt tired and harassed. But his host seemed to enjoy that, saying it was the only way to keep out the undesirable vermin that always milled around looking for handouts.

When the last gate swung open and the car slowly drove in, Ole Kaelo and his wife were not prepared enough to behold the imposing and splendid buildings that stood before them. They were humbled.

They were in a cluster of red-tiled houses whose tall outer walls painted in brilliant white, surrounded one large two-storied building that was also of the same colour. A few metres from the fence that enclosed the homestead, was the expansive Lake Naivasha and across it was a scenic sight of hills and a forest that covered them. As he watched the hippopotamuses frolicking in the lake water, Ole Kaelo thought of the grandeur of nature. He could not help but chuckle a little, amused by the fact that, Oloisudori and the hippopotamuses were two different kinds of animals that nature had brought to live side by side, each minding it's own business.

The house was awesome. Kaelo had more than once made to nudge his wife when she stood by the windy corridors of the magnificent house, mesmerized at the elegant and luxurious rooms that lay open wide ready for viewing. The living room was lavishly furnished and the furnishing must have been done by a person whose mind must have been preoccupied by the need to be showy, pompous, elegant and ostentatious.

When they were introduced to the lady of the house, who was simply referred to as *wife number three*, they thought she was as beautiful as her surroundings. She was taciturn but friendly and she served them with dignity and decorum.

At the end of the tour, they made a detour that took them to Nakuru Milimani area where Oloisudori had just completed the house he had been building for Resian. Ole Kaelo was speechless. His wife was stupefied by its grandeur and magnificence. They gazed with amazement at the expensively built double-storied house whose large windows glinted in the afternoon sunshine. In the leafy neighbourhood were other equally imposing and lofty mansions and apartments where the rich businessmen and women lived alongside the senior executives of large organisations.

When a servant opened the front door for them and Oloisudori ushered them in, they were greeted by a large beautiful chandelier that gleamed brightly as it dangled above their heads in the room that was obviously going to be the living room.

Oloisudori led them through the yet to be furnished but brilliantly lit rooms, across the smooth shining floors, up a ceramic tiled staircase that was guarded by a well polished mahogany balustrade, and into a spacious room that was self-contained and which was going to serve as the master bedroom. Its back door opened to an open area that held a swimming pool and a sauna. Standing by the swimming pool, one had a fine view of Lake Nakuru to the east, and a happy scene of school children playing in a nearby school to the west.

For a few minutes, minutes that fleetingly floated along like the morning fog that drifted in the wind, the would be father-in-law and would be son-in-law stood together at the poolside, their thoughts drifting into different directions. They were both thinking of Resian.

Looking at the distant hills to the west which was the direction of Nasila, Ole Kaelo stood there musing silently. He then made one decision: he was not going to allow his daughter's ignorance to destroy her future. As a father, he declared, he had a God given duty to guide her to a secure future; to lead her to the honey pot that would be part of her future. Whatever happened Resian was to be married to Oloisudori.

Before they parted, Oloisudori took them to a restaurant in town for another cup of tea. It was then that an idea on how to deal with Resian was hatched. Oloisudori was to come on the appointed day and time. Ole Kaelo would have prepared the ground so that Oloisudori would find Resian alone. Oloisudori would then persuade her to accept his marriage proposal, without alarming her. If she was agreeable, well and good. In that scenario, the rest of the plans would take their natural course. If she declined, he would leave it at that until the evening when his men would pounce on her and abduct her. They would then drive her straight to the house prepared for her in Nakuru.

The three of them, Oloisudori, Ole Kaelo and his wife

roared with rich laughter when Ole Kaelo equated the scenario to that of a goat's kid that stubbornly refused to suckle after it was born. Its owner would tuck it between his knees and forcefully open its mouth and tuck its mother's teat into it. He would then squeeze out the milk into the kid's mouth. The taste of the milk would make it suckle and removal of the teat from its mouth would be a struggle.

"So would be Resian," Ole Kaelo concluded triumphantly. "When she sees what you have laid out for her pleasures, she would rebuke herself for her procrastination in the first place."

To cap it all, Oloisudori had given Ole Kaelo and his wife his four-wheel-drive and a driver to take them back to Nasila. Mama Milanoi sat in her corner of the back seat appreciating with awe the spacious, splendid leather upholstered interior of the vehicle. She then turned her head to look out of the window, her mind and her heart in a turmoil.

Although she had laughed with her husband and with Oloisudori, the plan to ensnare her daughter like an antelope left a feeling of betrayal in her heart. Truly, the riches were in plenty, she argued to herself, but shouldn't Resian be coaxed and persuaded to accept them rather than being ensnared into them? The idea of ensnaring her daughter in a web like a spider did with a fly, did not appeal to her at all.

It was different for her husband. He felt on top of the world as he sat comfortably at his left corner of the immaculate vehicle. A happy mood pervaded his heart. It was a feeling of satisfaction and achievement.

They were driven smoothly and swiftly through the streets of Nakuru town and driven out into the flat wooded countryside past the gates of the Egerton University where their daughter Resian yearned to go. A strange pang of sadness twisted the nerves of Mama Milanoi's heart. How sad it was, she thought hopelessly, that Resian would miss to join that institution that seemed to have occupied her mind so relentlessly. Ole Kaelo also noticed the gates of the university and he recalled angrily his daughter talking foolishly of wanting to join the institution. It was that kind of frivolous talk, he thought nonchalantly, 'that made him dislike Resian with a passion.

Tossing the thought aside, he looked askance at a group of untidy peasants who walked by the roadside, leading their heavy laden donkeys. Some of them stopped momentarily to stare at the stately vehicle as it sped past them while they shifted from one shoulder to the other, the heavy loads they carried. He disdainfully looked the other way. He was in his element and he would not allow any unsightly view dim his spirit. Instead he looked at the waters of Lake Nakuru that glittered through the trees, reflecting the fire of the sunset through the branches of the yellow acacia trees and the evergreen *Ilourrurr* trees. Small mud-plastered houses, many of them with brightly painted tin roofs, stood in the clearing of the recently hived out forest, chicken pecking about the yards. Dogs sprang to life as they passed, barking furiously and chasing the wheels of the strange awesome vehicle.

And later when they got to the Nasila plains the road was rough and rutted. Even the powerful machine slowed down. There were few other vehicles on the dusty road, and as they were tossed up and down, Ole Kaelo questioned the wisdom of his own decision to move to Nasila in the first instance. He began to admire the luxurious life of the likes of Oloisudori; the urbanite.

However the notion that he was about to hand over his own daughter to a gangster revisited him and continued to gnaw at the conscience of Ole Kaelo relentlessly. It troubled him greatly and he felt guilty, especially when he recalled the atrocities that were known to have been committed by Oloisudori over the years. But another voice told him quietly that he was being foolish and unreasonable to question his own conscience over the matter of Oloisudori for he was just one among many who were enjoying the fruits of their labour. And it was hardly anybody's business to know how honest that labour was. After all, the small voice reassured him tauntingly, those who committed bigger crimes such as Goldenberg and Anglo-leasing, were still enjoying the 'fruits of their labour.' Had they not invested the yields of their ill-gotten money in housing estates, in shares, in import and exports in tourism, in transport and in other trades, just as Oloisudori had done?

When he went to bed later that evening, he remained awake for many hours pondering over those disturbing thoughts that went through his mind fleetingly, like water that churned violently in a turbulent sea. He thought of Oloisudori's impending visit and his intended marriage to Resian. He knew the event's success or failure would effectively determine the fate of his business. Even his continued ownership of that house where he and his family lived, depended on the outcome of that event.

Should Oloisudori fail to get Resian and recall the loan he had extended to him to buy that house, he was done. And knowing Oloisudori, he could very easily draw the rug from beneath his feet, leaving him vulnerable to all kinds of vagaries. And the thoughts gave him anxious moments.

At dawn when sleep overtook him, Ole Kaelo had a pleasant dream. Resian had consented to Oloisudori's proposal. After Oloisudori reported that to him, he was greatly pleased and relieved. His wife was rapturous. Although they were astonished at the turn of events, they were relieved to know that they would not have to live with the guilt of having forced their daughter to get married. What a wise child his once hardheaded daughter had turned to be after all! And how devious! After all those years of sullenness, awkwardness and tactlessness, she had finally brought relief to their life and ushered in a period of peace and tranquillity. But then, it was just that. A dream!

As the parents pondered over the dream that had given them false hope, their daughters were busy hatching their own little plan in their bedroom. They had been observing their parents, especially their father, ever since the arrival of Oloisudori and they were convinced that there was something fishy going on.

Resian came up with a two- pronged plan. They would find a carton and into it pack all those gifts Oloisudori had given them. They would then find a piece of beautiful wrapping paper and smartly wrap the carton and address it to Oloisudori as a reciprocal gift from the daughters of Ole Kaelo. When Oloisudori came to their home next time, Resian said she would personally hand the gift to him and ensure that it was safely deposited in his imposing vehicle. Once the gift was in his vehicle, she would then pretend to be docile and give him the impression that she could be manipulated. She would agree to go along with him, allowing him to lead her until she knew the direction of his thoughts. Once she got to know his intentions, she would decisively react. Woe to him if he thought she was a chattel to be secured by the content of a briefcase! Oloisudori would have Resian the daughter of Kaelo to reckon with! And they hoped that when Oloisudori got back to his destination and ripped open the carton, he would find all those gifts he brought them sitting there prettily, staring back at him. That would serve him right!

It did not take long before Taiyo and Resian had their chance to put into practice their plan. It was a little conspiratorial game they thought they were playing behind their parents' backs. The mission was intended to show Oloisudori that they were not on sale. And if he thought the prize of one of them was equivalent to whatever amount of money was in the briefcase previously handed to their father, he was mistaken.

They also wanted to show him that they were young modern women who had their own pride, self respect and self esteem. They wanted him to know that they were not rudderless objects drifting in the sea without direction. They already had their aims and projections that could only be enhanced by the lofty ideas they held and the desire for higher learning at the university and career development. It was therefore an insult to their intelligence, dignity and integrity to think that mere material things such as the gifts he lavishly gave them would sway them from the goals they had already set for themselves.

"Since he seems to target me in his demonic designs," Resian said determinedly, "I shall try to face him bravely and tell him what I think of him, especially if he shows me his ill manners."

"Well, I don't know whether I would be able to face him alone," Taiyo said apprehensively. "He looked rapacious to me and I can't trust him if we are left alone with him in a room."

"The man is a monster and I fear him too," Resian said balefully. "It is only the desire to right things that gives me courage to face him. To speak the truth, when I think of the monster, I squirm in my shoes with fear!"

"What you should never accept, little sister," Taiyo told her sister emphatically, "is to be left alone in the house with the monster. However brave you are, you cannot be locked with a boa-constrictor in a room and expect to survive."

"That I know, Taiyo-e-yeiyo," Resian answered timidly. "I would only accept to be in the living room with Oloisudori, if *yeiyo* is going to be in the kitchen. I can't take that risk."

Little did the girls know that their parents and Oloisudori had also hatched their plan. So when Ole Kaelo discussed with his wife Oloisudori's day and time of arrival, he was apprehensive. Knowing how stubborn Resian was, he was not sure how they would lure her and make her accept to be with Oloisudori in their living room. It had been agreed that Oloisudori would arrive the following day at ten o'clock in the morning.

After the visit was made known to the girls, and it was suggested that Resian was to receive and serve him with coffee, the parents were most surprised that Resian accepted the proposal without a fight. Ole Kaelo wondered whether the dream he had had was coming to pass. He hoped the rest of their plan would be as smooth and that Resian would accept Oloisudori's proposal without much ado. They had decided that Taiyo would be sent to their uncle's home to help their *yeiyo-botor*. He himself would be at the shop while Resian would remain with her mother at home to wait for Oloisudori.

The plan also suited the girls. They had already packed Oloisudori gifts in a decorated carton that was now awaiting delivery to the owner.

When Resian appeared for breakfast the following morning, her parents were astonished. Her father suppressed an alarming premonition that suddenly leapt and nagged his old heart. Her mother stared at her daughter speechlessly and confusedly, not knowing whether to appreciate or allow the astonishment take the better of her. She opted to keep silent and watched with amazement the transformation of their usually sullen daughter into a cheerful and jovial child. But what amazed them most was the apparent preparation she had made for that morning.

She was clad in her maroon taffeta dress whose stark neckline was softened by a cream and maroon silken scarf that fluttered about her neck. Her usually braided hair had been carefully made and piled softly upon her head. Her golden colour earrings glinted in the morning sunshine as they swung, emphasizing the graceful length of her neck. She carried in her hand a maroon handbag that matched the colour of her shoes. The effect of her attire was dazzling and contrasted sharply with Taiyo who was wearing her usual simple blue dress.

"*Sasa Yeiyo!* Look at me, I am ready for our visitor," Resian said cheerfully addressing her mother. "How do you like my dress?"

"Splendid," her mother answered cautiously.

"My little Resian-e-yeiyo, how lovely you look!" her father who was uncharacteristically emotional said. "You almost look like a grown up lady. What do you think, Olarinkoi?"

Olarinkoi who was present that morning looked up at Resian, grunted and snorted. He then grinned in grudging admiration.

"Not bad," he said looking at Resian sheepishly. "Not bad at all."

Oloisudori was time conscious. In the kind of business that he had done in the larger part of his working life, time was of the essence. As a gangster, he had to be punctual, precise and punctilious. A small delay, inexactness or careless disregard of the plan could not only result in missed opportunities but, could also prove to be fatal. Punctuality had therefore become his second nature.

That was how he approached Resian's issue. Like all other tasks that he undertook, he approached it with singleness of mind. He planned meticulously, putting a precise time frame to it. His retinue was well chosen and all details taken into consideration. He had hired an anaesthetist if the need to render Resian unconscious arose.

At nine-thirty in the morning, they were assembled somewhere near Nasila. Oloisudori was reviewing the detailed instruction that he had given each individual who was to take part in the task ahead. Except for him and his driver, none of the others were to appear anywhere near Ole Kaelo's residence before six o'clock in the evening. They were to arrive at six o'clock on the dot, pounce on the girl, seize her, carry her into the car and speed off. If there was need to render her unconscious, that would be done on the way. The next stop would be at her house in Milimani Estate, Nakuru.

The moment Taiyo left, Resian's confidence began to wane. She began to tremble quite literally. In order that her mother did not notice how nervous she was, she excused herself and fled to their bedroom. But on seeing the carton into which they had packed all those gifts that Oloisudori had given them, and which she intended to give back to him, her courage returned. She had vowed to face the monster gallantly, and it was foolish of her to develop cold feet at that point, especially after promising her sister that she would face him, come what may. She was in the battle front and success or failure was in her hands. She had to do it even if her father would never forgive her. If she rebuffed him successfully, an inner voice told her, a whole new world would open up before her. She had therefore to be stoic and face the monster bravely. She glanced at the clock beside their bed; it was a quarter to ten.

She mustered her courage, picked the carton and quietly left the bedroom. When the stately limousine turned up at their gate, she was at the steps holding the carton, as she prepared to receive the distinguished guest. She held her breath.

She saw him alighting from the vehicle. As usual he was immaculately dressed: a pair of white trousers; a flowing short-sleeved white flower-patterned collarless shirt and white leather shoes. Without his suit, his expensive golden ornaments were more conspicuous. The golden chain that dangled from his neck, the golden bracelet and the golden wrist watch, all glittered brilliantly in the morning sunshine. But no fancy wear could disguise the arrogant power of the tall, muscular individual who now stood there beside his powerful machine, surveying his surroundings. Before he noticed her, Resian watched that pair of large black, appraising eyes in that large brown weather beaten face. He beamed his glance at all directions of the home, as if to confirm that no dirty tricks were being played on him. She thought his well trimmed black moustache gave him the look of a bandit!

When he saw her, his facial features immediately changed. He smiled at her broadly and his rapacious eyes flickered dangerously. The skin of her body crept, raising goose pimples on her fore arms and neck. She knew she was playing with fire, but she had promised to be brave. As he walked towards her though, she nearly backed off, but he did not give her much time to think of other options. In a few quick strides, he had crossed the front yard, mounted the steps, and was now standing beside her.

"Good morning, sir, Oloisudori," she began tremblingly. "May I kindly, hand over this humble gift to you. It is a reciprocal gift from my sister Taiyo and I, our appreciation for your many gifts."

That little speech that she had memorised and rehearsed several times, nearly took away her breath. But it worked. It completely disarmed Oloisudori. He least expected that gesture and for a brief moment he was speechless. He took the carton from her, and looked appreciatively at the square label on it, on which was written, in a flowery female handwriting:

To Mr. Oloisudori Loonkiyaa
with love
from Taiyo and Resian

What he thought was going to be a battle of nerves, had turned out to be a walkover. But that did not unduly surprise him. In fact he nearly expected it. In the case of the other six women who were married to him, he hadn't struggled to get any of them. Actually it was the reverse. For him to accept any of them, each had to fulfill certain conditions and agree to live a certain pattern of life. One or two did not pass the test and he rejected them outrightly. The six who passed the test were happily married to him.

He had thought Resian was going to be an exception. He thought he was going to have a tough struggle and he had come prepared for it. He was a little disappointed though, for the anticlimax had robbed him off the anticipated adventure. He called his driver, handed him the carton and instructed him to take care of it for it contained items of great value.

"I can't thank you and your sister, sufficiently, for this kind gesture" Oloisudori said happily. "Rest assured, beautiful lady, that this will be repaid a million times. Just wait and see."

He took Resian's hand and carried it to his lips kissing her palm. His moustache was rough and wiry against her sensitive skin. She shivered a little as she opened her fingers, surrendering herself to the small outrageous intimacy!

"Would you come in, please," she invited him cautiously leading the way to the house. "My mother is in the house and she has prepared tea and tasty pancakes for you."

"Thank you very much." He followed her into the living room.

Hardly had they got in than the familiar paralysing panic rose in her. The moment he took his seat, his gaze deliberately dropped from her face to her bosom and lingered there. She decided to ignore that stupid look on his face excusing herself to bring his tea.

"Tea is not very important to me," he said pleasantly and added softly, "there are many things I know you want to know about our future. Oh, yes. Many things."

"What do you mean by our future" Resian asked petrified by his words.

"Don't be ridiculous, Resian," Oloisudori said his large eyes narrowing a little. "Must we repeat what is obvious, my dear? But if I may say, you will never regret taking the decision you have taken. You will be the happiest lady in the whole of East Africa!"

"What are you talking about, sir?" Resian asked trying to learn a little bit more.

"What I mean, is simply this," he said slowly like one talking to an obstinate child. "When you are married to me and you are settled in your palatial home at the Milimani Estate in Nakuru, you will be exceedingly happy!"

She stared at him speechlessly. His words did not at first make sense to her. But slowly it dawned on her that her father had already sold her. Yes, the briefcase that was handed to him contained her dowry money. What that meant was that, she was literally Oloisudori's slave. She was his playing thing. And as if to confirm her fears, he stood up and began to walk towards her saying, "our fate with you Resian is sealed. You can never escape. You are my wife and only death shall part us. You hear me, eh?"

"You are mad!" Resian screamed at him. "You are stark mad if you think I am your wife. I can only be your wife over my dead body. Yes, you and my father can kill me and carry my dead body to your palatial home."

He was stunned by those harsh words. He winced as if he had been struck. The already harsh line of his mouth tightened and he stood tense for a moment. Then he relaxed and watched her mockingly. "You can never escape Resian," he repeated quietly, smiling. The very normality of his voice as he spoke those monstrous words was most shocking and disturbing to her. "Whether you scream your heart out, or jump into the deep sea, Resian, you are mine. You are my wife from now henceforth!"

"I want to go now," Resian announced angrily, shuddering with disgust and terror.

"You want to go?" he asked, the contemptuous quiet of his voice a menace by itself. "Go! You want to be persuaded, coaxed and pampered to marry Oloisudori Loonkiyaa? Sorry I will not do that! If you want to go, please yourself. You may opt to go, but when you are mine, you will do as

I please. No one plays games with Oloisudori. Ask your father, he will tell you."

"Stop it! Stop it!" Resian screamed exasperated, perplexed and excruciatingly pained by the disdainful remarks of Oloisudori. Putting her hands over her ears, she made a dash for the door. He made no effort to stop her but she flung it open and turned to glare at him with tearful eyes.

"You are mad!" she screamed again sobbingly. "You are stark mad! You hear me? You are nothing but *Ol-ushuushi.*" She walked away and as she did so, she heard his soft laughter behind her.

Blindly she ran through the house, blundering into a table and stumbling over a chair. Banging the outer door, she ran and pattered down the steps ignoring the surprised looks of Olarinkoi and Oloisudori's driver who stood wondering what had happened.

Outside, she inhaled several gulps of fresh air before turning to run down the rough road that led to her father's shop. She ran without looking back, determined to put distance between her and that foul tongue of Oloisudori, his disgusting eyes and his intimidating threat.

When she neared her father's shop, she slowed down and her spirit quietened a little. But she was still angry. She was raving mad with indignation. Her eyes were twin rivulets from which hot tears streamed down continuously. Her young spirit was sore as she tried to come to terms with what had just happened. Although she had always known that her father disliked her, she never thought that he could go as far as selling her outrightly. How could he do that to her? Was there a curse for being born a woman that took away her right to her own body or her own mind? What did the monster mean when he asserted that she could not escape? Tearfully, she searched for the answers to those questions but they were not forthcoming.

When she met three old men walking down the same dusty road, she peered at them through the mist of her tearful eyes. They glanced at her curiously and one of them kindly asked her who had beaten her.

"*Na kerai, aingae likitaara?*" he enquired.

"*Meeta,*" she answered demurely her eyes downcast.

It was then that she suddenly became aware of her tears and her hair that she had carefully made in the morning but which was now blowing untidily in the dusty wind. She rubbed at her swollen eyelids, trying to wipe the tears with the back of her hand, but more tears flowed as if from an inexhaustible source.

She had to calm down and collect her thoughts before embarking on a fact-finding mission. She would have to behave as if nothing had happened at home so as to hear what her father had to say about Oloisudori and also know the fate of their request to enroll at the Egerton University in the forthcoming academic year.

When her father saw her enter his office, he was alarmed. He tried to read her face but she was not giving herself away.

"Where is our visitor?" her father asked her as calmly and as casually as he could manage.

"I left him at home enjoying his tea and pancakes," Resian answered calmly without batting an eyelid.

"And what brings you to the shop this time of the day instead of remaining at home to help your mother?"

"I'll go back there, *Papaai*, as soon as possible," Resian answered pleasantly, trying to be as calm as she could, "I thought I should come down here and ask what you thought of my recent request to enroll as a student at the Egerton University at the beginning of the new academic year this September."

"University?" her father asked astonished that the question of their enrollment to the university should crop up at the time when a weightier matter about her marriage to Oloisudori should presently be occupying her mind. He got confused and wondered what had taken place between her and Oloisudori. He cleared his throat portentously and said, "I thought about it alright, but decided that I am not sending you there!"

"Why not, *Papaai*?" she asked angrily as she stood rigidly before her father's desk, her hands clasped firmly to prevent them from trembling.

"Because I think for now, you have had enough of formal education," he answered eyeing her sharply, and then stretched his arm, took some papers from a tray at the far end of the table and leafed through them. "There is always time for further education later and..."

"But *Papaai*," she interrupted him.

"There is always time," he said, ignoring her interruption. With studied patience he tapped the papers back into order, laid them neatly before him, squaring them with the edge of the desk. Then he looked up, his face stern. "It is only that you children are at times stupid and have myopic minds. When we as your parents try to plan for your future, you refuse to see..."

"*Papaai* please," Resian pleaded. "If you can only listen to me for a second..."

"You refuse to see that we always have your interest at heart," he interjected. He waited until she lifted her head and met his eyes. He thought it was time he told her what Oloisudori had not possibly told her. And if he appended her wish to join Egerton University as an added benefit to marrying Oloisudori, he thought he could lure her to move to Nakuru immediately. He softened his tone a little and said "You see at the moment, there are a number of programmes at the university. You can enroll and stay at the campus, you can take a parallel degree programme or you can study by correspondence.

"All that I know," Resian said impatiently. "But..."

"If you do," her father added shifting in his chair and spreading his hands expansively, "then you can take any of the last two options for I have made appropriate plans for you, my daughter. I have been waiting for an opportunity to speak to you about them. In fact that was what I wanted to tell you the last time when I called you. You are a lucky child, Resian. A very lucky child, dear Resian."

Resian stared at him. She already knew what he was to say next.

"No," she said flatly.

"You are a very lucky child as I said," he continued, ignoring her protest.

"I am delighted to tell you that my good friend and business associate Oloisudori Loonkiyaa has approached me asking that he marries you. You know he is..."

At first she was stunned like one hit by a bolt of lightning. Then suddenly she began to shout. She threw her head back and screamed so loudly one would have thought she was engulfed in a ball of fire. She hollered, shrieked and shrilled, saying all sort of things to express her indignation, outrage and terror. She cried, accusing her father of hatred and betrayal by betrothing her to Oloisudori. Her father stared at her in horror. But she would not stop, she shouted even more and screamed like one possessed with demented spirits. After a moment of frozen immobility, her father suddenly pushed back his chair, moved fast from behind the desk and slapped her face, sending her reeling back so that she almost fell. She stared at him in disbelief. He slapped her again backhanded.

"That should teach you never to talk like that to your father," he said fuming, his nostrils flaring and his eyes glittering with anger.

"It is better you kill me, *Papaai!*" she cried out outrageously. "You'll better kill me than hand me over to your monster friend. Yes, kill me right now!"

He watched her with distaste as she heaved her shoulders and blew her nose. She tried to control the flow of her tears but she could not. By then there was a multitude of people, standing and milling around the building, peeping curiously, wondering what was happening inside.

"I may as well tell you, my dear child," her father said in a low angry growl, "I have taken dowry from Oloisudori. You are now his wife whether you like it or not!"

In silence, Resian turned and walked to the door opened it, and stepped into the corridor. Then as she walked through the shop, she lifted her voice, still hoarse and ragged with tears and screamed attracting the attention of everyone. She looked back and saw her father following her, his eyes bulging out with anger. He strode briskly and sharply towards her. She quickened her step away from him but as she walked, she repeated her words.

"You hear me, *Papaai*? I said I'd rather die than get married to a monster, who is an *Ol-ushuushi* like Oloisudori. Never! Never! If I don't die and I live to be eighty, I will still go to the university. I'll go to Egerton University, *Papaai*, I tell you! I hope you will be there to witness my graduation. But for now, I can as well reveal to you, that I have told your friend Oloisudori what I think of him. Yes, he is a monster, he is a gangster, he is a bank robber and an extortionist per excellence!"

"Resian!" her father's voice cracked like a whip. "Resian!"

She ignored her father's call, pushed though the outer door of the shop and rushed outside. Her cheek throbbing from her father's blows, her eyes red and swollen from weeping, she walked with an odd dignity down the road that led to Nasila river ignoring the stares and whispers of all those who stood by watching.

Nasila river– cool, smooth and silent – swirled quietly about the boulders that were half submerged in it. It was deep and wide. She stood at its bank for a long time, staring down, into the water. Could the answer to her woes be in that river? Yes, it could be! Just a swift, cold shock as she fell into the water and then there would be peace. Yes, peace all over, from her father, from Oloisudori and from the fact that she had failed to get admission to Egerton University. As the idea floated in her mind, she felt a tap on her shoulder. Shocked, she turned around. It was Olarinkoi.

"What are you doing here at the river side?" he asked with little interest.

"Nothing," Resian said nonchalantly. "I am just relaxing."

"Don't be foolish, little girl," Olarinkoi said seriously. "You may not want to tell me what is happening, but I am not foolish and I can put one and one together. Oloisudori's men are now looking for you everywhere. They have instructions to seize you and take you to Nakuru to be his wife."

"Just leave me," Resian said angrily, "Go tell them to come and find me here."

"Listen, you stupid girl," Olarinkoi said in his caustic language. "If you do not want to marry Oloisudori, I can rescue you the way I rescued you from those vagabonds who had accosted you and your sister. I know where Minik ene Enkoitoi the *Emakererei* lives and where she keeps girls rescued from the situation you are now in. There is no need to despair in life. There is always another chance."

That could be something to consider, Resian thought, new hope rising in her heart. Yes, it would be wonderful to be received by the *Emakererei*. And who knows, there could still be a chance to enroll at the Egerton University, through *Emakererei*.

"How could we ever get there?" asked Resian a flicker of hope lighting her heart. "I hear it is very very far from here."

"Yes it is far," confirmed Olarinkoi. "But where there is hope things always work out. The *Maa* people say home is never far for one who is still alive."

"Then find the way," she finally told him.

He promised to take her to a family he knew in Nasila where she would spend the night while he organised transport so that they would start off very early the following day. What she did not know was that no journey was ever predictable.

Chapter Fifteen

Resian was woken up very early the following morning. The kind-hearted old woman who accommodated her for the night cooked porridge. She served the scalding, hot and sugarless porridge in a big yellow enamel mug. Resian shook the mug gently to cool the porridge and downed it soon for she was very hungry having missed lunch and supper the previous day.

When an old battered and rattling ramshackle of a pick-up hooted outside the old woman's house, Resian rushed out eagerly, followed by the old woman. They were greeted cheerfully by Olarinkoi and the driver. Olarinkoi told Resian to climb onto the back of the pick-up while he sat with the driver in the front cabin. The old woman looked at Resian sitting there at the back of the pick-up and had pity on her knowing how windy and dusty such a ride would be. She asked the men to wait for a while as she went back into her house. She came out with a *leso* and an old blanket which she handed to Resian, asking her to cover her head with the *leso* and wrap her body with the blanket to keep herself warm and shield herself from the wind and dust. And truly, those two items proved to be invaluable to her, not only during the gruelling journey but even thereafter.

Resian was in very high spirits when the journey began. The air was crisp and refreshing. The notion that she was outsmarting Oloisudori and her father from what they must have thought was an inescapable situation, made her exceedingly happy. A feel-good sensation pervaded her heart and she regarded the journey as an exciting adventure. She began to whistle and hum some cowboy tunes earlier learnt in school, and that added excitement and cheerfulness to her spirit now that she was travelling to meet her role model, the *Emakererei*. She was no longer apprehensive the way she was the night before when she harboured the notion that she was plunging into the unknown.

The farther they drove towards Nasila the drier the land became and the dust was appalling. Instead of fresh green pastures that she looked forward to seeing, her eyes were met by a sprawling limitless stretch of brown bare ground with patches of tawny grass. In the distance were hillocks covered by desiccated bushes of *Oleleshua* and *Olkinyei* and stunted shrubs of *Olobaai* and *Oltikambu*. There was an occasional stand of trees and scattered species of cactus, such as *Irankaun* and *isuguro*. Save for that scanty vegetation, Resian saw an empty, lonely and nearly desolate land that stretched to as far as her eyes could see. Truly, reality had come to mock her cherished imagination.

And it was unbearably hot! Despite the fact that she was seated at the back of the pick-up she could still feel the heat. The sun beamed down from a clear blue sky with such torrid intensity that the metal bodywork of the vehicle became scaldingly hot to the point of being unbearable. The heat sapped her strength and the dust and the heated air burned in her throat and lungs. She felt hot, thirsty and very uncomfortable. But the men in the front cabin never for once bothered to look back to see how she was faring.

By five o'clock they were still on the road. The road

had by then become so rough that the driver had to stop the vehicle several times to remove boulders that were strewn on the road. Whenever the vehicle stopped the dust settled on Resian in several layers. But dust was a lesser nuisance. Flies and mosquitoes gathered around her eyes and mouth and crawled into her nostrils in search of moisture. The mosquitoes in particular gathered in shrilly droning clouds, attacking all areas of her exposed skin and even biting through her dress. When the vehicle resumed motion the flies and mosquitoes menace lessened as they were blown away by the wind. But the reprieve was only temporary until the vehicle stopped again and the cycle was repeated.

At one point the driver – a short thin man of forty or so with brooding eyes and a twitching mouth – stopped the vehicle glanced at the back and growled a rude remark at Resian. Like Olarinkoi, he seemed callous and irritated for reasons she did not understand.

"You, woman," the driver called rudely, "would you want to stretch your legs?"

Resian nodded silently and gathered the skirts of her dress, then stepped over the side of the pick-up slowly, placing her foot carefully on the wheel, then lifted the other foot over the side of the vehicle and stepped down to the ground. The men totally ignored her but that did not bother her. What bothered her then was the heat, flies and mosquitoes. The moment she stepped onto the ground, she began to sweat profusely. Her body reeked of sweat and dust. And the sweat attracted mosquitoes that bit her through her dress and raised lumps on her arms and legs which itched constantly.

She walked to the side of the road to a bush. But within seconds she came back running fast as she screamed at the top of her voice. She was shaken and panic-stricken, as she sobbingly explained that she had seen a snake. But for reasons she did not understand, instead of sympathizing with her, the men were enraged and they bitterly rebuked and scolded her for screaming.

Soon it was dark, and the temperature fell rapidly bringing her welcome relief from the stifling heat. But it also brought her a new terror. She feared that a leopard could easily spring from the bushes onto the pick-up and drag her out, especially when the vehicle slowed down as the ruts became impossible to cross at high speed. She therefore crouched at the center of the back of the pick-up, wide eyed, looking from side to side with terror, wondering how far they were yet to travel before reaching the sheep ranch where Minik ene Nkoitoi the *Emakererei*, resided.

She gave thought to that important destination that could change her life entirely. She wondered how *Emakererei* would receive her. Having seen the manner in which Olarinkoi had behaved towards her since leaving Nasila in the morning, she doubted whether he would be in a position to present her case adequately to the *Emakererei*. How she wished she had a clean set of clothes that she could put on after a shower, to give her confidence to face *Emakererei* and bravely put her case properly to her. But as it were, she thought she now looked like a sow that had been rolling in the dust. She had a layer of dust in her mouth, in her nostrils, in her ears and on her eyelashes.

She was thus musing when the vehicle suddenly slowed

down, turned and began to labour as it passed through a rough terrain. It creaked, rattled and swayed from side to side as it was driven over uneven ground. But she thought they had at last arrived at their destination. That diversion excited her and her heartbeats increased with anticipation and expectation.

Suddenly, the beam of the vehicle's light brought into view a small mud-plastered house with a rusty tin roof. Around the house was a thorn fence and beside the house was a small wooden gate that was shut. The vehicle slowed down and stopped in front of the gate. The two men conversed in low tones for a few minutes in the front cabin, and then Olarinkoi opened the door and came out. He walked round to the back of the vehicle and shot back the tower bolts that held the tailgate and lowered it. He pulled out two bags, one of maize flour and the other of sugar, and lifted a couple of large cartons and placed them on the bags that were already on the ground.

"What are you still doing on the back of the vehicle?" he asked Resian rudely. "Alight quickly, the driver doesn't have the whole night to wait?"

The moment she alighted, the pick-up reversed turned and was driven off. Within a few seconds they were left in pitch darkness and no sound was audible save for their breathing and the gentle rippling sound as the wind rustled dried leaves. The stillness was eerie and frightening.

Olarinkoi removed a torch from his pocket, beamed it to the gate and began to walk towards it without talking to Resian. He took a bunch of keys from his pocket, selected one and inserted into a dangling padlock and opened it. Resian still stood where she was left in the darkness, feeling sick from hunger and nauseated from the lurching and the rattling of the pick-up. Already, a swarm of mosquitoes was gathering around her and a cold wind that was blowing towards her made her shiver uncontrollably.

"Come on, woman," Olarinkoi growled. "Are you going to stand there until you are dragged away by hyenas?"

"Good Lord!" Resian gasped in shock. She hoped in God's name that what she was imagining was not what was in Olarinkoi's mind. What did she get herself into! Where was she and was Olarinkoi sincere when he said he was taking her to *Emakererei?* She hoped the house before them belonged to another family friend of Olarinkoi and that they were going to be there only for the night. In the morning, she hoped, they would walk to *Emakererei* place, which she imagined was close by. But it worried her that, other than rebuking her, Olarinkoi hadn't looked at her nor spoken to her since they left Nasila.

She followed him through the small gate across a small courtyard, to the front of the small house. He inserted another key into a padlock that locked the door. He opened it, left her standing alone and went back outside. In a minute, he came back carrying one of the cartons, shoved the door open with his shoulder and stepped in. Once in, he placed the carton on the floor, fumbled in his pocket, brought out a box of matches and lit a lamp. Resian entered into the room and observed with shock, disgust and utter revulsion, her new surroundings.

The house had two rooms. One was a fireplace whose dead ashes signified desertion. There were two three-legged stools that stood next to the wall and a rough wooden rack that stood at a corner, where unwashed dishes, utensils and pots with dried remains of food, stared back at her. The floor was caked with sheep dung while dirty clothes hung from pegs on the walls.

"Don't stand there staring like a fool," Olarinkoi rebuked her angrily. "Light the fire and let us make some food. If you want to know, food here is not a right, it is a privilege that comes with conditions."

Resian was numb with shock. For a moment, she did not even seem to hear what Olarinkoi was telling her. She just stood with her mouth agape, her lower lip hanging loose. Like one in a dream, she felt detached as if watching things happening to someone else.

Olarinkoi left her standing in the house and went out to bring in the provisions that he had left outside the gate. He dragged in the two bags, one after the other, then carried in the carton, untied it and rummaged about it fishing out a wrapped item, which turned out to be a piece of meat.

"You, woman, look here!" he shouted at her aggressively. "You can either cook or keep standing stupidly and die of hunger. The choice is yours. Should you choose to cook, here is a piece of meat. The knife is over there. Of course you are not blind you can see the *sufurias*. There is a whole bag of maize meal there and water is in that container. There is paraffin in that can and you can collect firewood from a stack outside the house. Any questions?" Resian did not answer.

She silently stared at the man who seemed to have suddenly turned from a person she had known for quite some time, to a beast. On his part, Olarinkoi glared at her and without uttering another word, picked up a knobkerry and a spear from one corner of the room and took two long strides that brought him to the door. He flung it open with a forceful yank, stepped outside and then pulled it shut with such a loud bang that the rickety doorframe shook precariously. She heard his brisk steps as he strode to the gate. He walked out and locked the gate from outside.

Resian realised fearfully that she had been left all alone in a strange hovel, in the middle of nowhere. She was scared and trembled with fear. She began to imagine that a dangerous animal could be lurking in the dark corners of that shack and could spring on her at any moment tearing her into shreds. Fear sharpened her sense of hearing so that any slight noise such as a rippling sound made by the blowing wind, sent her jumping in despair.

After sometime, she calmed down sufficiently to start reasoning. She wondered what had happened. Had she dropped from a frying pan into the fire? Was Olarinkoi a beast that had been pretending to be a human being while waiting for an opportunity to avail itself so as to spring a surprise on her? Or was the man just playing games with her and would turn up in the morning, asking her to get up and follow him as they resumed their journey to the *Emakererei's* place? She held onto that latter reasoning and it gave her a flicker of hope. And like a match stick that kindled and lit a fire that spread by leaps and bounds, that hope grew and pervaded her entire heart. Yes, Olarinkoi meant no harm and that was the reason why he left her alone in that shack while he went elsewhere to find himself a place to sleep.

She wrapped the blanket the old woman had given her around her body, covered her head with the *leso* and sat on one of the stools letting her mind float fleetingly into all kinds of fanciful thoughts. For the first time since leaving her home, she thought of the kind of turmoil her disappearance had created. Her mind focused on her father and she thought how mad he was at her for having disrupted his plans with that monster called Oloisudori. Then she thought of her mother and how sad she was on realising that she had disappeared. She imagined her moving from place to place looking for her desperately. Thoughts of her sister brought tears into her eyes. How she missed her sister Taiyo. Oh sweet loving Taiyo! Always ready to listen, always soothing her anger, stress or anxiety. How she missed her laughter, her argument and her reasoning. She thought of their warm, comfortable bed and wished she were there sleeping next to her sister.

She drifted to sleep. She was asking her sister to move over. Taiyo was a bit reluctant but eventually, she moved and she got into bed beside her although she had not washed her feet. Oh sweet bed it was! The sleep took her to a dreamland where she met the *Emakererei* who promised her all kinds of wonderful things. She promised to take her to Nakuru and have her enroll as a student at the Egerton University. She also promised to offer her a vocational job. But above all she promised to protect her from anyone threatening her with the pain of Female Genital Mutilation. She said it was her right to remain among *intoiye nemengalana*.

Her dream was rudely and violently interrupted by a thunderous bang and a loud roar of laughter. She woke up with a start, jumped up to her feet and stared at the door with wide panic-stricken eyes. For a moment she couldn't figure out her surroundings and called out the name of her sister Taiyo. She was terrified. The door flung open and Olarinkoi staggered in. He was stone drunk. Resian stared at him unblinkingly as he walked towards her and she backed off terrified, squeezing herself flatly against the wall. He followed her there and got hold of her shoulders and shook her violently glaring at her with his glittering eyes.

"You silly thing," he thundered angrily. "I tell you to prepare food and you refuse to do so, eh? Today you will know who is the owner of this home. If you are still in doubt, let me tell you frankly that from today on you are my wife, hear that, eh? You are my wife. For a long time you have been sneering at me, showing how highly educated you are. Today we shall see how educated your body is! Yes, we shall see!"

He got hold of her hand and began dragging her into the other room. At first she did not understand his intention until he began unfastening her buttons with his rough trembling hands. Then the truth came, and with it, terror and panic. She tried to get away from him, but he held her effortlessly as he brutally continued fumbling with her dress, trying to loosen it. She screamed as loudly as she could while she pushed him away and thrashed frantically about. But that did not deter him and he totally ignored her screams holding her more firmly with his strong arms. Against her loud protest, he tore her garments and began to push her towards the bed.

Then desperately she took the last chance of self defence and self-preservation. Mustering all her strength, she thrust his thumb into her mouth; sunk her teeth into the flesh like a ferocious animal and tenaciously held onto it, tugging at it fiercely like a lioness. She could feel the flesh tearing and she tasted the salt of his blood as it filled her mouth but she clung unto the thumb as Olarinkoi howled with pain. He tried to push her away but she held on. He cried out loudly, but she was relentless as she dug deeper and deeper into the flesh, nearly severing the limb. Then suddenly, he hit her so hard on her ribcage with his elbow, knocking the wind out of her. He hit her again on the side of her head and she passed out.

When she regained her consciousness, it came back gradually, like a remote recollection of a distant past incident. She felt as if a haze of tiredness had come over her mind in the form of a fleeting dream; floating like mist blown by a gust of wind.

The first thing she realised was that her mouth tasted bitter, was very dry and her throat was parched. She opened her eyes lazily and looked about and around her. At first she did not know where she was and how long she had been there. She was lying on a makeshift bed that was built into the corner of a room; in a desolate filthy house. The bed was covered with dirty bloody rags. And she was naked. Her head throbbed with an excruciating pain that nearly blinded her. There was a trickle of blood in her nostrils, indicating that she had nosebled.

Slowly by slowly, she began to regain her memory. She gathered fragmented pieces of information that were scattered in her mind and began to piece them together. She recalled the incident with Oloisudori, the quarrel with her father, the trip with Olarinkoi and her struggle with him as he tried to rape her and she had bit his thumb. She could not remember anything beyond that point.

She noticed that someone had removed a rag that covered a hole on the wall above the bed to let in some light from outside. She also noticed that someone had lit the fire and the room was full of smoke that drifted and found its exit through that hole above the bed. Her eyes burned with the effect of the smoke and they filled with tears which blinded her as she strained to familiarise herself with her surroundings.

She tried to lift her head but she could not. She tried to move her legs, but they were as heavy as lead. She could hardly turn any of them. She felt an excruciating pain all over her body as if some cruel person had mercilessly pounded her body, limb by limb with a heavy mallet. The attempt to lift her head or move her limbs sapped the little energy left in her body and she fainted, drifting back to unconsciousness.

When she later came to, confused fleeting impressions registered on her awareness. There were sensations of movement, of cold and of heat. And always there was pain, a continuous unending torture and from which there seemed to be no escape. Distorted images moved about her at times, and at other times there was only a cold and lonely darkness. Several moments of consciousness came and went.

There were brief moments when she imagined that Oloisudori had caught up with her. Then there were the longer periods when the fever that gripped her, coupled with the struggle of her body to recover from the massive loss of blood took away her memory. Images of Olarinkoi and Oloisudori merged, becoming one great block of terror like the image of a charging elephant.

In her confused mind, time was warped. Sometimes, a day seemed to stretch for an endless period, while a single twinge of pain jarred her nerves in what appeared to be an eternity. Impressions crowded together in rapid sequences and periods of light and darkness flickered by in a dizzying swirl.

The first day the lucid memory came, she realised that she was alone in the room and bright sunlight flooded in through the doorway. It was hot in there and she was naked, sweat forming and trickling down her face and the side of her body. That was when she realised that there was someone else in the room apart from her. For a moment, terror returned to haunt her. Was it Olarinkoi who had come back to torture her? She turned her head slowly, and her eyes were met by a kind stare from an old woman.

Their eyes met and held, and Resian recalled faintly the motherly figure that had been nursing her. Was it a dream replayed in her mind from the days of her infancy or was it the fever playing its cruel games in her mind? But she vaguely recalled the presence of an old woman in that room, who resembled her mother or her *Yeiyo-botorr*. She recalled her talking to her kindly asking her how she felt. At times she held her up, giving her drinks of water, or milk, or feeding her; putting bits of *Olpurda* dipped in honey into her mouth, or pounded pieces of mutton and *ugali* and urging her to swallow. Yes, she was certain that a woman had been in that room. And now, there she was standing beside the bed.

"Who are you, kind mother?" Resian asked weakly,

aware that those were the first words that she had uttered in along time.

"*Kaaji enkabaani*," the old woman answered quietly.

Resian knew *enkabaani* to be a nurse or a person who treated others. So she wondered whether that was her name or her profession. But the old woman would not be drawn to discussing names. She told Resian not to tire herself with unnecessary details. What should be of importance to her, she told her, was to regain her health. When she was back on her feet, she would tell her how long she had been lying on that bed and what happened to her when she was unconscious.

The old lady helped Resian to a sitting position and she braced herself on one arm. She was still very weak, sweat was breaking out and her arm trembled from the effort of holding herself up in a sitting position. But her head was clear. For the first time, she was ravenously hungry. And she ate her full meal unaided.

The following morning, Resian slowly raised herself to a sitting position. Then she lifted her legs one after the other, and with an effort, got out of bed. She fetched the *leso* that the Nasila old lady had given her and wrapped it around her body. Supporting herself with the walls, she carefully and slowly walked to the fireplace, and again, slowly lowered herself to sit on a stool beside the fire. The old woman was not in the room by then. When she came back, her eyes widened with surprise as she saw Resian sitting by the fire, then a brilliant smile spread across her face, her teeth gleaming in the morning sunshine.

"*Tagolo*," she said prayerfully and spat on Resian's face.

It took two days before she could get around the vicinity of the house. Even then, she was still weak and terribly emaciated and she could hardly walk except to drag herself haltingly with the assistance of a walking stick. Having entered the house in pitch darkness, the night they arrived she was now eager and quite curious to get out and see how the countryside looked like.

It was late afternoon when she got out of the house. Standing outside, she had a good look at what had been her home for the last several days. A small shabby structure of mud plastered walls and a tin roof that was spotted with pieces of bark where the iron sheet had rotted or fallen off, with a couple of rickety sheds and a tiny structure that served as the toilet, made up all what Olarinkoi called home. It was in the middle of a plain that stretched from the overgrazed hillside down to the winding river called *Inkiito*, at the bottom of the slope. The light breeze blowing across the hills smelled fresh and clean. It caressed and soothed her haggard face providing the much needed fresh air. In that damned place, it was only the fresh air that gladdened her heart.

As she sat on a log enjoying the cool fresh air, the light deepened as the sun started to set. The sky became a bowl of red which darkened to a thick combination of deep purplish red colour clouds. Those clouds spread toward the west, flooding all those extensive plains with a tinted crimson glow. Then she saw a few sheep, possibly fifty or so, being driven towards her. They too became tinted with varying shades of red.

The sheep were being shepherded by an old woman. And they seemed to know their home, because when they got nearer the small Olarinkoi's homestead, they ran towards it leaving the old woman behind. The old woman walked directly to where Resian sat and stood before her. Resian looked at her and fear crept through her weak body. Who was she? Was she a witch? She asked herself fearfully as she peered at the ugly woman who stood there glaring at her silently.

Resian could not estimate her age but she thought it was substantial. She must have been tall in her younger days, for she now walked with a stoop. She had bony arms, legs and shoulders and her long flat breasts hung pendulously down her thin ribs. Resian thought some kind of disease must have made most of her hair come out, and what remained on her head was cropped off in uneven patches. She appeared completely toothless and her face was a maze of crevices and wrinkles.

But what frightened Resian most were her eyes, or rather her eye for she was mono-eyed. She had a single, glaring, red-rimmed eye that resembled that of the legendary *enenaunerr*, the monster that was said to be partly stone and partly human: it was said to devour human beings. When they had visited their uncle's home at Nasila, the old woman story teller would narrate to them those fables that frightened children to obedience. What was before her now was no fable. The old witch was real and the sight was frightening. Resian thought the old woman didn't look very strong or healthy, but when she thought of her own health, the old woman could have been ten times stronger then she was in comparison.

"So it is you who chewed my son's hand to near amputation?" the old woman asked in a low rumbling and frightening voice. She sneered at Resian contemptuously and spat on the ground. "What were you guarding so tenaciously and valiantly when I am told you are not yet a woman? Are you not ashamed to be among *intoiye nemengalana* at your age? *Ptu!*"

Resian was shocked by the words of the old woman and she stared at her frightfully, a new hopelessness and helplessness threatening to wreak more havoc to her already wrecked nerves. But the old woman was not finished with her yet.

"I hear your father is stinking rich," she said mocking Resian derogatorily. Then roaring with a demonic derisive laughter, she said disdainfully, "I am also told, you, being his favourite daughter, was always fed in bed with a silver spoon. This is what we have been trying to do to you in the last few days. I don't know whether we have succeeded. We looked for a silver spoon in the whole neighbourhood but we could not find any. I hope the ordinary spoon we have used to feed you does not make you retch!" then she burst out and laughed uproariously.

"Oh my God! What is this?" Resian cried out silently unable to bear any more the detestable, stressful, and disgusting verbiage from the old witch. She found it offensive, repugnant and downright obnoxious.

The much she could do was to listen to the old woman as she spewed out her loathsome nastiness and foul grossness.

"Listen to me you daughter of *Olkarsis*," she growled like an irate bull, her irritating foul language grating on Resian's nerves. "I hear your father and that *Ol-ushuushi* called Oloisudori to whom he had betrothed you and

233

from whom my gallant and valorous *moran* snatched you are combing every bush, every cave and every river bank looking for you, as if you are the only *esiankiki* in the whole world. Anyway let them try for I know they are not going to find you. I am not going to allow it. That fool called Oloisudori does not deserve you. You belong to Olarinkoi, my son. As soon as we clip that erogenous salacity from you that destroys homes, you will become a respected woman worthy to be called…"

"Stop! I do not want to hear anymore!" Resian said weakly, her heart beginning to palpitate fast and irregularly. "I want to go into the house."

"Before you go in," the old woman continued relentlessly, "listen to me, you have to eat well. Get strong as soon as possible for the trek ahead is long. It is already arranged that you and Olarinkoi will have to move to Tanzania where you will remain until this fuss kicked up by Oloisudori and your father is over. If you like it there you can settle and build your home in that country. I have asked the *enkabaani* to engage the services of *enkamuratani* when you are strong enough to undergo the ritual so that we are done with it soon. It is a pity that we now have to do what Ole Kaelo ought to have done long time ago. Anyway, Maa culture will soon judge him harshly. Now go in for it's becoming chilly."

"O God of all creation!" Resian cried out bitterly and audibly as soon as the cruel ugly old woman left her. "What unending woes these are! *Taba! Kilome sogo*! What have I done to the gods to deserve this kind of punishment?"

Then she recalled the teaching of the Bible, and especially where it narrated the woes of those who went through similar or even worse tribulations, but triumphed at the end. She particularly remembered the wailing lamentations of Job and his railing against injustice, and she thought her problems were nothing compared to those he had suffered. He triumphed because he was stoic, focused and was able to persevere. Olarinkoi and his demonic mother may physically take her to Tanzania, Olarinkoi may physically take her as his wife, they may even physically circumcise her, but mentally she was going to resist. She was going to refuse to be subdued. Where she could, she was going to physically resist. She resolved to remain focused and she prayed for strength and endurance to be able to bear all those misfortunes.

She had wondered where Olarinkoi was, but she had now learnt from his mother that he was some place, planning more evil. She had also learnt that Oloisudori, the monster, was looking for her. She now wondered who among them was a lesser devil. She did not know what to think about her father. He was like the proverbial pig that was fried using its own lard. She thought he was suffering double tragedy: the loss of his daughter and the loss of his shop and home if they were financed by Oloisudori.

She thought of Joseph Parmuat and wondered how he had taken the news of her disappearance. Did he organise another *enkitungat* to comb the forests of Nasila the way he had done when they were accosted by those vagabonds?

She knew her sister Taiyo was inconsolable and so was her mother. But when she thought of her mother, some bitter bile rose in her chest. Yes, although she loved her mother dearly, she had failed her. She so much feared her husband that she was awed to silence by his presence even when injustices were being committed against her own daughter. She now understood a quotation someone mentioned to her once. It said at the end: what pained one most was not the injustices carried out against one by one's adversaries, but the silence of those who called themselves his or her friends at the time the injustice was being carried out. Her mother's silence pained her beyond words. Although one had to know which side their bread was buttered, she reasoned sadly, there was a time when the bread and the butter were not important. Even the hyena's greed spared its own young ones, she reasoned.

Resian was still sitting on the log outside the tiny homestead when the *enkabaani* returned from her errands. By then the moon had risen and it was high up in the sky. She saw her walk towards her moving slowly as the bright light of the moon that streamed through the few trees subdued the colour of her skin, making her brown complexion seem darker. She carried some luggage on her back that made her stoop a little. On seeing her approaching, Resian's heart leapt with joy. Although she did not even know who she was and why she took care of her, fed her and nursed her, she had come to regard her as the only connection she had to the sane world. She had promised to give an account of what had happened to her, what was happening and what was in the offing. She was very eager to know all that so that she could plan her next move. She knew she was still weak but she was grateful that she was steadily and progressively regaining her strength.

"Oh, poor thing!" the *enkabaani* exclaimed concernedly on seeing Resian. "You are still sitting outside this late?

Oh my God! The mosquitoes must have sucked your veins dry! Come now. Let me help you to stand."

The *enkabaani* helped Resian to walk back into the house. She made her sit at the fireplace as she lit the fire and made her some tea. They were taking the tea as the old woman prepared supper, when Resian asked who the mono-eyed old woman was.

"She is the mother of the man who assaulted you," the *enkabaani* explained coolly. "She is also a feared and respected *enkoiboni*. Most likely you have only heard of a male holder of that position called *oloiboni*. Female ones are there too but very rare. This particular one is famous for her prediction and prophecies that always nearly come true.

Take your case for instance, she had made a prophesy long before your father Ole Kaelo, moved to Nasila. She said your father would relocate to Nasila and bring along with him his *intoiye nemengalana*. Then she said her son Olarinkoi would move to that home, live with the Kaelo family for some time and eventually bring one of his daughters to his home to be circumcised and given to him as a wife. So when you came, it was not a surprise to us who had heard the prediction. It was bound to happen. What was not in the prediction was what Olarinkoi tried to do with you. Rape was not part of the programme. For his disobedience and defiance, he was rebuked, scolded and reprimanded by his mother. He is now in a hide-out somewhere in the bush recuperating from that wound you inflicted upon him with that vicious bite."

"Where do you come in?" a shocked and flabbergasted Resian asked, her eyes wide with disbelief.

"You see, if it were not for Olarinkoi's drunken stupidity," *enkabaani* explained nonchalantly, "you would have been circumcised the following day. The *enkamuratani* was ready and I was to take over from her and nurse you during your recuperation. My role was going to end after your shaving and handing over to your husband. The *enkamuratani* and I are paid handsomely to carry out our instructions."

"What is going to happen now?" asked Resian, stunned and frightened by the outrageous explanation.

"I don't really know," the old woman said, "Now that Olarinkoi had bungled the job by dipping his dirty finger into the porridge before it was dished out to him, he will have to suffer the consequences. The whole thing has aborted and the *enkoiboni* will have to go back to her pebbles to chart out new directions."

"Meanwhile?" Resian asked her heart in her mouth with fright.

"To speak the truth young lady," the old nurse said sympathetically, "the twelve days I have nursed you have made me come to love you as my own child. You are courageous both physically and mentally. In the first five days after the assault, I did not think you were going to live. You were very weak and you had lost a lot of blood through that nose-bleeding. But you fought on. You had a will to live. Even now I believe you have a will to go places. I don't know what *enkoiboni* has predicted but, I am willing to help you do what you intend to do or go where you want to go once you are back onto your feet, with or without *enkoiboni's* predictions."

That was music in Resian's ears! A surge of renewed energy spurted in her veins. She suddenly fell to her knees and hugged the legs of the old woman, washing them with her tears.

"My own God given mother!" she sobbed, "may God Bless you."

Chapter Sixteen

Resian's stay in that tiny homestead was not only stressful and agonizing but it was sheer torment; it was simply traumatic. While flies and mosquitoes were a constant torture, rats, lizards and snakes got into the house at will from outside the fence. And the walls of the house crawled with such insects like cockroaches, spiders, termites and crickets.

The worst torment however emanated from the old *enkoiboni*. For days on end, she railed at Resian complaining that she was deliberately refusing to eat enough food so that she did not gain strength soon to enable her undergo circumcision. On one of the days, she cornered Resian in the room she used as a bedroom. On seeing her, Resian quickly stood up ready to ward her off but the old woman ignored her. She glared at Resian with her powerful mono eye, stooped and got hold of the hem of her tattered dress. She pulled it up and then thrust her withered and callous claw-like hands under it to feel her stomach. Resian seethed with anger at the blatant intrusion of her privacy and total disregard for her feelings. But the mono eyed *enkoiboni* did not care about her feelings and Resian had to persevere the embarrassment as she probed and squeezed over her stomach, looking for whatever she thought she was going to find.

"I thought you are pregnant," she told Resian rudely as she pulled down her dress. "It is good you are not, for it would have taken us long waiting for you to give birth before calling in *enkamuratani*. It is even better so, for who wants *entaapai* as a wife to her son?"

Although it was of little consolation to her, Resian found that the old woman's worst epithets were directed at the rich people in towns such as her father, Oloisudori and leaders who she said decided where a road or dispensary were to be built. The *enkoiboni* held a grudge against the well-to-do whom she declared thieves, extortionists, robbers, poachers, swindlers and marauders.

"Take that *Ol-ushuushi* called Oloisudori for instance," the old *enkoiboni* would say disdainfully, her demonic red-rimmed eye glaring at Resian unblinkingly. "How many times did I cook for him porridge in this house as he hunted elephants and rhinos in this area? He used to stack ivory outside this house like firewood. Rhino horns were thrown onto a heap like tree stumps outside my compound. When big lorries eventually came and hauled the loot, we never saw him again. Today he calls himself a rich man who will not soil his hands by shaking ours. Where did he get his riches from? He is nothing but a thief and a poacher."

At times she would rail against leaders who she complained of neglecting those in rural areas and concentrated development projects in urban areas.

"Tell me, are we not people like those in towns?" she would complain bitterly. "You saw the rutted and dilapidated road that you travelled through the other day. Can you compare that road with the roads in towns? What about a hospital? The nearest one is two or three days walk from here. How does a sick person access it? You are lucky that *enkabaani* was around when Olarinkoi hit you. You would have died if it were not for her treatment!"

However, the *enkabaani,* whose real name Resian came

to know as *Nabaru*, did not approve of the old woman's foul language. In the old *enkoiboni's* absence, Nabaru told Resian to ignore her and not to allow her constant harangue to distress her. She encouraged her to continue eating well to regain her strength while she looked for a way out of her problem. She confided in her about the constant pressure the old *enkoiboni* continued to exert on her, wanting to know when Resian was likely to be strong enough to withstand the ritual. She complained that the delay was causing unnecessary anxiety. The sooner it was done, the old woman said, the better so that when she had recuperated the journey to Tanzania would begin.

Nabaru proved to be not only a kind nurse and a loving and caring foster mother to Resian, but also she became a valuable friend and confidant. Resian poured out her heart to her about her background, her growing up and the fact that her father scolded, rebuked and ridiculed her since she was a young child. She told her of her education, her fears and her aspirations, her ardent wish to join the university, to her forced marriage to Oloisudori and how the ongoing abduction by Olarinkoi and his mother had come to interfere and mar her progress. She sobbingly pleaded with her to help her get to where *Emakererei* resided; if she did that, she would never forget her for the rest of her life, she added.

She mentioned that the *Emakererei* inspired her and she was her role model. She however did not talk of *Emakererei's* loathe for Female Genital Mutilation. She knew Nabaru was of the old school and she still cherished the old ritual. The only grouse Nabaru had with *enkoiboni* was that she was interfering with another family's child.

She thought it was none of *enkoiboni's* business to want to circumcise Resian while her parents were still alive. And Resian knew that and so she decided to delicately balance her need to escape the forced marriage to Oloisudori and that of Olarinkoi, and her need to reach *Emakererei's* place in time to enroll at the Egerton University, without making her fear for the cut a major subject.

On her part, Nabaru demonstrated her motherly affection to the young helpless girl by extending to her all the help she could marshal. She knew she depended on her entirely for her upkeep, safety and possible escape from the snare. Even when she regained her strength fully, she knew there was no way Resian would escape on her own. Between *Inkiito,* the place where that homestead was situated and the next centre where she could get assistance, was a long distance within an area that was infested with dangerous animals and which she could never traverse alone.

Since food was provided in plenty by Olarinkoi and his mother—a sackful of maize meal, a sackful of sugar, tea leaves and a goat slaughtered after another—Nabaru's task was simple. She made sure that water and firewood were available in the house and that she cooked delicious meals. She brought her own two blankets and together with the one that Resian brought from Nasila, made her a bed after discarding those bloody rags. She also brought her own two *lesos* and gave them to her so that she could wear them as her dress had been ruined by Olarinkoi. With Resian's consent, she shaved her head for her hair had become unmanageable in the absence of combs.

Every morning after breakfast, that consisted of

tea and cold leftovers from the previous evening's *ugali,* Nabaru would leave to conduct her other businesses; one of which, was to find a way through which Resian could leave that homestead secretly.

As she got stronger, Resian began to venture a little farther out of the homestead. She discovered that there were two or three homesteads farther afield that were three or four kilometers apart. In one of the homesteads, she met three young women who were married to old men twice or thrice their ages. One of them who was about eighteen, was married to an old man who was probably seventy-five years old. She was carrying a baby of six months or so and a boy of about four years tugged at her *shukas.* The children were constantly crying, a dreary monotonous tearless sob, with swarms of flies encircling their eyes and crowding their nostrils as they sucked the mucus that oozed from their noses.

The other two women were even younger. They were probably fifteen or sixteen, but they had all prematurely aged due to poor diet and hardships. Resian was elated to meet them, for solitude had bred loneliness in her heart. But her happiness and the pleasure of meeting the young women did not last long. She soon found out that the two had an intense curiosity that propelled them into asking her questions she considered private, personal and confidential. They wanted to know whether it was true that Olarinkoi had fought four other men who wanted to marry her, including one giant called Oloisudori, defeated them all and he snatched her from them bringing her there to make her his wife. They also wanted her to confirm what they had heard; that she was among *intoiye nemengalana* and that she was expectant, and soon she was going to give birth after which she would be circumcised to become an *entaapai*. Resian's response and confidence surprised them and they became suspicious of her speech and mannerisms. Their visits at the hovel she called her temporary home helped to break the monotony in her life but, at the same time, she found them depressing. They however provided sound and motion in a place that was bleak and cheerless.

One day after the women had left and she had gone into the inner room to rest on the bed, she saw a looming shadow in the doorway; she raised her head to see who it was. She first thought it was Nabaru the *enkabaani* who had returned earlier than usual, but it was not. It was Olarinkoi!

He stood at the doorway grinning down at her sourly. She had not seen him since that night when he tried to rape her. He had put on some weight and his thumb was still bandaged. He took a step towards the bed and Resian quickly lifted herself and slid out of bed sitting up on its edge; her eyes wide open with terror. He moved closer and sat on the edge of the bed beside her. Resian silently moved away from him and sat erect and motionless. How the man stunk! she thought as she wrinkled her nose slightly. He smelled strongly of sweat, sheep and sour breath.

He threw a furtive glance at Resian, grunted and sighed. Then he heaved a gusty sigh and cleared his throat as if preparing to say something. Resian steeled herself to keep from trembling and she forced herself to breath with a slow steady rhythm. He cleared his throat again, licked his lips and swallowed saliva noisily. The seconds dragged by, each one an eternity long and Resian could hear rats racing from one end of the room to the other. He turned towards her and placed his heavy hand on her knee. She fidgeted and her face twisted with anguish while her lips opened in a silent wail of helplessness and desperation.

"I don't mean any harm," he said quietly as he looked about him sheepishly. "I'll not repeat what I tried to do last time and I regret having been forced to hit you."

Resian stared at him blearily.

"I don't blame you for having bitten off my thumb," he continued his monologue. "I know I was the cause of that for which I have been rebuked severely."

Resian said nothing.

"My mother tells me you are back on your feet and that you are now able to move around in the homestead," he said eyeing her stealthily. "She has arranged with the *enkamuratani* who will come the day after tomorrow so that we can clear the pending job and move on."

Resian began to tremble but stoically held on.

"This is just a small matter that would be over within minutes," he said nonchalantly. "There is nothing to be afraid of."

He released her knee and stood up. Without another word, he was gone. Resian's only hope was that Nabaru the *enkabaaani* would have found a solution to her problem before the *enkamuratani* came.

As soon as Olarinkoi left, Resian leapt from the edge of the bed where she was seated and dashed to the door, quickly bolting it from the inside. She however knew that door was not sufficient protection against any incursion. Nonetheless it reduced the element of surprise and afforded her some sort of preparedness in case she was confronted by those who were planning evil against her.

She knew her preparedness was of little use to her though, for chances of escaping the *enkamuratani's olmurunya* were becoming slimmer by the hour. The option of running away from that desolate homestead was out of question for it was in the middle of expansive lands that extended to the horizon in all directions, and were teeming with such dangerous animals as lions, hyenas, snakes and wild dogs called *isuyan*. Chances of outwitting the old mono eyed witch and her evil-minded son, Olarinkoi, could not be given thought, for the two were determined to have her circumcised and no persuasion of any kind was likely to make them change their minds. Even running to the nearby homesteads was of no use, she concluded, for they all supported girl circumcision and she would appear to be ridiculously stupid to want to run away from what other girls were proud to have undergone. She was ensnared. Her only chance of escape lay on one human being; Nabaru the *enkabaani,* and God!

She sat impatiently waiting for Nabaru to return so that she could tell her of the new development. Then she would plead with her, beg her, beseech her, implore her and supplicate for her help to free her out of that hell in whichever way she could. She could now understand how anguished Jesus was that night at the Garden of Gethsemane when He prayed that the cup of agony be taken away from Him. She found herself praying animatedly that the looming excruciating pain be taken away from her.

Evening approached and Nabaru had not yet returned.

Resian heard a stampede outside as the sheep rushed onto the small courtyard and into their enclosure, driven by the mono eyed *enkoiboni*. She also heard her yell at the animals and then locked them in their pen. Thereafter it was all quiet. The silence became eerie and frightening.

Dusk came and Nabaru had not returned. Then it became dark, still she had not come. Resian began to panic, then she became fearful. Doubt began to envelop her. Was Nabaru sincere when she said she was going to help her, she thought confusedly, or had she been fooling her by uttering kind words to mollify her and calm her nerves while evil was being planned against her? When it became apparent that Nabaru was not coming she disappointedly concluded that the kind old nurse was nothing but a shameless liar.

Then the moon emerged, its sad yellow light seeping through the cracks on the walls and the single hole above the bed. The sadness brought in by the moonlight made her cry. She could hear from afar the discordant howls of the hyenas, the monotonous groaning of the wild dogs, and the chirrup of crickets and cicadas outside the house that blended with the rustling sound made by the blowing wind. They merged into one major sound that closed in around her, like a physical force that was suffocating her and seeming to put a crushing pressure over her body.

Soon the moon receded into thick clouds and it became dim. The room was filled with a grey flat and lifeless monotony in which everything faded into hideous shadows under which, she imagined, all kinds of frightening and dangerous animals lurked.

The fear made her body numb and she did not feel the

mosquitoes bite. The shivering and chattering of her teeth reminded her of the cold. As she sat there on the edge of the bed, her mind drifted into another world where the air was cold and clammy against her skin.

Yes, it was early in the morning and the time of reckoning had finally come. A crowd had gathered outside the tiny homestead, and she was being led naked, to the spot where she was gong to get circumcised. She saw herself exposed to the eyes of 'others in her nakedness. The Nasila *enkamuratani* with her *olmurunya* was there and so was the mono eyed witch and the *enkabaani*, the shameless liar.

The touch of the mono eyed *enkoiboni's* fingers as she pushed her to *enkamuratani*, registered only dimly in her mind as the modesty and other sensibilities in her had fled to cower in a tiny recess in her mind to escape the torture of the *olmurunya*. The three – evil women nodded their heads vigorously in tune with the rhythmic sound of the hyenas, wild dogs and the chirrup of the crickets and cicadas.

Their lips quivered as they moved slightly as if singing in unison with the wild animals and the insects. She tried to scrutinize their faces but the flat dim light distorted their images and exaggerated their demonic dance movements. Her tortured senses tried to place the images transmitted by her blurred vision into proper perspective, but failed.

Then the struggle began. She was determined that the old *enkamuratani* would never circumcise another girl again. She was going to deal with her firmly and finally. She took hold of the old woman's bony arm. Her fingers were now laced firmly through the old woman's, gripping the shrivelled claw-like fingers that held the *olmurunya* and twisting the hand mercilessly. The old woman shrieked with pain. Resian pounded the old woman's head with a mallet she had picked from the ground and hit her repeatedly as the woman looked up at her pleadingly. When the old mono eyed *enkoiboni* came to rescue the *enkamuratani*, it was as if all Resian's energy had been reserved for her. Like a ferocious leopard, she descended upon her with vicious blows completely disfiguring her face and battering the one eye. The old witch tried to say something as if to curse her, but she would not let her. She hit her hard on the head like a snake and she sprawled flat on the ground, lifeless. Then she moved on to face Nabaru, the *enkabaani*, the shameless liar. She was about to hit her when she called out her name.

"Resian! Resian!" the sound was urgent and came from outside the house. "Resian be quick, open the house! They are coming for you!"

She woke up with a start and jumped to her feet. It was then that she realised she had been dreaming and that she had not slept under the blankets the whole night. A headache throbbed dully in her temples and she felt feverishly light-headed. Contact with her surroundings was flimsy and tenuous, requiring a concentrated effort to make out what was happening. And her entire body had swollen lumps caused by mosquitos' bites. Yes, someone was pounding at the door insistently and she wondered who it was. The person pounded the door harder and insistently, but when Resian tried to raise herself, she could not. It was as if some power was holding her back. She got back into bed.

"Resian! Resian!" the person outside called, banging the door and shaking it violently. "They are coming for you! Get up and be quick. Resian, Resian wake up! They are coming for you!"

Yes, she could now make out the voice to be that of Nabaru the *enkabaani*. It was loud and strong, the only sound that made a distinct impression through the mist clouding her awareness. It now struck a responsive chord within her mind. With a mighty effort, she pulled herself out of bed and struggled to stand. The banging at the door became more urgent and insistent. Resian took the first step, staggered and nearly fell. She supported herself with the walls of the room, walking slowly and haltingly. Each step was a tremendous effort as an excruciating pain throbbed in her head and chest.

"Open the door, Resian," Nabaru shouted from outside the house desperately. "They are about to arrive. Do you hear? They are coming to take you away. Resian! Resian! Resian!"

Nabaru shook the door so violently that it nearly broke. Just then, Resian reached the door. She raised her hand weakly and shot back the tower bolt and opened the door. Then she collapsed. Nabaru got in and seeing the state in which Resian was, scooped her like a little baby and carried her back to the bedroom. She laid her on the bed carefully and tried to diagnose her problem. She was an experienced medicine woman and within no time, she got it right. She was suffering from a fever caused by the mosquitoes bites. She was cold for having laid there exposed to the elements the whole night and she was hungry. Nabaru quickly went to her medicine bag at the corner of the room. Took out three containers whose content she tipped into a cup and mixed them with a cupful of milk. She came back to the bedroom where Resian still lay unconscious. She bent lower, putting her elbows on Resian's shoulders and holding her down. Taking her face with her strong fingers, she opened her mouth, pinched her nostrils closed and emptied the cupful of the concoction into her mouth.

Resian instantly regained her consciousness, sneezed and shook her head vigorously. She tried to spit out the bitter medicine, but Nabaru held her head straight and blocked off her breath from her nostrils, chocking her as the liquid ran back into her throat. She swallowed, gagging from the nasty taste, then breathed deeply through her mouth. Nabaru released her head and held her shoulders again. The concoction burned a trail of fire down to her stomach and it spread a glowing warmth through her body as a hard knot of nausea formed in her stomach. Within no time, life returned into her eyes and a surge of energy ran through her veins. It did not take long for her to regain the possession of her faculties and to understand the looming danger that Nabaru was explaining to her.

Nabaru scooped a tinful of *olpurda* and put it into a container while Resian quickly put on her *lesos* and picked the blanket and the *leso* given to her by the Nasila old woman. Holding the bundle in one arm, Resian walked quietly across the bedroom to the fireplace and got out into the small courtyard. She opened the gate, slipped through it and closed it behind her. Nabaru who was ahead of her urged her to hurry up. And truly, there was need to hurry up, for from a distance they could see the mono eyed *enkoiboni* approaching and with her were her son Olarinkoi and an old woman who Nabaru said was the *enkamuratani*.

For the first time since Resian came to that desolate village, it rained; a heavy downpour that came suddenly and drenched them as they ran down the path towards the road where Nabaru told her a vehicle to transport them waited. The downpour soaked her *lesos* through to her skin. Water streamed down her face in rivulets making it hard for her to see or to breathe. But she could see Nabaru ahead of her, also struggling to move forward, with the *shukas* that she wore clinging onto her body and water pouring down her face, blinding her. She followed her as she stumbled from side to side wading through the mass of deep muddy water. She moved on determinedly. She had to get there at all costs. Then the cold began penetrating her body and she began to shiver. Nabaru waited for her and when she got where she was, she encouraged her to persevere and press on for they were not far from the main road.

True to her word, they were soon there. Resian almost ran into the bodywork of a lorry that was parked by the road and which was invisible in the rain. Her heart leapt with joy on seeing it.

As they quickly boarded, they heard a voice from behind them.

"You, Resian, stop!" It was Olarinkoi.

Olarinkoi was in hot pursuit of the two fleeing women. His face worked with rage as he arrived to find the two clambering over a stationary lorry. They however managed to climb over before he arrived and they locked themselves inside the covered cabin of the lorry. On arrival, Olarinkoi realised that he had been outsmarted. Resian was now completely out of his reach. Frustrated, he angrily brandished his knobkerry as he wheeled confusedly around the lorry, his mouth frothing as he let out a wordless growl.

He stepped on the rear wheel of the lorry and peered into the cabin coming face to face with Nabaru the *enkabaani*. His eyes bulged with fury and his face turned black as he angrily stared at her. He lifted his knotted fist and shook it at her threateningly. "Where do you think you are taking my wife, you filthy woman? Wherever you are taking her, remain there with her, because if you ever come back to Inkiito, you will not see the light of day. But you are not lucky, for wherever you go, my mother's curse will find you there. Mark my words!"

"Away with you, you good for nothing, *osuuji*," Nabaru sneered at him in the safety of the locked cabin. She pouted at him, her lips tight and her eyes narrowed and sparkling. "You are like *embarie* the coward fox that waits for the lion to kill before it stealthily creeps in to steal the meat. How could you cheat this child who was desperately looking for help as she ran away from that villain called Oloisudori? You took advantage of her trust in you, just like *embarie* does. That is exactly what you are: *Embarie*. A good for nothing *osuuji*."

Resian too could not restrain herself. She glared at Olarinkoi and sent out a corrosive salvo from the safety of the cabin.

"You, stupid Olarinkoi, you are worse than Oloisudori," she told him acidly as she trembled with anger. "But the two of you have one thing in common: warped minds.

Thank God your weird ideas hit the wall. I pray that God's favour would continue to abide with me, so that a few years from today, you will be ashamed to realise what your stupidity would have stopped me from achieving. Good bye Olarinkoi and go and tell your mother to go back to her pebbles and attempt new predictions!"

"You have not seen or heard the last of me!" Olarinkoi declared in a thunderous growl that shook with impotent fury. "The *enkoiboni's* predictions always come to pass." The lorry drove away, leaving him standing there in the rain.

They embarked on a journey that immediately became a living nightmare. The road was nothing but a rutted cattle track with a series of connecting links made by columns of cattle travelling in search of water and grass. As they progressed, the terrain worsened and the lorry laboured as it climbed rocky areas and manoeuvred around boulders. The driver had to occasionally stop the lorry as the engine overheated and they had to wait for it to cool so that he could add water to the radiator.

Then in the afternoon, the climate changed. It became cooler and the vegetation also became greener. The road too improved. They began to travel through well established farms judging from the large, comfortable looking houses with gardens enclosed by sturdy fences. Resian admired the expansive lands with broad stretches of grassland, low stony hills, and areas of deep forest. Healthy cattle and sheep grazed contentedly on the farms. At one place where men were indiscriminately felling tall gigantic trees with scooter power-saws, she remembered the indefatigable Professor Wangari Maathai who continues to fight gallantly and tirelessly to save forests and thought how angry she would be if she saw that wanton destruction of trees. If there were two women she admired, she thought quietly, they were *Emakererei* and Wangari Maathai. They were her role models.

It came as a shock to Resian when she learnt that they had entered into the Sheep Ranch where Minik ene Nkoitoi, the *Emakererei* was the manager. Resian clung onto the body of the vehicle, in her dull detached state which had become her own way of preserving her sanity in the monotony of the journey, as Nabaru pointed out to some glittering buildings in the distance that shimmered in the afternoon sun.

"That is Ntare-Naaju station where we are going," Nabaru said quietly, pointing at the shiny buildings. "We are already in Ntare-Naaju Sheep Ranch where you said *Emakererei* lives."

The comment by Nabaru brought Resian sharply back into full contact with her surroundings. She learnt that they had been driving through the expansive ranch in the last fifteen minutes or so. She thought that to be the ultimate anticlimax. After the long time that ranch had preoccupied her mind, and after the effort to reach it and the hardships she had gone through in the last three weeks, she had hoped that her arrival into the ranch would be announced by something more significant than just a turn at a corner.

It now dawned on her that she had arrived at the place in which she expected to find her nirvana and she had hardly known it. She tried to separate what she had seen before from what she was now seeing, and in her

mind, it was all the same. If there was anything about the expansive plain of deep grass, spotted with clumps of low scrub stretching away to the horizon in all directions, that distinguished it from the rest of the terrain they had crossed, it was the presence of
thousands upon thousands of tawny woolly sheep that grazed contentedly in their paddocks.

The lorry had just completed climbing a steep hill when it began to lose power. The engine sputtered for a moment and then stalled. The driver and his companion climbed down and lifted the bonnet. Suddenly, a hissing sound emanated from the radiator and a spurt of scalding hot steam spewed out of it as if from a geyser. The engine had overheated again.

The lorry driver walked to the back of the lorry and told Resian and Nabaru that they could climb down too and stretch their legs as they waited for the engine to cool before he added cold water into the radiator.

Nabaru took out the container that had *olpurda* in it and climbed down followed by Resian. They sat down on green grass on the side of the road. Nabaru opened the *olpurda* container and gave some to Resian. They chewed silently as they watched the breathtakingly beautiful undulating pasture lands that stretched out in all directions. The breezeless hot afternoon hours that they had known back in the semi-arid lands of *Inkiito* were unknown in those highlands where a cool breeze of fresh aromatic air from the hills soothingly caressed their nostrils and filled their lungs. Even the blazing sun that usually burned down from the blue skies with a vengeance, was amazingly heartlifting.

"This is a beautiful country," Resian said excitedly as she looked all around her with a cheerfulness she had not known for along time. "I am so happy that the ordeal is finally coming to an end."

"I am happy for you, young lady," Nabaru the *enkabaani* said quietly, "and I thank God that I have been able to fulfil my promise to save you from the hands of Olarinkoi and his mother. But I must say you are a brave girl. It was your bravery that inspired me to walk the whole way to the next shopping centre where I knew I could find this lorry driver. It was not easy persuading him to take a detour from his usual route and pass by to collect you. I will never forget the way you bravely wrestled with that brute called Olarinkoi and bit his thumb so severely that he was unable to rape you as he had intended. You are a great young lady and I am sure you will go places."

Resian was humbled and reduced to tears when she learnt that the old *enkabaani* walked the whole way through the dangerous terrain to look for means to remove her from Olarinkoi's snare. She tried to find words to express her gratitude, but she found her heart too full to speak. She got up from where she sat and knelt before the old woman and tearfully hugged her as she buried her face in the old woman's bosom.

"*Yeiyo ai! Yeiyo ai!*" Resian cried passionately. "Only God the Almighty can repay you for your surpassing love and kindness. I am but a poor girl and I have nothing to give you as a token to show my gratitude. But rest assured, *Yeiyo-ai-nanyorr*, my heart shall forever be grateful."

She went back to stand at the middle of the road and began to review, in her mind, the events that took place ever since Nabaru the *enkabaani* came into her life.

She was musing when they saw three motorbike riders coming from the direction of Ntare-Naaju station. Nabaru stood up and shaded her eyes with her hand as she looked into the distance ahead of the lorry. Resian shook the remnants of *olpurda* off her hands, and stepped off the road staring at the approaching riders with an expression of curiosity. The driver and his companion also saw them and they too looked at the oncoming riders though with little interest.

The three motorbike engines roared loudly as they made the approach. On reaching the stationary lorry, they slowed down. The driver rubbed his hands together, as he looked up at the approaching riders, a wide smile of greetings on his face.

"Are you all right, Lebutu?" one of the riders asked.

Resian stiffened with surprise as the driver replied in a cheerful, ingratiating tone. The voice of the rider was that of a woman. Resian wondered how the lorry driver came to know the woman rider.

"I am very well, thank you," the driver answered. "How about you *Daktari*, how are you?"

"Can't complain," she answered. "Did you deliver all the sheep or you lost some on the way?"

"I lost none, *Daktari*," the driver answered in a defensive tone. "I delivered all of them safely. The delivery notes are here. Would you like to see them?"

"No, take them to the office," she said authoritatively and began to rev the engine again, ready to go.

"Is there some more work for me?" the driver asked meekly.

"Yes, there are four hundred bales of wool…"

Resian no longer listened to what she was saying. Her heartbeat quickened sharply and her mouth dried as anxiety gripped her. She rubbed her eyes anxiously and stared at the woman. Could that be Minik ene Nkoitoi, the *Emakererei*, the woman that she had longed to see and meet for a long time? She was an exceptionally tall woman of slight built. Her shoulders and back were straight, and there was the subtle softness of femininity about them compared to the stocky masculine features of her two male companions. Her shirt and trousers were loose and shapeless, but the front of the shirt had the fullness of a woman's bosom. Her face had a smooth chocolate brown complexion and she had big solid, gleaming black eyes. Her lips were full and when she opened them, she displayed pearl-like sparkling white teeth planted on black gums. She had an unmistakable aura of superiority and authority around her: she was devastatingly beautiful.

Resian was still observing the lady when the trio revved their engines ready to go. They roared louder and they began to move. Then the lady's large black eyes turned to Resian. When she neared the spot where Nabaru and Resian stood, she stopped and looked at Resian. Her eyes questioning and reflecting curiosity.

"Are you Resian *ene* Kaelo?"

"Yes!" Resian answered wondering what was happening.

"I guessed right," she said delightfully, her eyes glittering with excitement. Turning to her two male companions, she added, "other than her clean-shaven head, her face is exactly the same as the one that appeared in the newspapers."

Resian was shocked and stressed. What was the advertisement all about? Could it be that Oloisudori and her father were still pursuing her? Anxiety began to show on her face. That alarmed the lady who quickly began to reassure her.

"There is nothing to worry about young lady," she said in a pleasant soothing voice. "We have remembered that about a week or so ago, your father and a man called Oloisudori put an advertisement in the papers reporting that you had disappeared. They promised a reward of a half a million shillings to whoever would find you. And by the way, may name is Minik *ene* Nkoitoi. People around here call me *Daktari* or *Emakererei*. I am the manager of this farm and these two men are my colleagues. Let the driver bring you to the station and we shall talk more."

She turned to the lorry driver, "Lebutu, bring this girl to the station," she said and jovially added, "and don't you lose her for she is worth a lot of money!"

Resian immediately began to walk back to the lorry, a mixture of emotion churning and swirling in her mind. She still could not believe that she had seen and met *Emakererei,* her saviour and role model. It was too good to be true. She however thanked God prayerfully for enabling her to escape the dreadful *enkamuratani's olmurunya* and for rekindling afresh her hope of enrolling as a student at the Egerton University. However, the mention of Oloisudori and the advertisement her father had placed in papers regarding her disappearance, had slightly dampened her spirit. But as she climbed onto the lorry, she reminded herself of her resolution: she would not allow other people to sway her from her charted course. She remembered the *Maa* adage that said: home was never far for one who was still alive. So as she watched the three motorbikes speeding off, and as the lorry reared into life, she knew she was now on the final home stretch. She recalled the wise words in the Holy Book that said:

Now we see but a poor reflection as in a mirror,
Then we shall see face to face!
Now I know in part, then I shall know fully.

And she thought: How true!

Chapter Seventeen

The lorry driver drove the last few kilometers to Ntare-Naaju station with ease. Resian sat at the back of the lorry watching the breathtakingly beautiful scenery all around her excitedly, with a blanket wrapped around her. The lorry drove across expansive paddocks on which Resian saw such large flocks of sheep as she had never seen in her life. They were seas of tawny woolly animals flowing and rippling around as they grazed or as they were driven from one paddock to the other. At long last, the lorry came to stop by a long low building in which stacked bales of wool were visible from its open door.

The driver and his companion leaped from the front cabin of the lorry, laughing and greeting the men gathering around, shaking hands and slapping shoulders. Resian climbed down slowly, carefully looking around, followed by Nabaru.

Minik *ene* Nkoitoi, the *Emakererei* sat at the veranda of her spacious house and watched Resian and her old woman companion walk from the godown where the lorry had stopped. She wondered who the old woman was. Then her eyes moved back to the girl. She noticed that Resian was taller than the old woman, had long slender limbs and high firm breasts. She had a narrow waist that tapered down, swelling out to bulging hips. Her arms and legs were slender but shapely. She moved with a natural gait and pride.

The confidence in her beauty was reflected in the line of her chin, mouth and the way she held her head. Although she was tall, her features were small and almost delicate, with high wide cheekbones, large eyes and full wide lips. She thought she could detect an atmosphere of distant wilderness about her, something free, wild and untamed. But she seemed to have liked her instantly. She got up from where she sat and went down to meet them.

Then Resian saw Minik *ene* Nkoitoi, the *Emakererei*, walking along the path from the large house towards them. She was now wearing a brilliant, pink silky, dress patterned with white silken lace in the neck and sleeves and matching pink shoes. Resian noted that she had long shapely legs and her long black woolly hair that curled upwards at the nape, accentuated the brightness of her beautiful face and the sparkle of her big black eyes. She walked with a dignified graceful gait, with her chin up and her mouth slightly open, as she smiled at them. Her eyes were fastened on Resian and their gaze was like a physical force. Resian suddenly felt very much in awe of her. She had an authoritative aura like that of the principal in her high school days. The scantiness of Resian's attire made her feel even more insignificant in front of Minik. When she was about two metres from her, Resian stopped and in the most respectful voice she stated her case.

"If you allow us a few minutes of your time, madam, we shall explain what brought us to your place and you can thereafter decide our fate," she added humbly. "This *entasat* with me is called Nabaru," she said humbly.

Minik's eyes moved over Resian for a long moment, studying her. Then she smiled slightly and her eyes pleasantly warmed as she slowly moved forward to where Resian stood with Nabaru and put her hand on her shoulder.

"No, you don't have to state your case outside here," she said as she patted Resian's shoulder, her smile widening. Looking right into Resian's eyes, she added pleasantly, "you are welcome to Ntare-Naaju Ranch and to my house. Please come into the house, you two."

They followed her back to the large house through a smooth tarmacked driveway that ran between tall leafy trees on both sides and squat robust shrubs underneath them. From the driveway, they could see a sprawling garden in which clusters of flowers blossomed into all shades of colours. On fences and hedges, a blaze of bougainvillea's bright pink, scarlet, amber and cream petals added beauty to an already breathtaking scenery. The lawn around the house and beyond was a smart, soft green mat that seductively enticed one to cross over, sit on it and relax.

When Minik opened the door to her living room and ushered them in, Resian was intimidated by its glamour and elegance. Its fitted soft, thick carpet of deep maroon colour – tastefully interwoven with cream and amber colours – was soothingly cool to her tired and thorn pricked feet. Its colours were deliberately chosen, or it seemed, to match the pale orange colour of the walls and the heavy maroon curtains that flowed voluptuously to the floor and fluttered lazily in the wind that blew through the open windows.

The seven-piece lounge suit upholstered in glowing black leather; the wall to wall bookshelf that was book laden with paper backs and hard-covered volumes; the glass-faced wall-unit that held trophies, souvenirs and other oddities; were all completely overwhelming especially

265

to someone who had just emerged from that poverty-ridden hovel that Olarinkoi called home at Inkiito. She had not only been awesomely impressed by the grandeur of that living room, but it had taken her breath away.

It was after she dipped herself into the gigantic bath tub filled to the brim with steaming hot water, that Resian realised what she had missed in the three weeks that she had been in that stinking hovel. She soaped several times, washed, scrubbed and rubbed herself, repeating the process many times before she declared herself clean; having got rid of the many layers of grime that had accumulated over her body during that period she was in the wilderness.

It was only when she peered into the full length mirror on the dressing table that she got shocked by what she saw. She was emaciated, her eyes were deep-set and she had a haggard look on her face. Without her black flowing hair, she looked as if she was a stranger even to herself. She however accepted that as a temporary situation. What was most important, she reasoned, was that she had come out of the ordeal with her mind, soul and body whole and intact.

It was only after they had eaten and gone back to sit on the comfortable sofas in the living room, did Minik allow Resian to state her case. She eloquently gave in full details the account of the events that had bedevilled her and her sister Taiyo ever since they relocated from Nakuru to Nasila. Their *intoiye nemengalana* status had been a cause of innuendoes about them. She spoke of the constant harassment by vagabonds, all trying to discredit them for not having undergone the cultural rite of circumcision.

Together with Nabaru, they gave a detailed account of the torture Resian had gone through while held hostage at Olorankoi's home. She narrated her escape ordeal from an early marriage and Female Genital Mutilation.

Resian hastened to give further explanation. She told Minik how she and her sister Taiyo had for a long time longed to meet her. And though she had not met her until then, she added, she had always inspired them. Her ardent ambition to enroll as a student at the Egerton University was influenced by the course Minik studied at the University. She told Minik they had heard of her relentless struggle to end the abhorrent practice of F.G.M and the shameless giving away of young girls to old men in those underage marriages that were prevalent in Maa.

They had also heard and admired the way she single-handedly rescued girls from the *enkamuratani's olmurunya* and organised for them to go back to school. Like her, she and her sister Taiyo abhorred that archaic culture of female circumcision which they considered obnoxious, repugnant and a threat to the health of the young girls. Resian declared that as soon as she was able to participate, she would join Minik's lobby group to fight the hazardous tradition.

When Minik began to speak, it was to Nabaru the *enkabaani* that she directed her discourse. Looking at her with charming warm eyes, Minik told her she thought she was her mother's agemate. She would not therefore begrudge her if she found out that, like her own mother, she supported the traditionally favoured girl child circumcision which was said to have been handed down to the people dating back to the time Maa people ascended the Kerio Valley. That was said to be in accordance with Maa culture – a culture that she too loved and respected. She said she even lauded the Maa culture for the tenacity of its fabrics that enabled it to hold its people together long after others had disintegrated. She however said culture was supposed to be dynamic and it ought to shed off aspects that had outlived their usefulness. She argued that in the past such archaic aspects had been discarded and forgotten.

She gave an example of *emuata*, a horrible and outdated cultural practice that demanded that young brides called *isiankikin*, wear heavy copper wire tightly coiled around their limbs, legs from ankle to knee, arms from wrist to elbow and from elbow to armpit. The copper wire coils were so heavy that they impeded the young women's movement. They were also so tight that they constricted their veins and wasted their muscles. Besides, they harboured flies and fleas underneath them resulting to incessant itching. Eventually, that injurious tradition *Amaut*, was discarded and the women were freed from that harrowing experience that was ironically meant to enhance their beauty. Similarly, she said, *emuratare-o-Ntoiye*, which referred to the girl child circumcision should be discarded in the same manner, for its time had passed and it had outlived its usefulness.

"The name of *intoiye nemengalana*, should stop being derogatory," Minik said triumphantly. "Instead *emuratare-o-ntoiye* should disappear from Maa language and should be regarded as extinct."

She said much more that, at the end, Nabaru was convinced that F.G.M did not add any value to the lives of its young victims. Instead, she agreed, it traumatized them and it was hazardous to their health. And having been *enkabaani* for a long time, she said she could testify to its devastation, having witnessed the way young lives were ruined by the practice. She vowed to join Minik in lobbying against it.

Minik thanked Nabaru for her understanding and welcomed her into the lobby group and hoped that when she went back to Inkiito, she would tell people there the dangers to which girl circumcision exposed their daughters.

Turning to Resian, Minik congratulated her for having bravely stood firm and resisted the pressure to have her circumcised. She acknowledged that there were very few girls who would have resisted the lure of Oloisudori's riches. And even fewer would have wrestled a brute like Olarinkoi in a remote house where no help was expected from any quarter. She welcomed her to join the five hundred girls who were in that Ranch who had refused to undergo the cultural rite. There were still many more, she said, who were still out there in the villages who needed to be rescued from the obnoxious rite and be taken back to school. The battle was still far from being won.

Resian was thus musing when Minik uttered the magical words she had waited to hear ever since she left Nakuru and landed in Nasila. Minik promised her that she would do whatever was possible to see that she and Taiyo enrolled as students at the Egerton University as they had wanted. It would have been impossible for her to believe that she was not a victim of hallucinations hadn't she repeatedly convinced herself that Minik was real and that what she was telling her were not fairies that belonged to the realms of the imagination. The excitement that was caused by those wonderful words exploded in her mind, and the resultant ecstatic feelings overwhelmed her. Tears streamed down her cheeks as she blissfully said, "your voice dear *Emakererei* is truly the voice of God. This is a true case of a dream come true. And only God alone makes such things happen. *Meisisi Olaitoriani!*"

There were more good tidings on the way for Resian. Minik told her that Ntare-Naaju Ranch operated a scholarship that benefited young talented girls who had excelled in their school examination and who were unable to continue with further studies for lack of fees. Under the prevailing circumstances, Resian would qualify for the scholarship. In addition, she told her, her gallant fight against the evil designs of Oloisudori and Olarinkoi on one hand, and her definite stand that she took against the archaic obnoxious culture of F.G.M on the other, had set her on a pedestal, and made it a joy for her to want to help her. And for the duration of her studies at the university, she told her, she would be regarded as an employee of the ranch, drawing all the benefits enjoyed by the employees, including half of the salary that she would be earning during the vacations. She would also have a fully furnished house. Meanwhile, she was going to pay her an advance on her first salary to enable her buy a few dresses and help her settle in her new house.

The sun had set by the time they left Minik's house, and only a glow of red crimson touched the horizon in the west. A rosy light illuminated the fences and the trees as Minik led them to the house she had allocated Resian. They followed her, Resian carrying in her hands a bundle of the only possessions she had in the world: the three wet *lesos* and the dusty blanket the old lady in Nasila had given her.

When they got to the house, Minik inserted a key into the padlock and opened it. And as they got in, a chilly night breeze blew through an open window as Minik lit a lamp. It immediately cast a yellow cheerful light around the room they were in, giving it a comfortable atmosphere. Before Minik left them, Resian requested her to allow Nabaru to stay for a few days as she thought of an alternative place to go, for Olarinkoi had threatened her with death if she went back to Inkiito. To her delight, Minik consented.

The two bed roomed house was another wonder that Minik had surprisingly given Resian to use and which was far beyond her most optimistic expectation. She could hardly believe that the house was hers. It was simply luxurious! It had a living room cum dining room, kitchen and two bedrooms, all of them spacious and appropriately furnished. The living room had four armchairs and a settee, coffee table and a set of stools, and two empty book shelves. And it had a fireplace. The dining corner had a table and four chairs and a sideboard. The two bedrooms were furnished with beds, dressing tables and wardrobes. In the kitchen stood a wood stove, charcoal brazier, a cupboard and a meat safe. A neat bathroom with running water completed the first round of the tour. She took Nabaru back to the living room, and left her there. She then walked back and forth through the house, looking at things, touching them to assure herself that what she was seeing was real. The furniture had a pleasant, gleaming, clear, varnish finish.

When Minik returned later with two workers carrying bundles of blankets, sheets and cartons containing utensils and foodstuffs, a poignant wrenching stab of feelings which she had never experienced before, overwhelmed Resian. She quickly put down the bundle of blankets she was holding and passionately hugged Minik, kissing her with a sudden fierce affection that brought stinging tears to her eyes.

"Here, the days begin early," Minik told Resian in a formal tone. "Tomorrow you will rest, but in all subsequent days, you must get down to work. Note that workers get up about five in the morning. A block away from your house, you will find a hall where early morning tea is served to senior members of staff. We all meet there and as breakfast is taken, chores and tasks for the day are shared out."

In the first few days Minik watched Resian carefully, taking her to every paddock where she worked. As the two were together most of the time, they developed a warm working relationship. Occasionally, Resian contemplated asking Minik some of the evil things she used to hear about her while in Nasila. She recalled that men used to call her a wasp and women a witch. But she found that Minik was often taciturn and always maintained an air of officialdom about her which precluded unlimited intimacy. She therefore gave up her intention of asking any questions and instead devoted all her time in learning as much as she could about the practical management of the sheep ranch. Minik noted Resian's undivided interest in her work and her desire to want to know more and that pleased her immensely.

Chapter Eighteen

It was midmorning of her fifth day in the ranch and she was working with Minik and a handful of workers in the mustering yard where they were separating female lambs from male lambs. Resian noticed a trail of dust as an approaching vehicle drove along the top of the hill, east of the home paddock. Minik noticed it too. She straightened up and shaded her eyes with her hand as she tried to identify the fast approaching vehicle.

It was the vehicle that she had sent out to Nasila on a rescue mission to the distress call from a girl who was said to have been forcibly circumcised and whose would-be husband was said to be hovering over the homestead like a hawk.

Turning to Resian, she told her to continue working while she went home to assess the condition of the rescued girl, if at all the rescue team had managed to come back with her. Resian wondered if the girl would be as traumatised as she was when Olarinkoi terrorised her at Inkiito. She also wondered how old she was.

An hour later, Minik sent a worker to fetch Resian. The tone of urgency in his voice as he delivered the message somehow alarmed her. She quickly released the lamb that she was holding and straightened up, wiping her hands on the seat of her trousers. For a moment she stared at the man who delivered the message as if she expected some more information from him. When she did not get any, she excused herself from the workers and began to walk towards the home paddock. For reasons she did not understand, she was gripped by sudden anxiety and apprehension.

And when she got to the house, there were foreboding hints. Minik was at the door to receive her and quickly led her to the living room where she put her hand on the back of a chair in a token gesture of seating her. Resian noticed that although her tone and manner were extremely courteous, she appeared angry. Resian's apprehension over what was in Minik's mind intensified, especially when she seemed hesitant in broaching whatever matter that seemed to be troubling her. She hoped whatever had angered her had nothing to do with her.

Minik looked, with sadness, at the young innocent girl seated before her. She felt pity for her and her agemates who lived in constant fear of stalking predators. She felt very angry and bitter bile sizzled inside her and the acid burned her heart searing it the way fire would sear dry bushes. She knew her anger stemmed from the realisation that at the time when she thought she had began to see the fruits of her five year struggle against female circumcision and forced underage marriages, new daring cases of arrogant predators were emerging to sneer and jeer at her, challenging her to match their monetary prowess.

Yes, there was a neo-culture whose driving force was wealth, she thought, ire blinding her. What chance did the young helpless girls, like the one who had just been brought in by her rescue team, maimed, traumatized and her future destroyed, have when pitted against those giant predators who dangled their riches to lure them and when they failed, abducted them and had them circumcised in order to enslave them and destroy their self esteem? She thought there was need to plan new strategies to battle the new monster that was rearing its ugly head.

Resian raised her eyes and looked at Minik. Her black eyes were hard and cold. She stood legs astride and hands akimbo, looking down at Resian with lips tightly pursed in a thin impatient line. Resian cleared her throat nervously. She was puzzled. What had she done that seemed to have made Minik so angry to the point that she was unable to speak?

"Something totally unexpected has happened," Minik said in a flat voice. "We did not receive sufficient information regarding the girl who was said to have been forcibly circumcised. When I sent my rescue team to Nasila to trace the girl, I thought they would go straight and find her, but it was not easy. The team eventually traced her at a place called Esoit, about five kilometers or so from Nasila. But unlike other homes where my team has been before, this particular home was guarded day and night by fierce armed men."

Poor girl, thought Resian. She imagined the person who wanted to marry the girl was probably a senior *moran* who commanded his junior *morans* to guard the home, to ensure his would-be bride was not snatched by rivals from another village.

Minik explained that on finding the home guarded, the rescue team had to retreat. They went back to Nasila to look for their contact man who initially directed them to *Esoit*. He was very helpful and he agreed to accompany them to the village where the girl was, and help them rescue her. They were about to give up the rescue mission after several attempts to distract the guards had failed. But the man from Nasila was able to lure the whole team of guards to a beer party at a nearby village, leaving the girl unguarded.

It was then that the rescue team struck! Amidst screams of terrified women, the barking of fierce dogs, braying donkeys and mowing of cattle, they entered the hut where the weak and sickly girl lay. They carried her and scampered away fast, like men fleeing from a burning village for three kilometers, to the spot where they had left the vehicle. And they were lucky to have escaped, for immediately they put her onto the vehicle and they themselves had jumped into it, the fierce-looking guards arrived, breathless, but fuming furiously and brandishing all sorts of deadly weapons.

On seeing that they had been outsmarted, they resorted to throwing stones at them, but by then the four-wheel drive vehicle had shot past the range of their missiles.

Regrettably, they learnt later that the man who assisted them so much and enabled them to rescue the girl, was speared to death by those thugs who accused him of tricking them so the girl could be stolen. The girl had however arrived safely and she was in fair condition although she was shocked, traumatized and terribly emaciated. She said the girl still found it difficult to walk, for the injuries inflicted to her by the *enkamuratani's olmurunya* had not yet healed.

Minik was thinking of how best to broach the matter in her mind. For a moment she wondered if it was the right time to bring out in the open the matter which she knew would be very painful to the girl who was just recovering from her own trauma. But she knew she could not hide the truth for long. It had to be revealed sooner so that counselling sessions could be put into place soon. Bracing herself appropriately, she quietly and coolly dropped the bombshell.

"I didn't know until the rescue team arrived," she said flatly, her face furrowed, "that the rescued girl is your sister, Taiyo, and the man that was killed is called Joseph Parmuat – a teacher."

"What are you talking about!" Resian asked in a shocked and trembling voice that was raised into a shriek. "And where is my sister right now as we speak?"

"She is in your house," Minik said sadly.
"But be calm as we handle this delicate situation!"

Taiyo at first did not know where she was nor did she know how and when she got there. What was still fresh in her mind was the disappearance of her sister Resian. The anguish and turmoil that she suffered had never subsided, and the pain was still raw in her heart.

She could still remember some incident in the distant past when her mother called her into their house in Nasila one afternoon to greet three women visitors whom she had not seen before. The trio told her they were from a village called Esoit where her sister Resian had found refuge after running away from home. They said she had become obstinate and for about three days had eaten nothing. She had gone on hunger strike. They said they pitied the hapless girl and enquired from her who in the whole world could persuade her to eat and save her life. That was the time, they said, she mentioned her. It was for that reason, they said, that they had come to Nasila to see whether she, being her sister could accompany them to save Resian's life.

Taiyo knew that Resian had depended upon her

all her life and that she had taken her to be her own responsibility. It was therefore very much like Resian to want her to go wherever she was and rescue her. She felt compassion for her sister and she was gripped by an immediate compulsive urge to go wherever she was and see to it that she was brought back to safety. She did not even give it another thought. She told the three women she was ready to accompany them. They had started their journey immediately, happy that her mother had assured her that their father had vowed never to try to marry them by force to any man.

It was dark when they got to Esoit village. She was shown a dingy dark hut where a smoky smouldering log glowed dimly in the fireplace. Nobody attended to her or even spoke about Resian who was the reason for their travel to that village. She just sat alone turning the matter over and over confusedly.

She had just dozed off at dawn when suddenly pandemonium broke loose at the entrance of the small hut. Many women struggled to enter amidst excited chants, arguments and banter. In no time, she was dragged out, despite her fierce resistance. Once outside, about twenty litres of very cold water were emptied over her head. She shivered and tried to clear water from her eyes and ears but, strong hands held her and wrestled her to the ground. In the dim light of dawn, she saw the face of the *enkamuratani* who she had once seen in their house at Nasila. She screamed and screamed, but nobody came to her rescue. Then she fainted.

When she came to, two days later, she was sore, bitter and angry. But she was no longer one among *intoiye nemengalana.* From then on, she had a hazy recollection of what had happened.

In short moments of lucidity, she recalled faintly seeing people carrying her on a stretcher. She had imagined that she had died and they were taking her to the burial place. She remembered thinking it was the best thing that had happened to her as she was going to be relieved of all her problems, including that of forced circumcision.

Instead of going to purgatory she had ended up in paradise. She remembered seeing green lawns, beautiful flower gardens and tall leafy trees. She had been taken to a house where she was received by an old woman who she suspected could be another *enkamuratani*. She had felt afraid, but she was helpless and decided to wait stoically for whatever was to happen.

But the woman in the new house spoke to her soothingly. She settled her on a comfortable bed and soon brought her a black liquid in an enamel mug which she asked her to drink. She gulped and swallowed it once. It exploded in her mouth making her want to retch, but she fought it, swallowed another gulp and gave back the mug. During all the days of her ordeal she had intermittent periods of sudden attack of sickness that left her wincing and gasping with pain. They were proceeded by some restlessness and followed by an excruciating headache in her temples that left every single muscle of her body sore. The heat in the bedroom intensified after she took the medicine and her neck grew weak until it was unable to hold her head. Then she dozed off.

She was getting deeper into sleep when a sudden shrill

and agonized scream rent the sleepy atmosphere in that bedroom and snatched her from drowsiness. She quickly opened her eyes wide and looked around her in a panic. The only thing that seemed normal and natural then was the bright sunlight that streamed into the bedroom through the window. She listened. Again the scream rang in her ear. She turned and looked at the old woman who sat by the bed enquiringly, and she looked troubled too for she fearfully looked here and there confusedly. Was she dreaming? She thought the scream voice was like that of her sister Resian. She listened more carefully and she was positive that she had identified the voice to be that of Resian. She was puzzled and at the same time fearful. If it was her, what had made her scream?

She did not wonder for long for within no time the bedroom door burst open and Taiyo saw her sister Resian tumble in, wailing and weeping wildly, followed closely by an older woman who was trying to restrain her.

Before Taiyo could comprehend that rapid succession of events, Resian was all over her on the bed hugging her tearfully and kissing her passionately. She gripped and held Taiyo's head between her hands and stared hard and straight into her eyes, her own red-rimmed swollen and tearful eyes wide open with panic and bewilderment. Looking as if she was seeing a ghost, Resian screamed once again, a penetrating animal like shriek as she buried her face under the neck of her sister.

Minik and Nabaru, being mature and experienced women, understood the anguish of the two young sisters who had been separated and suffered immensely in the hands of brutes. They therefore handled them carefully and delicately. They knew the turmoil and the mental torture they were suffering. For Taiyo, it was particularly difficult as she had yet to come to terms with the fact that she had been forcibly circumcised. The situation was not however strange to Minik who had handled similar cases in the past and had employed a teacher trained to counsel such victims of trauma.

Slowly by slowly, Taiyo recuperated and regained her strength. The nursing care of Nabaru the *Enkabaani*, Resian's excellent cuisine and Minik the *Emakererei's* encouragement, coupled with sessions of counselling given by the guidance and counselling teacher from *Intapuka-e-Maa* school, all made her begin to recover her physical strength and her memory. Then she began to heal.

After two weeks she struggled to get out of bed. It felt strange to be on her feet again, and the floor felt cold under her bare feet. Resian held her up as she slipped her feet into her sandals. The pain and soreness that had lingered with her for quite some time was less than she had expected, and the feeling of wellbeing was returning to her rapidly. She walked weakly but without assistance. Resian walked with her from the bedroom to the kitchen, her arm resting loosely around Taiyo's shoulders, and Nabaru followed behind them closely.

The kitchen was warm, bright and cheerful with a roaring fire in the wood stove. As they sat warming themselves while enjoying mugfuls of tea, they discussed past events and the hardship they experienced during the period they were separated. They both found fault with their father for wanting to please Oloisudori to the detriment of his own children's lives. They concluded that Oloisudori must have ordered for Taiyo's circumcision with the aim of marrying her after Resian ran away.

Their mother did not escape their ire. They knew she was in awe of their father who held her captive and never for once allowed her to express her own opinion on any matter however small it was. She was an example of a wife they never wanted to become. They concluded that if ever they were to get married they would only enter into such a contract if they were considered as equal partners with their spouses, and had a say in all matters that affected them. They declared that they would never accept to be subservient to their male counterparts. They would never lose their liberty and their rights in exchange of marital accommodation.

When Resian told Taiyo what she had heard about Joseph Parmuat's death and that he died as he struggled to have her rescued, she was inconsolably sad. They both cried and grieved for him for long. They hoped his death would be avenged and that it would not end up being police statistical data: filed and forgotten.

Nabaru the *enkabaani* found fault with the women of Maa. She thought they were the perpetrators of the obnoxious and repugnant tradition of female circumcision and its perpetuation. She argued that no man had ever taken up the *olmurunya* to circumcise a girl. The *enkamuratani* had always been a woman. What would happen if the *enkamuratani* threw away the *olmurunya* and refused to wield it again?" she asked.

"But it is the men who force the women to perpetrate the obnoxious tradition by insisting that they can only marry a girl if she is circumcised," argued Taiyo angrily. "Take my case for example; if the demonic and hellbent Oloisudori did not insist that I must be circumcised before he married me, I would have been spared the damage."

"It is true what you say, dear sister," Resian answered soothingly to mollify her angry sister. "But suppose all the women said no to the detestable culture? What would men do? Nothing! I am proud to be among *intoiye nemengalana* and I would not trade my position for anything!"

"I envy you dear sister," said Taiyo sadly. "It will take long before my conscience reconciles with what happened to me physically. The damage that was done to my mind, is indelibly printed on my memory."

"No, no, no! That should not be the way this matter should be treated," Nabaru said forcefully. "Minik and I and many other women have undergone the ritual, but it has not made us different human beings. What you have to do, Taiyo, is to accept that it happened to you. The most important thing is that you will discourage others, and you will not allow it to be performed to your children. If we all did that, the *emuratare-o-ntoiye* would come to an end!"

Chapter Nineteen

One day in August that year, Minik sent for the girls. She had never called them to her office and they had never had any reason to go there. The man who had been sent to call them walked ahead of them to the door and opened it for them.

The office was large, clean and tidy with a large oval desk with a glass top taking up most of the room. There were six or so comfortable arm chairs, filing cabinets and shelves around the walls. There was a small fireplace in the corner and the fresh air that gently blew through two large open windows brought in a pleasant aromatic scent of the blossoms of the Savanna. Minik walked to her door to welcome them in.

"Come in my dear girls," Minik said happily. "Come in and take your seats."

"Thank you." the girls replied in unison as they sat apprehensively in the armchairs.

Minik's tone and manner were extremely courteous. She walked around the side of the desk, and sat down in the chair behind it, picking two envelopes on the desk that she toyed with in her hands as she cleared her throat. The girls' apprehension intensified as Minik appeared to hesitate in telling them the reason for which she called them. She pulled out a neatly typed letter from one of the envelopes and scrutinized it closely, her eye-brows knitted. She turned from one page of the letter to the other and then she carefully put it back into the envelope and cleared her throat once again. She picked the other envelope from the desk which she similarly opened and pulled out a letter and peered through it, all the time keeping her eyes away from Taiyo and Resian. Then she suddenly sat back in her chair and raised her eyes to look directly into the girls, a faint smile appearing on her lips.

"My dear lovely girls," Minik called in a trembling emotionally charged voice." "The moment we have all been waiting for has finally come. These two envelopes here contain your letters of admission to the Egerton University! You are required to report at the campus on the fifth of September!"

The announcement of the good tidings came in such stunning swiftness that it caught Taiyo and Resian unaware. It left them dazed and dumbfounded.

At the end of August, Minik the *Emakererei,* organized a farewell party for the girls. She had noted that they had become popular with the workers and she knew they would like to bid them farewell. She therefore invited many workers from all paddocks, and also invited the girls from the Intapuka-e-Maa school and their teachers.

On the day of the party, the younger employees laboured over large fires built in a long line near the wool godown, roasting mutton from the ten sheep slaughtered alongside a bullock, and cooking large pots of potatoes, peas and cabbage. A king-size pot of *ugali* hissed cheerfully at the side.

The feast began at two in the afternoon and the workers around Taiyo and Resian laughed and shouted merrily as they consumed great quantities of food and drank many bottles of soda and fruit juices. Taiyo and Resian were very much a part of the scene around them, as they ate, drank and enjoyed themselves, frowning with feigned disagreement with a comment here and laughing in response to a joke there. The girls from Intapuka-e-Maa enjoyed themselves too.

After all the people had eaten, the girls from Intapuka-e-Maa said they were going to sing a song. They stood up, straightened and smoothened their skirts and formed four lines, one behind the other. Their voices were soft, pleasant and melodious. And the words of their song brought tears into the eyes of Taiyo and Resian.

We are the blossoms of our land,
We are the cream of our generation,
We are the future of our nation,
We are *Intapuka-e-Maa.*
Where are those who used to doubt us?
Where are those who thought we were not worthy?
That for us to be worthy we must be cut?
Let them come out and see the Daughters of Maa.

We are proud to be *Intoiye nemengalana,*
We are proud to be the blossoms of the Savannah,
When you come to look for us, we shall not be there,
We shall not be found in the dingy, dirty huts.

We shall be doctors, engineers and teachers,
We shall stand side by side with the men,
We shall be building our nation together,
We are the blossoms of the Savannah!

As the girls sang, a procession of vehicles came from the east. It raised a long column of dust as it rapidly approached. Everything came to a standstill as all attention was shifted and directed at the unfolding scenario. Minik stood up and shielded her eyes with her hand, peering at the unannounced visitors. They did not take long before they arrived and loud revs rent the air as the glittering vehicles reversed and were parked carefully and systematically. All the people stared silenty at the magnificent vehicles, wondering who the strangers were.

Minik rubbed her hands together nervously as she walked cautiously towards the parked vehicles. As she walked, she counted the vehicles and she thought she saw ten of them. She was not sure whether she got the figure right.

When the man in the first vehicle saw Minik approaching, he alighted. Minik, Taiyo and Resian recognised him at once. It was Oloisudori Lonkiyaa!

"How are you, madam?" he greeted Minik as he walked towards her his hands outstretched, "we didn't know you were holding a party!"

"You did not announce your coming, so that we could tell you we were having a party." Minik answered acidly, "besides, we do not have to inform anybody when we have to hold a party. Anyway, what can I do for you?"

"Since you seem to be rush with me," Oloisudori said in a fit of pique, embarrassed by the way Minik rudely addressed him, "I'll come straight to the point. I am told you are keeping two of Ole Kaelo's daughters here. For your information, I have a choice to marry any one of the two. Choose the one you want to keep for I have come to take one of them. I have already paid dowry enough to cover the two!"

"You will be advised to get out of this place fast,"

Minik told him in a quiet angry tone, "the two girls are under my charge and none of them, I repeat, none of them would be taken away from me, not even by their father, Ole Kaelo!"

She steeled herself and looked up into his eyes with an unwavering stare. Oloisudori's nostrils flared as he walked briskly toward her with an angry snarl, pointing his finger at her.

"Who are you to talk to me like that?" he bellowed trembling with fury. "Do you know Oloisudori Loonkiyaa? I don't need your permission to pick a wife, do I? Who are you by the way? You are nothing but a mendacious spinster who has lost a chance to get married and now masquerades as a crusader against the so called F.G.M. Let us not waste time, call either Taiyo or Resian, then you can go ahead with your miserly party peacefully."

"You are getting none of them," Minik snarled, walking toward him menacingly. "For your own safety and the safety of your expensive machines, leave this place this instant."

Oloisudori uttered a strangled sound in a wordless growl and his eyes bulged with fury. He called out his men pointed at Resian and told them to get hold of her.

The pandemonium that broke loose was unprecedented. Oloisudori must have underrated the loyalty of about four hundred energetic workers who had just eaten to their fill. As the girls retreated, the men surged forward and in no time, Oloisudori's convoy was reduced to smouldering shells and acrid smell of burning tyres. Oloisudori and his men had to run for dear life. But not before each one of them had been clobbered thoroughly.

The following day was the fifth of September. It was the day that was to be etched in letters of gold in the hearts and minds of Taiyo and Resian. They could not find words to describe the sensation that enveloped them and pervaded their hearts as they climbed into the four-wheel drive vehicle that belonged to Minik the *Emakererei* and sat beside her. It was hard to believe that their long cherished ambition and aspiration had at long last become a reality. It was truly a day of victory and exultation. It was a day of anticipation and expectation as they imagined entering through those gates of the university. How would they ever repay Minik the *Emakererei* for her kindness?

The workers came out in their hundreds to see them off. Nabaru, the *enkabaani*, their friend and foster mother was there too. They watched and waved as the vehicle drove past the desolate shells of Oloisudori's burnt vehicles that resembled the destroyed armoured vehicles of a vanquished army.

"*Meisisi Olaitoriani,*" Resian said prayerfully as the vehicle went past the waving workers. "It is all well that ends well."

"*Esaai,*" concluded Taiyo excitedly.

And they were off to their Nirvana, that was Egerton University!

_____ **E N D** _____

289

Glossary and Notes

The meanings of Maasai and Swahili words which are not clear from their context are given here, together with some explanatory notes. Unless otherwise stated, the words explained are Maasai. Words included in the glossary are italicised whenever they appear in the text.

Angam	-	To notch or nick for the purpose of blood letting.
Atasaiya tomituoki siake	-	I beseech you, please rescue me.
Atulutoiye Papaai	-	A cry of an anguished person that says "I have taken shelter under you, my father."
Daktari	-	Swahili for doctor
Doi	-	Insistent demonstrative assertion that is used to signify urgency.
Enkai Aomon Entomono	-	Invocation made by women to God for the blessing for an offspring. Occasionally women congregate and collectively say this prayer to God to open women wombs.
Enkai Supat	-	Good Lord!
Eitu aikata adol	-	I have never seen.
Enkaini (singular)	-	Co-wife
Enkaitoyoni	-	Midwife
Enkamuratani	-	Circumciser (feminine)
Enopeny Enkang	-	The owner of a homestead (feminine)
Entagoroi	-	Wasp or any other stinging insect. A sharp-tongued woman.

Entaapai	-	Name given to a girl who goes against tradition and becomes pregnant before she is circumcised.
Enjore	-	War, raid, battle or clash
Enadua Kutuk	-	A woman with a bitter sharp tongue.
Esosian (singular)	-	The stick of a palm-tree that is used to clean calabashes.
Enkilelo	-	Crab
Elangatare	-	Love affair
Elangata	-	Girlfriend
Enkaputi	-	In-law relationship
Esongoyo	-	Aromatic shrimp plant that young people use as perfume and exchange as gifts.
Enchilaloi or encilaloi	-	A natural gap between the two upper front teeth.
Erankau (singular)	-	An acacia tree or whistling thorn tree.
Enkebaani	-	Nurse, healer or lady doctor
Enenaunerr	-	Legendary monster that was said to be partly human and partly stone.
Esiankiki	-	Bride. Newly married young woman.
Enkitungat	-	An armed group of able-bodied men that hastily forms itself in response to a distress call to pursue cattle rustlers, raiders or other marauding gangs.
Enkoiboni	-	Female ritual expert, medicine woman, prophetess or diviner.
Embarie	-	Fox. In Masaai folklore, the fox is the most cowardly of all animals.
Entasat	-	Old woman, especially one past childbearing age.
Emuata (amuat)	-	To coil around or to enfold.

Esaai	-	Amen.
Intoiye Nemengalana	-	*Intoiye* is plural of *entito* which means girl. *Nemengalana* means who has not been cut. It is a derogatory description of girls who are not circumcised.
Intalengo	-	Festive occasions where sacred rituals are performed.
Iloirienito (plural)	-	A brown wild olive.
Ilkilenya (plural)	-	Shrub or bush of the vine family. The sap of its fruits is used to treat wounds while its tubers are boiled and the liquid added to milk given to infants to forestall colic pains.
Ilnyangusi Age set	-	Made up of two age groups. Ilkamaniki and Ilkalikal who were warriors between 1942 and 1959. Ole Supeyo was a member of this age set.
Iloirraga (plural)	-	The name of a hardwood tree that often grows at river banks and yields sweet purple fruits. It is called the Mshiwi tree in Swahili.
Iloponi (plural)	-	Red – hot poker or flame tree. Its tiny read bead-like berries give its name of oloponi (bead).
Ilmiintoni (plural)	-	A pair of large colourful beads that dangle down the pierced and extended earlobes of elders. It is also the name of an orange flower.
Inkilani-e-papaai	-	Swear words used by girls to emphatically state their strong feelings for or against a certain position. The words, literally mean my 'father's garments.' It is taboo for a girl too touch

	-	or get near her father's garments.
Ilterito	-	An age set whose morans were warriors from 1926-1948. Old Ole Musanka was of this age group.
Ilmintilis	-	Animal intestines, tripe or sausage.
Ilmasonik	-	Fictional religious cult.
Ilarinkon	-	Legendary giants who fought many battles with the Maasai until they were finally defeated and driven out of Maasailand.
Ilkurteta (plural)	-	Scoops, spoons, spades
Ilkipiren (plural)	-	A wooden implement for stirring milk, soup or porridge.
Ilmeekure kishulare	-	Those with whom we no longer intermingle or interact.
Igo	-	The response to Entaguenya
Intapuka-e-Maa	-	Blossoms of Maa
Isurutia	-	A married woman's scrolled ear-rings that are also worn by newly circumcised boys. They signify harmlessness.
Isuyan (plural)	-	Wild dogs
Kokoo-o-sein	-	Sein's grandmother.
Kitenge (singular)	-	Swahili for dress material.
Kaaji enkabaani	-	My name is enkabaani
Kachumbari	-	Condiment of chopped tomatoes, onions and red-pepper that is served with roast meat.
Morans	-	Correctly called Ilmurran. Young circumcised men between the ages of 18 and 25 years.
Menye Resian	-	Resian's father.
Meeta	-	Nobody.

Meisisi olaitoriani	-	May the Lord be praised.
Ngoto Taiyo	-	Taiyo's mother
"Ne yeiyo-ai nanyorr"	-	The beloved daughter of my mother, an endearment name that a father uses addressing his beloved daughter.
Nyama choma	-	Swahili for roast meat.
Na kerai, aingai Likitaara?	-	Child, who has beaten you?
Olmorijoi	-	Title used to address a male senior member of the family or distinguish brothers using their ages as a criterion. Olbarnoti is the opposite.
Olkunchai / Olkuncai	-	Cattle trader
Olobaai	-	Name of an erect open shrub with bright shiny green leaves and bright-yellow flowerheads.
Olkilenyai (singular)	-	Shrub or bush of the vine family. The sap of its fruits is used to treat wounds while its tubers are boiled and the liquid added to milk given to infants to forestall colic pains.
Oloirragai (singular)	-	The name of a hardwood tree that often grows at river banks and yields sweet purple fruits. It is called the Mshiwi tree in Swahili.
Oloponi (singular)	-	Red – hot poker or flame tree. Its tiny read bead-like berries give its name of oloponi (bead).
Olosiro	-	A plant of the bracken-fern species that grows in forests, on wasteland and on hill slopes. It becomes a rich red brown colour during the dry months of the year.

Olkirrpanyany	-	A name of a plant that grows in the highlands and has pink stems and greyish green leaves.
Oleleshua	-	A common shrub or bush with silver grey leaves and grey hardy stems that dominate the semi-arid Maasai scrubland. Its wood is used as fire-wood and its leaves placed under armpits to soak sweat and act as a deodorant. The distinctive smell of the wood smoke from its burning is the ever lingering smell in all Maasai homesteads.
Osinoni	-	An aromatic herb or shrub with small red and yellow flowers in dense clusters.
Oloirepirepi	-	Name of a weed whose tiny leaves are sticky and when pressed together make a mat that is used to hold meat.
Olkirikoi	-	A vagrant. A man without home, cattle, wife or children and who lives off others.
Olmurunya	-	Razor-sharp blade that Maasai women use for shaving heads and is also used by the girl-child circumciser.
Olkurtet	-	Scoop, shovel, spade or spoon
Olkuenyi	-	Stupidity, folly or madness. It also refers to the general malaise where the afflicted person behaves abnormally, and is said to be contagious.
Olokesena	-	A leather wrap around garment that women wear around their loins and flows down to their ankles.

Oloiboni	-	Ritual expert, medicine man, prophet or diviner.
Oltaika	-	Moran's plaited hair that flows down to his shoulders.
Olbitirr	-	Warthog
Olkipire (singular)	-	Wooden implements for stirring milk, soup or porridge.
Olangata	-	Boyfriend
Olkuak	-	Character, behaviour, or way of life
Olkuak le Maa	-	Maa way of life
Ologol	-	A log that keeps the fire smouldering for a long time.
Olmilo	-	A disease (listeriosis) which infects some kind of madness among cattle and wild animals.
Oerata	-	Valley or stretch of lowland between hills.
Olourrurr	-	A softwood tall tree, with an orange-coloured trunk that grows without branches and whose large thin leaves cluster at the top forming a head. The leaves tremble with the slightest wind-blow and the head sways from side to side.
Ol-ushuushi	-	A reckless person.
Olkinyei	-	The maba tree whose stem is boiled and put in soup and given as medicine against stomach trouble.
Oltikambu (singular)	-	A thick greyish bush that grows in dry grassland
Osuguroi (singular)	-	Aloe, the stout perennial herb that the Maasai use as medicine and also used for spicing beer.